ANDREA OF HILLETON

Writing by Dale Taylor.

Andrea of
Hilleton

D S Taylor

Initially Produced:
October-December, 2009 Anno Domini.

Editing Completed: August-September, 2025, Europe.

Electronically authored by D S Taylor, Sydney, New South Wales, Australia.
Original electronic self publishing by the above stated.

Inquiries to: dlvtnsrv@gmail.com

Foreword.

At pains of repetition, yet to make abundantly clear, the following information is stated.

Any book is a package of information and entertainment. So too, is this one. If this tome happens to inspire, then good. Fair critics are always endless and both they and any defenders are treasured contributors indeed to the lesser aspect of here and the greater of the whole world of all things. However the process and result which is this product is a testament to the owner-author, who would remind the audience that this is what he had to say, whether it is judged praiseworthy or unfavorably in the passage of time.

The key aim of any writing is to spread ideas and dreams, whether figments of imagination or fact. Indeed, all information can be useful, providing it does not wilfully lead to the destruction of life, liberty or property. To add to the collection of ideas that humankind has, is indeed a worthy thing in itself, apart from any opinion or consequent writing productions.
It would seem to the author that ideas spring from each other, build and change, then fly free, to take on meanings that are beyond that which was thought possible a little while prior. By such doing, perhaps new dreams will be forged and even crystalised to the world. So to these thoughts and prospects, the author offers this literary work as an addition to the world's trust of all items made, which may we urge to be an influence for the betterment of the good.

For Elsa

The Question we all face is why?

Why here, why now, why not some other place?

Andrea of Hilleton:

-Seeing Through Dreams-

Andrea sprayed the hair spray methodically onto her half-wet hair. She loved her Deneby's, it gave just the perfect amount of hold whilst still allowing some body and clarity and movement. Of course hair was her life, having worked in a salon for so long before trying her hand unsuccessfully at story writing just earlier in the year. It was now July, and nobody had really been interested in her work, not even her publishing acquaintance through Jon, her hubby. So now she decided her stint away from the salon had to end. She got her old job back, and so it became just like being an out-of-teens young adult, trying to make that golden impression. Again….almost, anyway.

"Where are my razors?" She asked a still-dozing Jon.

He snored a little in reply. "Probably where you last left them" she auto-replied to herself. He was a good man, not in the least for suffering her recent work crisis of epic proportions. So, many family sit-downs engaging the line of " I want to be more than just a beauty consultant in a salon..." followed by his sincere rebuttals that he "loved her, never judged her by silly capitalistic values of work anyway, thought her profession quite honorable" and, besides all that, she was also a mother and a very good one; this was no mean set of feats.

She didn't disagree with him, and besides his work was horrendous by comparison to her station and its duty. Starchy collars and impressing his peers was dreadful at best, even if he was only of minor peerage stock. Those odd occasions of being invited to business dealings or banquets were like a labour rather than the always-suggested "delightful chance to meet and greet". Luckily they were apart from that most of the time – for the balance of the year in fact.

For what it was worth, were they becoming too bourgeois? Jon had always liked Marxian readings even though it didn't quite befit his position and status. It was a theoretical interest as he said. Is two times three seven? At least with Ben in boarding school he didn't have to endure all their crazed antics as parents that were, at best, "not quite there" as some relatives had joked. "Character building" though, as Ben's uncle Friedrich had said many a time, "adds to the family flavor", even if he said it always with an air of confidence that couldn't be surpassed (and a stiff lip)? Anyway, she hadn't always been agreeable to the idea of sending poor Ben away for the most part of the year, but educationally it was for the best and the family was paying for it after all. If the royals studied hard and even gave military duty of service, then surely even their "minor" relative members should also consider likewise, so had been said repeatedly...

There was a light on the horizon just away from the sun's gentle rising over the mountains in their Hilleton district. She had seen it some days ago and it was really getting to her. "I'm going to see that a little closer," She thought to herself as she finished putting lipstick on. Star and sky phenomena had always been a little side interests of hers. Astronomy was one of her better sciences at school. Lots of stargazing as a child had left its mark thanks to many wishes made on shooters.

Zoom forward and after some upstart customers and an early dismissal from the day's duties in "La Upper Crust" salon (her alma mater), thanks to Judith the new co-owner with Mark and Guinevere, she was setting off home in the car, picking up the miles per hour down the old cottage road when once again, now with dusk falling, the strange light puzzled her and teased her once more. Having time on her side today, she couldn't resist discovering what it was in that ultra-remote wooded mountainside that was doing all that glowing. A lighthouse she had never heard of? Festivals, some camp-out? It couldn't hurt to peek a little closer, so off she shuttled the car, careening the wheel down a new side street, almost childishly and with lesser care, to the beep of other annoyed drivers from nearby villages going about their simple lives.

It took quite some time and gear changing to approach. It was quieter but much damper and fogged as the car groaned up the slopes of the only approaching road anywhere near the direction of the light. Or lights. As she parked the car and trekked off into the wild blue yonder of leaves and twigs and damp dank forested grounds, she felt a feeling of freedom in a sense that had been dormant in her since who knows when? Luckily she always had spare joggers in the car because work heels just wouldn't cut it in this brush, with the air congealed around her. Not a soul in sight anywhere, just the glow of what now revealed itself to be many lights, perhaps ten in a polygonal circle of points...This is surely something of note, if only for the camera now... That would be for next time, notions of tourist fervour overtaking her senses.

The thickest of thick trees and foliage were around her now, very dark, brown, ancient all around, she was probably well lost now but pushed on, it was too far to give up now. Husband would think she had just stayed behind to clean up as could happen, perhaps a rush of ladies wanting to look prepared trichologically (in hair) for some gown needed for a ball or what-have-you. It had darkened, but the hour was only 5pm or so. It was hard to even see her wristwatch, and a little tremor of fear traversed her spine upon hearing a scratch here or there for a moment in the wooded surrounds. Still, nothing much could survive up here in these harsh terrains, and such landscapes had always fascinated her; She had trekked similarly so many times as a child with delight, glimpsing stars and night-owls hither and thither with glee so wistfully, so many times. "I just wonder now how I will get any stains out of my work robes, 'probably need a scrubbing..." in this way she thought over so many things at once, all competing for her brain energies.

The lights won.

It was a craft or building of some sorts, vaguely circular but with stilted edges and surrounded by shadows and unknowns. A silvery figure crept up behind her and politely asked if "madam would accompany her a moment." His masculine voice was ever so slightly crackled, but she said nothing and dutifully followed. It was a workman, informing her that the local council chamber had ordered some building work to be constructed, but that men had in the main taken fright, and that he was on night watch solely, to tend to the council's interests—just in case. "It's so remote though", Andrea replied thoughtfully and apologetically. "Why would any curious child wander so far?"

He didn't know himself. He seemed a straight-forward man, and gave her a cup of tea and the suggestion that she go home, offering to accompany her back to the town's street lamp vicinities. Gratefully she accepted without delay or forethought. "I suspect my family is concerned by now surely, dear sir" with a hint of apprehension in her night-crackled voice. The older man, perhaps 20 years her senior hopped up off his milk-crate chair and proceeded to go first, but with her close behind as was more polite. The clatter of twigs, branches and leaves, like strange percussion and rhythm began up again, now doubly with his heavy work boots adding to the chorus. It wasn't unpleasantly loud however.

Bob, as he had given his name, had turned a corner in the woods around near a great stony rock that she had not really seen on the way up, which made it plain their track back was ajar from the original path up. "I'll walk you to the car you say is parked on the down-road, don't worry at all Mrs. Levison." He whistled by an occupational habit she suspected, their pleasantries having now allowed them to address each other on a friendlier basis.

As he turned momentarily out of site around the rock, a little extra silence fell. She huddled downward, over some stones crudely forming a path of steps if one imagined well enough, quicker to ensure she did not lose site of her proxy-for-a-real guide. Approaching around the viewing side into the open below, it was so dark it really didn't seem they were any closer to escaping the no-man's-known-land. "Bob?" She called out, then waited breathlessly. No reply came in a minute's long wait, eternity almost, to the now cold Andrea. Or was it fear that was bringing out the shivering in her? She called a little louder. Then again more desperately as a cry of hope. Then a silvery figure held out a hand, which she took unthinkingly. Then out cold unconscious, all became misted in her present memory.

A voice whispering awoke her in a chamber. His voice crackled similar to Bob's, but in a more youthful way, and a more slender upright body. He sat on a chair and a colleague (for want of another word) with a robe obscuring his face and body left down a hall through the oh-so narrow doorway. A little light blipped next to the door, perhaps a security mechanism or simply to alleviate passage or nay through to wherever else the place allowed one to go into.

She had looked about in such input in a mere moment before reflexively rising in a flash, and demanding "Who are you? Where am I?" Bob escaped her memory a moment, then, "Where is the other man?"

Quietly the man said, "I am not a man, but a Zordant. Of the other man we do not know." He remained motionless, and looked pale though intelligent.

"How do you speak like I then" she blasted back, suspiciously. She got up, brushed herself, as though waiting for an answer impatiently before she would depart, as she did indeed intend.

"I heard your voice, and learnt your vocal wave patterns. We have heard your language at previous times. You are Andrea, is that right? I apologise for my having looked over your belongings to ascertain that fact." He moved his lips only slightly, and seemed timeless in posture and demeanor.

"Yes I am, and I find it disgusting that you think you can invade my privacy of person like this. I'll report you to the police unless you let me go NOW!" She said it with all the courage she could, hoping nerves didn't sound too detectable in her strained voice. She was tired and thirsty now too.

"Time does not pass here" announced the cloaked man who had returned into the doorway. "So you need not concern yourself with your family missing you. We will let you go freely, but hope we can learn from you and help each other."

"I want to go now! Now! Let me go!" She insisted all the more so.
"I have no reason to believe anything you say!"

The two Zordants projected an image into space as she looked insistently for a way to escape and then back to them. There was no way out conceivably except the doorway, not even a window. Then what showed on the projected image horrifyingly amazed her. It was her life, from early age to present. These two knew too much about her.

As she began to protest, the hooded one spoke quickly:

"We profess truthfully, we are not of your planet. Believe us not as you will. The imaging you see is based on our intellect of investigation, based merely from what we observe in your physical character and your belongings and our computational instruments. We are a people similar to your own, but yet also different. We have visited your planet with great interest before, but are careful to not impose. We are more concerned with sharing knowledge, for we have all we could want or need in the way of life means. This is a space traveler you stand in. Or, transporter, you may say. Please let me show you, and then we can arrange your departure back to your home without too much of delay."

Knowing there were few options and that for want of no choice, if they meant harm there was little she could do to prevent it, she nodded quickly, complied reluctantly and was lead out into a hallway, to see a night-sky like space, with stars and emptiness all around. Lights blazed out at the command of the first being/Zordant one, but still nothing revealed outside excepting the blankness of the outers. She came to slowly realise that she was nowhere, but in a capsule craft.

Even more reluctantly she decided to take them on their word. She was fed and given drink as time marched on, but somehow not like in her natural surrounds. Time was so less relevant, and more indistinct. Things seemed almost dreamy.

They spoke at length on many things, but they seemed to want more and more, on any topic from philosophy to psychology to general statistics of earth and more. Even her hair salon work was not off-limits.

She was given a book, which she placed in her handbag even though she did not believe in it or trust them greatly.

Out she stepped of the object of decagonal lights, and in another eye-blink only remembered herself back in her bed. As she awaited the drift into sleep, she recalled the evening with her husband questioning anxiously and rightly so.

"Where were you? What happened?" he had begun. When she began to relate to him, the flurry of more questions came out, as well as admonitions that she shouldn't have gone after some strange light.

"What did you think you would find after all? Didn't you think to let the police investigate the light instead?"

He gave her the benefit of the doubt, marvelous husband as he more often than not was. He didn't question her information about the craft either, but she figured he couldn't really believe it in his innermost core. They slept it off and away it went as a concern. She spent half the night in his arms and awoke to mundane bliss.

As she was driving to work, somebody else had joined her for a car ride, as it would turn out. She didn't really feel like going back to the salon today, but how could she really ask for time off after all they had done for her in taking her back without a second thought? So off she had trooped, just having a large orange juice at the breakfast table hurriedly, comically like the magazine of modern life "Your Day" had said in the article she had speed-read. She felt like a paradigm of the modern woman, teetering at the edge of super-mum status, yet altogether at the same time just really feeling average. The glossy pages were to no end filled with articles of dream rooms and interior decorations and couples from cover to cover that didn't seem at all to be like reality.

Or was it reality but she just wasn't looking through the right glass prism? Off should come the dust giving the roses an opaque indistinguishable nature.

She focused again on her driving, casting dreamscapes aside a moment, but a bit unsuccessfully.

Once more, as she thought along all these tangential lines, as was the normal morning routine, it was at that moment that a spider appeared out of a corner to give her a surprise and land on her hand. She startled, and in more surprise than her, it bit. Hard. She squealed with pain like a little girl, but with more right than absurdity, and wailed at the top of her lungs. Spiders weren't as bad as snakes to her, but not THIS close. In a flood of pain the car decelerated as she slammed the brakes and pulled over very roughly on the lightly busy street.

In her mind, time stopped. Next thing she knew, she was on the move. Through the double doors only some paces up, under the guise of a couple that had seen the plight and led her along, into the doctor's waiting room but not for long once the receptionist had seen her hand. It was just on the adjunct of her wrist to her arm in actuality. Swollen red.

The doctor, a man of uncertain older age, wrapped it and placed various treatments on it before giving her an inoculation, "Just in case of spreading effect, which we wouldn't want would we Mrs. Levison?"
He had said it so drily, almost scoldingly as to a child, but she could defend with nothing in the circumstances. Especially not when he helped to ensure the car was now spider-free after consoling her in counsel. He even arranged a neighbouring businessman to have the car cleaned then and there with vacuum and brush. He was an antique dealer, observed by looking at his sign and displays.

After many thanks, off she went. The doctor had also said that her abdominal pain of some days was by no means related, but more to her normal cycles, which she agreed was relevant and had taken his medicinal script-offer.

Yet alarmingly, it just kept on swelling and looked black. It was atrocious to behold. The anti-venom seemed to make her a bit woozy to make matters even far worse. No work or driving now, one of her pleasures normally.

Watching television comfortably in bed as hubby busied himself cooking and waiting on her (for want of no better explanation) to her smiling delight, though pained by her ailment, she watched amazingly as the "resignation of a nation" unfolded. "The PM has just resigned due to retirement, on no prior warning!" She called out to Jon.

"Really?" came the surprised reply. He was reading the paper as her chicken soup boiled frothingly a few feet away. "But he just announced new tax reform measures and a whole wave of bills to go through..." he continued. "Seems most odd, after working so hard to gain office from the conservatives."

Then as he finished and his voice trailed off from her immediate attention, she recalled the Zordants, though not by name, when they had spoken of their observations as they called them, and how they had said with great certainty that they believed the Prime Minister would resign within 48 hours or less. "We gather information and analyze, draw conclusions from myriad composures and factors, it is what we do in our kind, and what makes us achieve" had said the hooded one. She began to wonder as she watched on, still pained by the injury the spider had caused.

Eventually, after some days, she made it back to the salon amongst great compassion from Guinevere in particular. The wound still hurt but not as much as before. She wore a thin full-armed silk top to hide the worst of it as she busied herself in sweeping up, and serving the ladies who came for appointments, many glad to see her return, having known her for quite some time and even by husband. There were those that scoffed at what she did, but others who took delight in it, and showed real interest.

"Morvan, is that you, Hello?" said Doctor Myers on the telephone to Virologist Doctor Morvan. "Good, good" he continued as the line improved. He didn't trust telephones much himself, his father had shown him the telewires which he thought were much better for official business, but as he was told, telephony was the way now. A very conservative man he was at best. In some future decade he would surely be laughed at for being so technology-anxious.

"I see, I see" replied Doctor Morvan. Doctor Myers told him of how after a third visit that Mrs. Andrea Levison was still not showing the normal recovery signs with the treatment, the most powerful known in anti-inflammation and poison-and-bite curatives.

Doctor Morvan was puzzled by the situation also. "The lab results through and through are that she will recover, but it is indeed taking longer than usual. It's a relatively normal bite from all evidences. Has she had any underlying stresses lately? Best look into that, Doctor."

Andrea took the call in the little backroom, which served as the room for paperwork and lunch alike during quiet break times. Dr. Myers had been delicate so as not to alarm her, but she still could see through the veil of "all being well." It throbbed and ached, but she hid it well with painkillers, much to the discomforted opinion of husband Jon. The doctor had agreed that work was better for her, in order for her pattern of living to aid her immune recovery rather than hinder it now. He kept up well with the latest journal findings, he had assured her and husband both. Poor Jon, how much more could he take in the way of misfortunes for his dear wife?

She decided impulsively that she would return to the lights, crazy as it sounded. The drag of their correctness in regards to her past and the prediction of the PM made her curious. They seemed innocent enough and not willing to harm her on that previous chance meeting. They had insisted it was not altogether chance furthermore, but rather fortuitous. Was she crazy? It almost seemed as though she was being called, called, called.

So intrepidly she drove out, withstood the mist and scoured around the stony hill. Sure enough, despite having not seen them from home in her hobblings about the house and past the window of first sighting, there stood the craft. Dimmed by mists? It's stony look served the surroundings well, treachery it spelt out to any that would attempt to know it. Camouflage.
Inside she was directed, then a-gasped into the starry heavens again in no real passing of time as her mind saw it. This time there was only a voice at first, but then the hooded one came and inspected her wound after they had exchanged papery tomes, her contribution being a world atlas and a student dictionary. Their sketchy English was improving and would more still. They learnt fast, as testament to their knowledge-acquirement leaning of hearts.

In an imperceptible way the Zordant had waved a hand, and his cloaks with long loose sleeves did not completely disguise a kind of humming device and violet light that appeared to glow at her hand.
"Be at peace, child of human kind," he urged her through mind as she started to move head to look closer at his ministrations.

The hooded one now having left, and after some quite considerable time alone in the room, the first man came back, somehow a junior to the hooded one, who was addressed as a kind of commander though semi-informally.

The lead Zordant raised an eyebrow to find a paper fell out of the book marked as a dictionary.

Sweeping it up with almost unseen motion, he regarded it carefully, wondering to its content, if perchance it had special meaning.

"Stone upon stone, bone to unyielding bone,
the wordy ones would wander on,
willing to greatness from gentle beginnings
None to conquer what stood to seem prey."

Curling his lips at these words, he deemed them some art of play perhaps, or a code. It would require further reflection with his equal of race, on case and assumption it were pertinent to proceedings now or venturing forward. Another thing to processes and assess, no doubt.

What was the human suggesting by this inclusion?

Things had a wear of finding place where needed. At the time he did not and could know glean at the human word for it, that of serendipity, or perhaps, coincidence.

Carefully he folded the paper and returned it to inside the book, at a random leaf page.

Then with only cursory regard more, he turned on heel, to quest after his computational work at the technology machines of their craft. Other matters would have to wait a little. With a sigh he thought of his own kind, both his colleague here and those of beyond, hoping that their fortunes were still in the good way. Yet he needed to shun these emotive meanderings. They were dangerous to dwell on. Decorum and dedication, diligence and duty. The all imports, he self-reminded.

Snap! She woke up. Home. Comfort.

Had it all been dreamed?
Her hand was bandaged and healed almost now, with only a
slight-to-the-eye skin-folded line, curious to behold, that no man
surgeon could have so precisely hoped to copy with such
beautiful elegance. She looked down at it, wondering about Jon;
Poor Jon who'd suffered a lot in all of it and with a letter and
telephone call about Ben's having had to be placed under Sister
care after an accident. He'd driven 43 miles to ensure his son was
okay before coming back, and knew how it had pained his wife to
not be able to come along due to her own recent ill health. He
was hoping for things to calm down though as he said it now, for
all concerned. He wished it more than it wished itself, she
couldn't help thinking, but basked in his comforting chest until
she arose. He'd arisen to eat after asking if she wanted hers yet,
but as she declined, he quietly read and wrote intermittently in his
study chamber aloft. He had checked on her to find her drifting
back into delicate gentle sleep before at some time, but now she
was more than awake and quite surprised.

At some point she scratched her head with her opposing hand and
then as she rested it back down on the covers saw the ring on her
finger. The one the man she loved had given her, and all the
compassion and freedom it gave in its very special way. Then she
thought of her son and family, her deceased mother and other
relations, and her place in the world. She reached out to the
bedside dresser, careful to not hit the bed's heavy oaken headpiece
as she wafted through the screen curtains femininely surrounding
the bed, and in her dress felt a bump in her side-pocket. Puzzled,
she felt it then reached in to find: The rubesque ring.

The words silently came back to her with a smile of knowing
proportion on her unmade-up morning face. "When you need us,
it is your contact to us. It has special properties. We are very
grateful for your having entrusted us and for sharing with us your
world's wisdom as you could."

Could a pair of strangers ever be truly trusted, and did it really matter? She told her husband who showed some fascination and seriousness to hear her further revelations. As understanding as the day she had married him and even before.

-Un-dreaming.-

A 'blinding' jolt of pain seared in her forehead.
Though remarkably then, Andrea took to bearings. Here. Yes.
This is where she was. Short breaths. Chest heaving. What was
that? Vivid envisionings broke her mental focus. Shutting eyes
and hastening a shake of head. She stilled her racy air intake, let
out a big gasp and then sobbed bitterly. Tears streamed salt on
her soft cheeks. When had she fallen asleep? How had she lost
control?
A time later she thought to jot things down on writing pad. No
need for it: but she really needed to talk to someone who would
listen. All the things she'd done! Yet what, when, how... Oh, it
was hard to unjiggle the thoughts. These 'memories' were all over
the shop as they say. With a gasp again (this time of more shock),
it dawned on her that things made no sense at all:

For in truest fact, she had no son, and certainly no husband to
speak of!

Yet staring down, after pushing away hair from her face and a rub
at her puffed black-ringed eyes, the glint of rubesque remained.
On the digitalis, sturdy. She played with it. Turning and teasing
it in horizontal and vertical wavy offset rotations. In fear mixed
with pride, she thought to be off with the thing. Sudden impulse.
Yet slow wriggle lent itself to full-scale panic wrenching. Off it
would not come.

So indeterminate an hour it being, so silent, Andrea just sat at
bedside, devoid of sentiments.
In twilight was her humble uploft room, old wooden chair at side.
Cold, lonely yet familiar.
 Pressing a tasse of cold tea to her lips, she drank a sip. Placing it
down, the leaves blackly sat down in the cup's base with rings of
soiling where water once lay within. She sank down and let lead-
heavy eyelids carry her to the brink of unconsciousness.

She really couldn't sleep. Thoughts drifted with dull coherence in
that steel trap we all know as self. Thoughts, thoughts. No desire
to fight them just now. Energies at a low, the now soft rhythmic

rising of her torso stood as revelation of her now dreamless queasy deep slumber. It eased the heady pains. Blank of all pains, for now.

What cruelty had it been to dream all this weird stuff? People in her life that did not exist!? What on earth was happening in her poor little head?

-Mundane: Awaking In-

Andrea of Hilleton, born of humble, mediocre parents, looked into the round hair mirror. In early prime, she was, soft of feature. Golden tresses weaved beautifully amongst pale chestnut strands in a wondrous and completely natural effect.

She felt sad and had just awoken again. The unassailable truth of the ordinary glared all around, a display of the real here and now. Were it not for the slight chill of the early air, it could have been mistaken for a shiver of fright, as her spine tingled and the hairs on the back of her neck stood up.

Alone, she thought wistfully as she picked up her brush and set about straightening her locks more nicely. Now casting off mundane concerns, she blissfully became blank to other ideas, she gazed dreamily on her own image and found long hairs to caress with the bristles down, down, finding the ends and then starting again to new strands. Straights, curls, waves all washed over her mind in a lovely symphony. The corners of her mind embraced the womanly wonder of the moment and the dance of inner happiness. Gently she surrendered to the finery and sleek attentiveness of self adornment in all its subtlety.

A slow rhythm slid the strokes this way and through her tresses, gracefully glistening the goldy brunettes as she felt the sleek subtle softness. With a woosh, woosh, the still air carried distant vague music of songbirds sweetly whistling, while the brush, at her guidance continued fine swirls, swooshes and gatherings of her silk threads, trailing hither and thither, brought silent suggestions of grace and ever-contentment.

The soothing movements provided oh-so tranquil calm to her, as she delicately blinked while regarding her reflection and white cheeks, as loose threads found place in waves at her sides, though fading away to a nicer grouping, stroke by stroke.

This section, that section, gently her hand found way to side, back, all in good stylistic sense.

Time stood still as she strove to align well the sections of her fairness and groomed a nice parting line, playfully holding some hair and thinking this way or that, twix-between the notions of braiding, staying loose-locked or perhaps allowing an easy ponytail to keep her in place that day.

The cool of the room allowed the essence of this moment to seem heavenly eternity.
Thus on she caressed, softened, played now with fingers and allowed her whim to decide on sleek pony-hold with yellow ribbon, in that feminine touch of youthful girlishness.

A hint of smile reached the corners of her mouth as she continued to breathe quietly, noticing all details and lost in the moment from the world around. Perfume mist adorned the room with sweet pleasant aromas to warm the heart and she lay her hands to rest on her lap for a final visual appraisal. Patting away almost unseen dusts or such, she felt satisfied with the arrangement.

Her dress for the day was a white-and-pastel with green leaves sparingly highlighted all over. Her favorite brown woollen button coat, home knitted, was on her. She was almost ready to depart for the day. So much to be done and things had not even totally entered into her mind, but given a brief time, they would indeed.

The room was simple, her dressing table with polished appearance, perhaps melamine, and walls surrounding her of an off-white shade. She simply loved the chandelier, small if it was, but hanging proudly just ajar of centre in the ceiling over her. Strong of height but not overwhelming was her stature as she knew it well, but she was a slender woman and she took care of course about her habits and actions.

The chandelier was not precarious but hung over her, perhaps but a metre beyond her crown of head.

It was a lonely room and there was only one sugar-coated `Nice` biscuit on her simple silver serving tray. The Earl Gray had run cold with a gentle amount at the base of her good tea-with-handle cup. It was rose and vine adorned, this porcelain epicurean pleasure of a goblet that she had allowed herself to purchase, despite her inner sense of modesty. It could make her sigh with pleasure whenever she did imbibe the beverage aromas. She nibbled at the biscuit and finished the tea, just as her mother would say to do, not wanting to incriminate by extravagance of waste. Although to her it was ill to use things that did not taste right, because her stomach was a delicate thing prone to queasiness.

The musty air around her must be dealt with. The lemon at the window should need a replacement to give back a palpable fragrant atmosphere. Or onions, sizzled by fire, yes! Later. For now that must keep as a thought. Myriad thoughts she could keep of course, as can anyone, but she smiled a slight crease to think how silly other people might think her, even for being able to juggle so much.

She felt a little chilled and trusted her sixth sense. Intuition was everything, even for men, or women, who tended to put it away. It was her conviction and something she'd felt ever since she could remember but anything whatsoever. Sensing was her, it might be said.

She thought and thought timelessly, but actually not many moments passed in the opinion of the world. It was less than 10 am.

Scrambling through traffic, finding a nice parking spot...Andrea dashed into the salon and put on her apron. Judith and Mark, the owners and financiers of the business, both happened to be in. They were going over numbers in the backroom. The kettle in the corner was just slowing to a muted whistle. Judith gave Andrea a considerate frown and Guinevere, dashed from around curtain door to the front of salon. Pulling Andrea to the balcony outside the rear, Gwin (as she was also affectionately called) said her piece, giving a mild 'dressing down.' "When it was clear you'd be late again Andrea," Gwin started, "Mark started to lecture me that "the idea of the business is to make money, not just be a place to drop-in like some social centre whenever Andrea feels, even if the customers adore her as they do." The conversation went on. Gwin was a good supervisor but always understanding and not good at looking cross. So anyway, after apologies and explanations, both women set back to the task of meeting customers at the front and attending to things with speed and good technique.

As usual Mrs. Hutchens wanted a perm, and in fact today old Mr Hutchens came in for a beard trim. Andrea could do it, but Mark, an avid beard wearer himself, would pride himself on his abilities and preferred to be called upon to give that "personal touch" and keep "in the loop" with regards to his business' clientele. He kept apace of business management books and whilst some were curiously odd, they did give small edifices of useful information at times. Even Andrea had to admit so, when she had looked one or two over at Mark's insistence.

The Hutchens both quipped as usual that "La Upper Crust" was more suited to a bakery than a salon, but they couldn't argue at the service—especially Jenny, as there were always keen to say, and of course Andrea too. They had trouble remembering Lucy, usually. Nobody could figure out why, considering how fast and how much work Lucy could trail through (she was still an apprentice but it was hard to tell by looking at her, except for her dyed hair colors). The shop was almost guaranteed to be busy most of the day, until late afternoons would come around. Gwin did quite a job of ordering and all the practicalities of presentation and almost anything that would happen, while Andrea was doing more cashiering today.
When a moment became spare for everyone, Lucy took a break outside the front and Jenny was coming back in with some baked pastries for her "fruity filling" lunch. She always kept things simple and ate at the rear of the shop, regardless of Mark's and Judith's presence. As it was they were about to leave soon to their cars anyway, parked in the rear street. The salon had amazing size in the rear room and direct access to a lane way through a cloth-curtained door. When Andrea had first begun at the salon, it was some time before she even realised the rear door actually existed.

Guinevere and Andrea spoke at ease, mostly about Andrea's life lately.
"Lucy knows a Doctor Crystal...and before you say anything, he's said to be a very good analyst, from what I've heard. One or two customers have let on about him too. You know how Mrs. Aldrom likes to gossip. Don't take her speaking alone though. Lucy might be young but she's very cluey for her age as we all know. You really can't go on like this Andrea."

Andrea smiled meekly and could only agree.

"I know Gwin, I know. It's all so messy in my mind. However I don't talk to myself, not much anyway, and you know how I like being at work."

"Huh!" said Gwin..."well I know you do, but we'll have to work on that for the sake of Mark and Judith. Now don't worry I can get you some time off, or even see if Lucy can put in a word for you with Dr Crystal so you could see him at his office on a Saturday. Anyway despite your coming in late you've done well enough today so far. We're all worried about you Andrea."

At that point Jenny came back out and started sweeping. All the girls were trustworthy no matter what the conversation. It was a perk of being in that great parlour of parlay, the hair salon, where many gossips and truths could be told in confidence befitting a confession booth or better.

"You'll be right Andrea..." said Jenny in a higher tone, raising her voice over the radio as she swept some more in a corner, a difficult spot. She was a practical one, with deep brown hair neatly parted at the center and tied down to hang over her shoulder blades. She didn't much believe in doctors, treatments or anything—not even aspirin-- but she knew Andrea had been suffering and had been cajoled into agreeing that Crystal might be worth a try at least as a release-valve for the strange pressures and goings-on in Andrea's life.

Andrea herself wondered if people thought she was a sad case or something, too lonely or whatnot. Was that the image she projected and which now reflected back off others for her mind's eye to see?
Jenny was the kind of woman that boys at school had always overlooked. She was plain, ordinary, boring, dark-tressed and dull somehow. Perhaps too confident and again, that pragmatic nature. She was actually close to Mark the owner—they were second cousins-once-removed. Together with Gwin, who had really built the hair salon from the ground up as an idea, far beyond the financing and input of Mark and Judith, Jenny was like a pillar of the business. She could actually work or laze around with complete impunity, being in Mark's kin, but she didn't usually mis-use the privilege.

Andrea and Jenny were half-friends. Inasmuch Jenny was an independent person and had many friends away from work, Andrea was perhaps also the cautious one, not wanting to cross the line in work relations too far with Jenny. It was complicated, multi-level stuff. An outsider wouldn't be able to work it out for a second. Jenny and Andrea could be laughing off the day and even at a restaurant after work occasionally but their professional sense of distance was still mostly there. With Gwin it was different. Anyway Gwin was the clincher in this case, because really, she and Andrea were the best of dear friends. Very close. Judith had never known what to make of it, having a supervisor and subordinate so much in good association, except that nobody could deny it did wonders for the jolly atmosphere of the salon. Lucy had once said that it was one of the reasons she had turned down other offers for apprenticing after her first year of work. The story was that Lucy was such a speedy cutter that a big-city salon had spotted her and offered her a big salary improvement. Judith, Mark and Gwin were unbelievably relieved that Lucy was so loyal. All things paid off for all and now Lucy would get bonuses each year.

Andrea for her part was colorist. She had done Lucy's locks the several times when the young one had gotten temporarily fed up with her own self-creativity of colors. Andrea kept very good note of trends in coloring, technique and so on. She could advise on shading, alteration and natural vegetable-based alternatives, in addition to repair and shade removal.
The salon itself had stumbled, in some ways by luck onto a winning combination. Gwin and Judith wanted to keep it that way, and Mark, who had a good accounting background, was the one who worried constantly that things could one day change. Unlike some other number-cruncher types, he had a way of beating down suppliers on prices. This meant staff and salon could be well maintained alike. Judith wouldn't have it any other way, on Gwin's instructions anyhow.
When Lucy returned, smelling fragrant, Andrea asked about the Doctor Crystal. Gwin was in ear's range. Mark had already agreed to some time off for Andrea, on full pay. Andrea was worth every iota of money, just as much as the other women. Andrea still had doubts and sighed as she was helping close shop at the day's end.

Mark and Judith were long gone. Andrea didn't like everyone knowing about things. Mark didn't know that much, only that it was about de-stressing.

It had been a quieter afternoon and perhaps it wasn't such a good thing, in that it let Andrea's mind wander incessantly. She stared onto the street at the pitter-patter of rain. Lights out and she said good bye to Gwin, and took Lucy back to her apartment. Jenny rode on her bicycle, with anorak and boots, well prepared for the gushes of water and not at all perturbed by the thunderclaps. Not that her home was far anyway.

It was Thursday. By that evening, Mister..., or Doctor Crystal, rather, was still in his medical office. He took the call himself and advised Andrea he could fit her into a slot tomorrow afternoon due to a cancelation. He was delighted to hear about Lucy and asked after her boyfriend's father. Apparently her boyfriend's father and he played tennis together. Andrea hadn't realised that Lucy's boyfriend was around ten years her senior. The doctor was probably ten years that again, judging by his voice. Dr Crystal advised that his nurse Ms Leah worked alongside him in sessions and would this be okay. Andrea felt better about this and said a quick affirmation.

Lucy might have been 11 or more years a junior to Andrea, but it didn't really show. With the talk of seeing Doctor Crystal, there seemed to be a new kinship developing between the two of them. Lucy was quite a bouncy person and this uplifted Andrea's spirits. Lucy described the doctor as not like the other dry, unemotional kinds of physicians...but not so much that he had outright humor, rather that she was impressed with his line of work as she explained more fervently. He was a hypnotherapist and sleep specialist, but also just a counselor, a "listening ear" that had helped Lucy's uncle cope with his wife's death recently. Lucy was curious about some of her own dreaming and after looking into dream interpretations (amateur and Freudian variants), had seen him in her own right too. She had developed the habit since of documenting her dreams in a diary but was all assured nothing was astray and in her opinion the "committing it to paper" helped amazingly to brighten her day to day living. As had been confirmed by Crystal, it let her tap into sub-level mental thinking and processing of the mind, a kind of untapped potential. Anyway, enough of over-read books and Andrea couldn't help but passingly wonder (privately) if the doctor was being diplomatic in concurring with some of Lucy's ideas. However she didn't want to pass judgments and it was all giving her mind a flutter with possibilities. It was not overwhelming and reassured in a complex way--

Andrea was playing with her own hair at times, curling and twirling this way and that, ruminating over Lucy's chatter on the telephone. Perhaps the conversation was 70 percent of the time Andrea listening. It made Andrea chuckle to herself later when she recollected it.

As Andrea's thoughts and disturbances of late seemed linked to a solid place, at Lucy's insistence they agreed to both go again to the forest to look around and work through some events. Retracing steps was supposed to be cleansing somehow. Lucy hadn't seen the ring and Andrea didn't mention it at any point. "Should I really be going back to that place where my troubles seem to be from?" Inquired Andrea to Lucy.

"What troubles?" beamed the effervescent Lucy. "Maybe you just know the forest from a long time ago, maybe as a child."

Andrea was shaking her head in the negative. "I don't recall that I do at all," she said politely.

"Andrea, I can help and I'm curious to see the place...I wish I could connect my experiences, dreams, anything...to one big place, one significant event. Don't you see? What was it like up there? Is it pretty? I'm sure I've been there a few times myself on nature treks."

"Have you actually? So what do you remember of it?"

"Dense scrub mostly. Squirrel sounds. Dry rocks, stones. How many times have you been there?" So went on Lucy.

"Oh, twice, thrice...I think that's all. I would like to go back, maybe it would help but then another part of me is apprehensive Lucy...I...oh don't mind me, it's just hard sorting out what from what. Am I getting everything muddled up?"

Lucy quickly replied: "Don't think it for a second! There's nothing wrong with you Andrea! You're stressed! We'll work it out! You're good with the customers, good with everyone. So mature...I've never told you that before have I? Don't let it out or there's my reputation for coolness gone!"

Andrea laughed. It had been a while since she'd allowed herself that mirk of lightness. Lately everything was fraught and weighted to gravity.

So they went.

-Fire-

The car was parked at the base of the hills but so as to be away from civilization enough that they needn't worry about curious people being near.
It was twilight time but they were together. Andrea wondered why they had gone in rush and not left it for another day, but it was that happy impulsiveness of Lucy and her vigilant will to help that settled the doubts. They held hands and had good flashlights with them to scare away the shadows that would come soon.

Up the crackling stems of fallen brown branches, crisp leaves and little pebbles cast around, they scaled the gentle slopes upwards in the general direction Andrea now knew as almost 'her path.' Just thinking of it, she hinted then espoused the notion to Lucy. Path can mean many things, as they agreed. What was the power of the mind that could be called? Lucy didn't press the comments too much though. She could see Andrea was anxious and still fragile from it all. Lucy shared some mint sweets with Andrea as they walked. Both chewed thoughtfully.

To anyone who would have seen the two, Lucy looked the less prepared for the trek upwards. Her heels were a little too tall for good walking. Andrea couldn't really suggest otherwise to the unstoppable energy of Lucy. "Stop fussing, Andrea!" The comment had said it all. Lucy had her floral white, and faded pink skirt. It was above her ankles and swayed with the movement up. To her, it allowed for more free movement than any trousers could and anyway she had her silky stockings on, brilliant creme white.
By contrast Andrea had her dress on but, a sea blue-green (a favorite color of hers), with a black gem pendant hanging on the finest thin silvery gold chain. It balanced on her neck and front as though perfectly fitted to just her. She had leggings of much thicker fiber to Lucy, warmer and stronger against any kind of elements (she wouldn't tell Lucy she feared to be bitten again). Her sleeved arms where white, the color of her blouse under her dress and most of all it has to be mentioned that she had her flat-soled good brown boots. Something like a rider's with zipped

sides, they were of finest craftsmanship and had softened graciously with many wears.

Somehow in the midst of more chatter, Lucy stumbled after catching on a vine of some sort. The stones, hillside and clearance were very close at hand now.

Andrea could see them and almost feel something. Something strong. Vibratory in the air itself. At the very moment Lucy fell, a large raven called out in voice "arrr arrrrrr" and it obliterated Lucy's sigh from the fall to the ground. Andrea was oblivious in the confusion and took a few more paces forward, before realising Lucy was not talking. Nor walking. Nobody was beside her now. She turned, looked about in all directions. She called and began to walk at fast pace, backtracking where she'd been. Nothing. Oh no! What was happening? She got to panicking fast. Imagining Lucy was lost or caught up in foliage. Hurt? Abducted? Or left to go back home? No. Why would she do any of those things? She had to be near. Andrea leaned her hand on first one tree, then other branch trees too. Crisp branches and leaves crunched under foot. She wasn't trekking in any good straight line now. Or was she?

An image struck her mind: Of a woman, maybe Lucy, screaming but with no voice emerging from her larynx. Was this the stuff of imagination?

"Come on, snap back to it!" thought Andrea to herself.

She then saw Lucy, ahead but not moving. Sleeping? She ran forward, waving and yelling at Lucy. Only metres to go now. Her waving hand was shining almost unbeknownst to Andrea. The ring. Rubesque and brilliant. A gap in the ceiling of trees broke through and shone at the ring. Almost stabbing at Andrea's eyes, she cried out in pain. Blood singed from her pupil and burnt down her frame but she nearly didn't know it and her body froze to a stop. She couldn't move forward and time seemed to suspend itself still.

Lucy was up, or heaving of chest and beginning to stir. Andrea imagined her rising erect but no, it was just haze, and the ring made a sweep, a whoosh, and this thunderous zap struck like a clap that would break the ear-drums of even the dead. Totally deafening. A ring-beam burnt through trees and Lucy was down again. Down but not hurt, just out of it, cold, down, knowing nothing except the one instant of time she had locked eyes on her work-friend. Yet later Lucy would barely know even of that moment recording in her memory. Dark and black, Andrea was only shadow as the ring of flame from the Rubesque ring just kept pulsing out continually, burning, and now a towering flame of fires was all around. They were trapped. Oddly no smoke came. A moment passed, then Andrea felt herself, felt more, more perception. Smelt more. The smoke of burning timbers brought her back, back, tunneling like through a sea of seas, endless seas in her sweep of mind and she saw all before her, the mundane normal all, the scene of what she and Lucy would call now.

Far down in the civility of town, tinges of angry orange on the hill were seen by a man buying a paper. Derrick ran to the fire brigade house and in record time engines were mounting and great men of action were a-topping themselves in a scramble. Whole swathes of the forested hill were ablaze like nothing seen in recency.

What on Earth? Thought one firefighter captain Brennice. Engines parked, calls to order, hoses and packs readied, teams in coats and boats focused upward in good marching patterns. The man led the charge up the difficult pathways and one of his men heard screams, pleas. They fought off deathly smokes and putrid burnings of ash, out-of-place green shoots, deadened bark and dull sands, a mish mash of many smells and burnings, cinders. An hour had passed. Andrea was clutching at Lucy, protecting her, feeling her so cold. Her eye pained yet the fires were ablaze so near. Thorny cuts were at Lucy's ankle. Andrea's good remaining eye would not lie to her about this. Then a man bolting through saw them. They could not know it, but in a shy lost thought he found it hard to compute why a definite circle around the females was completely aglow but otherwise untouched by the singeing flames. Doubts cast aside, there he was, yellow jacket, coughing more than even the two of them were, hard hat on head and a look of great strength, he didn't wait for his comrades but literally picked them both up in a bear hug and charged through a temporary gap in the ring of fires. The ring of heat and flaming walls that were creeping closer to their protective enclave. They had been nestled in a tiny patch. Andrea had dragged Lucy, almost half-dead to the open patch in the trees. The stones were higher up. Andrea thought of them, neutrally, wondering. Praying. Hoping that somebody, anybody, would come. Even THEM. It wasn't a good time to name them. She thought of the ring and something told her to remember them. Ring, them...same....what?...good or bad or else wise...? Oh this pain...it was burning her and blinding her with headache, nearly more than she could take with her slender frame. Mark the firey and his comrades helped them down and into coats and helped them breathe finer airs, sip cooler waters. Both were assessed by hospital staff. The night went long and the smokes would clear.

The ring...Andrea paid it no attention. Had she tried to throw it off before? She was unable to quite recall. This was getting to be too much.

She wanted so much to rest.
Her eye was patched up. Seen to. A doctor and nurse had already taken Lucy home. Minimal sprain and no other apparent concern, they reported, aside from mental shock. Andrea insisted to know even as she lay there. The hospital made her edgy. By early morning's break she pleaded to be released. The doctor (whose name she didn't catch at this time) relented after giving her advice about the eye. It was clearing already with the drops and rest from light. "You're very lucky, madam. It will heal, but I would not want you to try your fortune again on that lens."

Later that day Andrea felt more herself. She felt even more linked and in friendship with Lucy. They'd endured an unimaginable experience. Down to earth. A fire. Lucy saw only the realistic view of it, when she visited her at home. "I have seen better days, but we had an adventure and we live to tell the tale. I'll be fine, just like your eye will be too, my friend."
Nothing else would she even entertain apart from natural phenomena.
"Accidents, crazy careless people," she said. Any thing like those or a myriad other plausible explanations.
Andrea knew better but couldn't relay it. It didn't matter.

The appointment with Doctor Crystal had to be rescheduled seven days. Completely understandable, his assistant had said after Andrea's duplicate apologies for the late notice.
Andrea unable to work again, by contrast Lucy carried on in the job working even the harder. Not thinking, just working.

In newspaper report the fire chief was quoted. His report was filed with an inconclusive finding. The investigation was hampered by no evidence, no weather reports to explain the forest's "towering blaze." "Some kind of energy. Possible reflections of light or stray lightning strike." were the chief's words, seen on TV evening news.

-Counseling at the Chambers: Dr Jack Crystal-

"Good morning Andrea," said Dr Crystal, hand extended as she entered his room. Ms Leah was behind him. His white lab coat gleamed as though it had only just emerged from a clean and iron. Crystal's desk was quite a mess with stethoscopes, blood pressure meters, many hand written cards, notes, and a large pen caddy. This was definitely a place of activity, Andrea thought to herself. That was somehow a good sign. He had a large filing cabinet off to the corner, a basin opposite and a door leading off to another room. Ms Leah was dressed in white nursing gown and Andrea was invited to seat herself on a low-lying couch. This left her head and shoulders raised but the rest of her lying almost in sleeping composure.

He had a pocket watch, Dr Crystal, and Nurse Leah took a damp cloth to her head and asked her to close her eyes. Crystal went through telling her how things would work, questions and descriptions he would give on how to relax herself and trying to breathe deeply and slowly. This would just be a talking session and if Andrea felt fine here afterwards, it would be possible to try some stronger "talking" therapy. He also told Andrea how he had helped even some government ministers, including one who was now retired and didn't mind being mentioned by name. The idea was, when taking out all the misinformed views some people had, to just relax. Then the patient could think more clearly and cast their mind back. Under guidance the mind could peer and forget about all distractions. A soft, silent environment was important for this.

He sat himself on a side chair and Leah was positioned on a chair at the opposite end of the room. She had a clipboard and also a tape machine on a tray table near her right-hand side. Dr Crystal turned it on and invited Andrea to the idea that they could begin to have their 'resting chat.'

The account of Andrea's experiences to date only emerged slowly.

Andrea began to breathe faster and it was getting nowhere. After an hour of trying to remove tensions and focus things better, Dr Crystal let out a sigh and told her "Don't worry." "There's next time and we can go further."

He consulted with nurse Leah and asked if she would like to return tomorrow, because in his view she could make faster progress and understand better her own situation better this way. As she upped and left, he was stopping the audio recording tape and attending to some notes.

Leah indicated with her hand and guided Andrea out to the reception leading to the outside. She smiled. She hadn't said much in the room itself, obviously being an officious and respectful type of woman, deferring to the well-renowned Dr Crystal. "You'll find it all settles into place. Would you like to come in the morning?" The woman had dull unpainted lips, medium brown hair down to the collar loose and comfortable flat white rubber shoes. The smile on her face was subtle, albeit sincere.

Nodding, "That should be graciously fine," Andrea agreed to the idea without much reason to not agree and that was that.

She slept deeper, kind of more at ease. Dreamlessly, it seemed. Andrea's hairbrush was at her bedside table where she had set it down. Her tresses were neatly plaid around her pillow as she dozed the hours. The new sliced-open lemon at her window wafted a sweet aroma into the air. The fastidious cleaning she had done certainly paid off, but when she woke she did recall Leah's words and tended to agree. Her hand-mirror indicated her eyes were not nearly as black-ringed this new day. Sun shone faintly in the window. The blinds were drawn. Andrea loved the pearly lace and as she sometimes did, was hesitant to disturb their cresses to see the light of the new sky. Overcoming this feeling she pulled back and took a deep breath to see nice life around and a gray bird floating in the high breeze afar off. Now she raised herself fully out of bed and fussed over the creamy sheets. The chandelier above was her pretty inspiration as always. She tiptoed on the coolish floor until slippers slid into her petite feet. Even in gown she had the slim sense of beauty about her, but she didn't like her 'out of bed' look at all!

The tick tock of the clock made her realise that eminent force in daily life: time. There was time. She wanted to bathe herself in the tub this morning. It was a fortunate delight to have the day away from her job, in one sense at least. She wanted fresh warm water for her skin, bread with warm butter and some green tea to give her nose the chance to smell fine aroma and think clearer, clearer. She wanted to wish away the shadows in her mind. The ring didn't bear much thinking as she set about her morning preparations. Now where was her perfumed bottle? Expensive but sweet of sweet it was. Fit for a fine lady, she liked to tell herself!

She was thinking now of her time, back in that dreadful boarding school. Just one year but it was enough...long dreary white halls and floors that always needed polishing. Andrea never could understand what she had done wrong until one of her room friends basically told her that everyone got punished simply because cleaning had to be done. What an eye opener that was on the ways of the world! Anyway as luck would have it, the costs were simply high and so she ended back up at a regular daytime school.
Looking back, arithmetic lessons didn't bode well for her, but literacy seemed almost fairy-like. As a twist, she liked to write, but often included curling numbers and alphabetic letters, artistically on the pages. Her teachers would smile or admonish her to try and stay more focused. Later on she was able to study much better but then came all the crass rivalries, hushed comparisons in the hallways. School's passing to an end was really the best time for her. Real life began. Adult seriousness.

Getting back to Dr Crystal's office reminded her of school days. On his couch again, with Leah once more at the far end of the room, she could just vaguely hear his voice, calling her into more and more relaxation. He had gotten her to look into the swing of his pocket watch this time. Full on! Surely this could either be a waste of time or give some relief. It was worth a try.

Forward some days, it was truly de ja vu. Andrea was getting even more school dreams.
She imagined she was in assembly meetings, then other times in the headmaster's office. Just like her real scholarly experiences, they never made sense and the moral angles she was supposed to take note of just didn't reach any good formation in her mind. Didn't those latest flashy books say that some personalities were...what was that word...kinaesthetic? More wholesome, or holistic, yeah. That must have been her. It fitted well. She had

to experience more directly to learn anything at all. It was why
she had loved her apprenticeship and the first time she'd seen a
color-kit for hair, what a grand impression that had presented to
her! She always thought her mother colored her hair for the sake
of father, but it just wasn't discussed. So many things were like
that. On the verbal banned list and there to stay. Mind, Andrea
was the same herself as she would freely admit.

Again visiting in the office of Dr Crystal, she saw he looked more
lifted in spirit and his studious-as-ever assistant Nurse Leah bore
herself ever ready: Andrea fell asleep this time but had apparently
said quite a lot. The next day she was rushed into another
appointment. The doctor was enthusiastically keen. Andrea had
heard the tape of the previous session for herself. Leah had
jumped at the idea as good even if initially Crystal wasn't so sure.
Yet to his credit, he had relented without much of a furrow of
eyebrow. Andrea thought his coat looked a bit more dusty and
the edges of his sideburns were a bit more gray against his
otherwise brown temple and crown. Occupational hazard? She
had noticed his gold ring before; he was aware of her Rubesque
band.
As he rose to shake her hand again and do some initial idle chit
chat on the weather, he brushed his desk one moment in animated
gesturing. He was talking about his new automobile but his
notepad fell carelessly to the ground. "Sword" had been scrawled
a little larger than some of the other notations. Andrea asked
about it and he, and Leah, said she had indeed mentioned it in
connection to the gem on her finger. Leah and Crystal hadn't
thought the ring so extraordinary. Leah herself had no jewelry at
all except her turquoise and silver earrings. Dr Crystal knew
about various art fairs and had seen some bejewelled items at
shows.
"It appears very old, like some of the collections I've seen,"
inspecting it closer, leaning over, "though I don't see anything
blade or sword like. It might be some mental false association.
Probably nothing important."

Andrea couldn't put her thoughts perfectly on it, but the ring
seemed so dull these days. Was it more so during her time in this
very office and consulting room?
Almost drawing on her thoughts, Crystal said, "Maybe it needs
some careful polishing and jewelry fluidisation."

"Oh," said Leah "I've heard of that too...but maybe I'm not much of an expert. How about you Andrea? Best we'd choose a time to begin anyhow, Dr Crystal." She seemed to say this without giving grace to Andrea's reply.

In all honesty Andrea was curious about all the things being transcribed as she made recollections under relaxed state, but in another way she was dearly missing Gwin, Jenny, Lucy and even the inextricable team of Mark and Judith. Her job was her purpose, and her creativity. She loved the balance from door to door: At home she had the balance, the puritan air of simple surroundings and then at work, it was a buzz of action, color, change. Unlike some other people, Andrea's feeling was that this was life, living between planes of existence.

It struck her that perhaps the forest was now adding to her repertoire. It was adventure and the lure of that former unknowable. It reminder her of her colleague. Lucy had the discoverer in her. She'd even been sailing...but now Andrea had to think back to the now, the words shimmering from Crystal and asking if she was "still there, ready," etc.

So the questions began and setting the scene.

"Now," the doctor said, "What are you doing? What can you see?"

The click of a tape as Leah moved to another blank. "Fields, bloomings, there's a creek and so much peace." Andrea had begun.
The visitors were not here. "No, no." Andrea with eyes closed, insisting. Crystal had asked her again about the place, the Sword people (his interpretation, somewhat bad, of 'Zordant'). Sometimes as things would progress beyond an hour, Andrea would be drifting off, losing volume of voice and consistency. Words would slur. It was a problem with these sessions with others too. He encouraged her to use the hypericum tea. It was light and good in between sessions as a way to encourage and open up calmness in the patient. Not a drug, just a balancing point. A floral plant, just as in the photo book he had in his cabinet.

Crystal hoped and wanted to see how the Swords linked to the fields Andrea could see, and what of this rock, stone, forest, whatever. To his inquiring mind, Andrea was an unusual visualist, and patient. She connected to anchored things in this real world. He thought it might be a traumatic earlier life, a holiday gone wrong that she was remembering. Anything. Clearly she wasn't mad. Regular job, good life, friends, albeit very work-centred. She wasn't so old as to be a spinster. Besides, Leah herself, his assistant, showed that not all unmarried women were unbalanced. He was liberal enough to see that, even where normally speaking his profession was firm in conservative thinking, caution and the familial life. He'd read all the cases and seen so many of his own, where if only people had been in concrete relationships and sturdy lives, their psychological forays would have simply fizzled out of the picture. Productive life was the chief good, this was the premise in medicine and indeed, he would argue, society itself. It didn't mean trappings of money, but just having a life where one could feel good in whatever one contributed to the world, whether small or greater. The thoughts zapped about him.

It was hard to get connections in the story Andrea told. He wouldn't bother seeing the forest in person. Clinically purposeless. He read the newspapers and saw the photographs. There was nothing remarkable in any of the locations and was already seeing plain explanations in the forest fire.
Andrea just needed to open up as she was. Professional discussion could uncover fears and lost emotions, incomplete thoughts in the synapses. Then the pieces of the puzzle would let her go on. He admired her courage to keep coming back, in all forthright audacious primacy.

"That will conclude today's session, Andrea. I should thank you for coming," he ventured and clasped her a handshake with both his hands, followed by a nod to the head and a look to Leah, who in turn assented a tilt of her head almost in perfect congruence. "Miss Leah," he clicked his thumb silently and opened his palm. The latter instinctively took out one of the duplicate tapes and then upped to move across the room and give it to him.
Thus he again handed her a tape of the previous session. Whether it helped move things along or not was difficult to guess. Her

stories were remarkable but then dulled to a murk. There didn't seem to be much more.

Telephoning her the next day, early in morning, he said he couldn't find a further need currently for their sessions. With rest and her life as it is, tea and all, he told her "I feel you've made great progress and we can discuss later any points I can summarise. I'll send the final tape to you and call your employer. Do you want to return to work again next week?" he invited her to this idea. He was thinking of other patients with varying other studies to do but also of Andrea's better interests.

Andrea was still in bed when the call came through and she cocked her head to the side when he asked about her reattending to her job. She smiled and instantly the next moment said "Absolutely!" After grace and thanks, that was that.
Later on she heard the tape. If anything it was boring. She had other thoughts in her and it all made sense. She wasn't convinced whether things were dreamt or accurately described what had happened to her.
After dialing on the telephone, the call connected. "I know I'm being a pain perhaps, but can I speak with the doctor a moment?" she asked Leah.   It was done after a pause of some minutes.

Apparently he was taking a lunch break still "Yes, connecting Doctor Crystal...ah Andrea, yes, that's fine, do tell, what is on your mind? How was the tape?"

They spoke for several moments. "I can put together some notes if you like to help you get a feel of it all. It's not a problem at all, to my mind to do this. These studies can be very useful.   The more knowledge the better for everyone, for other patients."

"Was it dreaming I had, only?" she had a lilt of doubt and innocent questioning in her voice.

"Oh. I'll put it to you in writing to better surmise it, Andrea. I like to reflect on these things to gain a picture after letting the possibilities settle. Professionally it's a bit like what a judge on a court case does. You understand. Let's think at this point that you have learnt more about the memories and this is what is really good: drawing out and balancing the thoughts. Putting pieces

together. Like completing a jigsaw. I know you'll work better.
Keep talking about anything and if your night sleep gets sour
again you know where I am."

"You've been very obliging, doctor." In side thought she tried to
imagine him younger, only to momentarily brush away the
imagery. For truly, his demeanor was too clinical to appeal
beyond medical halls.

"You're welcome, Ms. Levison." He replied courteously after her
thanks, and then cleared his desk. He thought a little and wrote a
word then filed away her details. Summarising could wait a bit
and then he could consider the sessions a success. The great joy
of the job was just helping people. He had many patients and an
excellent life, full, with lots of academic pursuit available. He
could write another paper soon for the university. There was no
doubt about it and Andrea's case would be another component of
wider research. Results...that's what his professor supervisor used
to say..."assisting lives."
Yes. There was the matter of the upcoming conference. He had
told Andrea at the end of their last session. It was not
unprofessional to do so.
Their sessions were friendly, with good professional distance.
Leah helped immensely with that and in turn it helped his
academic standing.
The crux of matters though, was that in one particular note,
Andrea's marital accounts (on tape in sessions) were so intriguing.
Figmented imagination, yet even so, the content invited for
catharsis' sake some use in psychological conference with his
peers and medical colleagues. She could be guest speaker at a
"hallmarks of marriage breakdown and long-term illness"
government-funded society conference. He gave assurance that
she wouldn't face questioning of any kind; although due to her
shyness she settled on her semi-friend Jenny (the hairdresser)
stepping in to do this. It had been agreed and now Crystal called
the convener to finalize the arranging of it. All was going well.
Clockwork. A diligent man, in prime, a leader in his work field,
pioneering. He knew it.
Marital matters were a new angle for him. Using Jenny for the
presentation gave it a sense of common personage and this gave
more reality to things. It was well practiced that substitutes could
be used where it was in the best interest of clients, patients,

others. With a twitch of his nose he pondered a moment if disclosing the fact it came from figments of imagined memories was vital, or not.

Leah was in the next room busy taking calls, notes, and sipping her tea. Dr Crystal's wife had called earlier. Leah didn't expect another call, but by the looks of it, the doctor was having another long day. He was behind schedule seeing another patient and busily making calls and writing files.
It seemed she would miss her evening at the cinema again. Prudent sense of mission took away her sigh of disappointment and she fixed again the bun of her hair. Her cheeks as always had a whitened glow to them.

The next day passed without anything of note. As did the next. Andrea had only a few clients and went home early from her workplace at the salon.

Up again with a bounce out of bed, Andrea set to her brushing of hair and had a sense of purpose this morning. She left the bedroom, almost in rush, dust and all. She didn't like doing that, but she wanted to be down the stairs and out to her good ol' job. The quaint spaces there gave her an "everything." She had toast with honey and tied back her hair, laced up her dress, put on her best soft blue cardigan and practically pranced out to the car. In she got and off at a steady cruise. Only minutes later she was parking and after the gravel, strolled in the door of the front way.

With a smile she saw Jenny. Today was good, because yesterday evening had been that conference. "How was it? That meeting?" she so eagerly asked Jenny who was brushing up chairs and spraying some frothy polish on the customer mirror screens. Was it going to be a fully occupied day? Everyone seemed in high swing. Later Lucy showed Andrea her bound up ankle. Underneath it was actually healed but Lucy had become affectionately attached to this latest "fashion" accessory. Both women giggled at it during the morning break.
Jenny told her it had gone well. Tricky questions were avoided afterwards. The doctor had actually given her some prepared notes and Jenny thought it was a nice occasion, although afterwards she felt a little out of place, so she hadn't stayed. As a guest speaker it didn't matter. The doctor was thoroughly in

discussion with colleagues and dignified peoples from every direction. The doctor had also given her a note as she left, thanking her and he followed it up with a quick telephone call telling her that indeed, everyone had thought the experience remarkable, that a dream could be that deep in content and detail.

Andrea was in her own bounce of things and feeling light-hearted. Maybe good was coming from it all and life becoming simple again.
Oh simple was so good, she could kiss the air! From the time of being a little girl, she adored simplicity, happiness, little pleasant feelings like the new toy in her hand, her mother's kind gaze, a cool day breeze after summer noon's rise. Yes!
The day whizzed by with a zest. Andrea had worked in tandem with Jenny on a woman that hadn't been in before, who wanted a cut and color but keeping the straight look. Perhaps for a date? Lucy, from the corner of Andrea's eye every now and then, wasn't working quite so fast but still doing amazing stuff with women, boys, and men. The takings were excellent this day, business wise—but this was more a matter for Judith and Mark, of course. Gwin had been in but had to leave early with something like morning sickness. The remaining women wondered about that! Baby news? Likely not, but such was the first thing that was instinctual for them to think possible.

With Gwin off, each of the women took a longer and lazier kind of lunch break. Andrea spent hers looking in nearby gift shops at all the delights and displays. She felt strong and like weights were lifted off her. Even the ring felt good this day—nothing could match its dazzle. It was like a child's secret, with brilliance she could see much more than anybody else! She did think in tiny moments about past events of late, but with a zillion thoughts in her head most of the time this was expectable. It was just that this time, they didn't matter, they shot in and shot out, 'sans souci' as the French would say? She supposed that was right. She arched on her heels and hurried back to complete the afternoon's work.
Home time in the door for her today was 4.30pm sharp. Great! She could try a new curry steak recipe.

Time zoomed to the next day. She'd bundled up the leftovers in the cooler. Yeah, as soon as she awoke that was front of mind in her. Looking at the jewel on the finger, after her obligatory morning stretch, her head lifted. Between slits of the blinds she caught daylight: A good sunny one today, she thought! Nobody would see it, but seeing as she'd awoken refreshed but early, she set to cleaning up: dusted the wardrobes, floors, everything. Sheets changed, put out to clean. Watered over. Kitchen spotless, more than she would even endeavor. She liked balance, not obsession. Her hair washed immaculately and brushed to include bouncy waves today. She hair-pinned the sides near above her ears and felt so feminine and soft. Her hand mirror at the ready and she allowed herself a smile. She could never be haughty and just did it for her, but she was happy and glad anyways, overall.

Still slender. She'd dreamt, but then forgotten it. Good sign?
Gwin would probably say just that, helpfully.
Now. That curried steak. She'd offer it to the others. Lunch wasn't important. Just a biscuit again. She made tea. In spite of all she'd done, her efficiency was immense when she felt this good, so barely any time had passed. She reached work before the nick of time.
A good day ended well and while Lucy didn't like the curry inspired dish, Jenny and Gwin had both gleefully completed the contents.
None went to waste, which to all was a good thing. Gwin had been wondering when Mark would be in again, or Judith for that matter. Perhaps they were off with families respectively or vacationing a day or two. It was that way sometimes and so it was with proprietors: They were a different pecking order with a variant pace of life and responsibility beyond.

Then at home, Andrea felt good and tired. Pulsing nice feelings. She looked over the newspaper that had been handed to her earlier and then closed her eyes to kind of reflect and meditate. Deep breaths. On a soft living-chair. Sleep overcame her and unknown dreaming enveloped her...

-Lights Out-

Andrea was tossing and turning, heaving with breath on the
sheets. Wrestling with linens and whites. Hairs tangling, then
sudden calm and murmur. It was happening again, she would
think it later in the day-wake. For five straight nights, this dream
would envelop her after sweet regular days. Why?
Now this night, she was gasping at air, struggling, fighting for her
will and mind. She was draped on the bed, a tall-off-the-ground
one, with banisters at the corners, a brass golden headpiece at the
end. Beautiful red-trimmed lace pillows sheltered her head,
under, beside, both sides. Under a single sheet on a balmy night,
all messy, parts of her legs and arms splayed uncovered. Sweat
and masculine smell starts to waft into her nostrils unstoppably.
There is no resisting. Dull piano tunes are lost to the choral past
in this mindspace she was living. Living in living. He is strong,
husky and grunting. Muscular and bold. Like a pirate, drips of
sweat as his arms are coming down. One moment he was just a
bystander at the bed, looking her over, elegant and white. Then
now, whipped where in time so fast, making no sense, he climbs
on, invading her space, knees on bed, arms checking to her throat.
One arm, then the other comes around, he is twisting and then
straightens. She feels her pulse under his vice grip. Pulse of life
flushing blood up her neck to temple. Her chest beating, he is not
interested and his look is undecipherable in meaning but intense.
He stares out of hazel stark eyes with huge whites now lining fast
with blood lines like a tingle. The frown is there, bristling hairs
on his brows that she is noting as she finds consciousness. She
turns her head, she cannot speak, unknown forces preventing.
Him? Paralysis? The ring is on a table, too far, but why is she
wondering this as her invader looks her over? What could it do,
what is calling her to such a notion in utter moment of calamity.
He grunts something inaudible, or unintelligible, then shakes at
her. He is lifting her head, will he shake and strangle the life out
of her? He panics, she panics. Whoosh, whoosh. It is her own
body, it has to be...she is draining away. Then a clap of hands
and she is up! Bolt up.

There is no man. She is out, free. Wind blows at the white
curtain, as though somebody has just vanished out. A cruel
wheeze of wind enters, chilling her, but she is in cold heat. Head

pulsing, and the ring—in her right hand. She undoes the pressure. Her hand was holding it so tightly, it had left an impression on her palm, awful red gushes. She drops the ring to the bed near her lap and shakes her hand, moving it in and out, spinning it. Trying to let the circulation bring it back. Ewww, it looked horrible. The ring. The ring. Back on the table. Wait. It wasn't on the table, was it? Her eyes layered out of foggy vision. What white curtain? Her breathing was returning to calm and her thumping chest was reclining itself more softly now. She had blinds, not curtains. Oh, details! Thank goodness dear me, at least she could see where she was now. She pulled at her dress with fingers, straightening out the creases and folds. Above: the chandelier. She smiled just a tiny nuance. At least some matters were a constancy. Andrea happened to want to do her hair. She turned to the side, put her legs on the floor to get up. Then decided to adjust her hair. Up the hand mirror, to her face, oh my goodness! Marks at her neck? What is going on?

Enough of doctors. The pale black and red could be attended to. She had pale shades of makeup to use. No. A high collar was called for too. It didn't fit with her style and much of her clothing generally, but nothing much to do about that. She didn't doubt she'd be conscious of not letting anyone see her neck the whole day and hoping that by home-time it would be faded at least a little.

She cried in the car, tears streaming all the way to work. Nobody paid attention in the rushing hour of the day. Absent-mindedly she nearly struck another vehicle. This was the last thing she needed. It wasn't her best time of month. Everything was disastrous. Who did this man think he was, waking her slumber? She felt venom, a little rage, which wasn't like her at all. Yet she also couldn't work out what this recurring vision meant. She went over all the details. Knowing it all by heart now, it really did seem hard to know if he meant to see her breathing and well, or if he was her killer. Lurking, preying, at a moment of weakness. Was she ill? Would she be ill? Is she ill now? Omen? No. No, no, no. Reality check needed.
She worked the day in silence. It was quiet and she thought a lot. Her colleagues gave her space. Either they sensed she needed it, or they were being polite because of everything that had been before. Andrea imagined they were hoping she was recovering

and were on eggshells around her. With a sigh, it seemed to her an icky thing to be an object of pity. She could be strong, she had her home, her job. Keep on thinking, she told herself, good things, real things, true things.

-Delivery-

Andrea finished writing her letter to Bridgette. The latter lived much further north, somewhat almost in mountains but a very pretty area when the fog would lift for a time. She put on a fluffy coat and got out the door. Stamp at the ready and glued on (she always kept spares to save on post office trips at inconvenient times), the post office drop-off pipe was only a few skips away from her downstairs access to the main pavement. Uneventfully she clumped her way with heels a little too high for the trip and her pretty pink skirt showing under the big coat. It wasn't the warmest of days and this was late day cool. The sun was already disappearing from behind horizon. She so hoped Bridgette was doing fine in her northerly retreat, where she took in guests sometimes who were looking for a farm homestead experience. The chickens and cows outnumbered the people! It was quite a world away, in Andrea's image of it.

This was how the earlier part of the day had gone: She'd worked, it was a quiet day with perhaps the highlight being the drive home and a soft paper and sofa waiting for her with some warm vegetables and lentils from the kitchen's cooking efforts. Gwin hadn't been there at work, Lucy was off with a headache and so Jenny and her had taken a leisurely day. Jenny had been at a shop and posting some documents to the accountant on behalf of Judith and Mark. Andrea had been just with her thoughts and a soft music piece. Classical. On the old radio set. Blissful. She was sweeping, dusting, humming as she worked. Even a little whistle to the silence of the room. Could it be always like this and feel wonderful? Andrea wondered a moment when Jenny came in the door, making the entry bell tingle as it always would. "Back." Jenny merely said. Andrea smiled to her colleague. They'd only seen two more customers that day and then written a note in case Gwin came in early next day. It wasn't so unusual for some quiet days, however it was good to let their supervisor at least get a feel for what had happened.
Jenny took her bicycle in Andrea's car this time. It was so windy outside and Andrea thought, but didn't say, that Jenny was worried about being knocked over!

-Self Again-

Anyways, now that Andrea had done her postal 'duty' it was time
for some green tea with honey. She wrote a diary entry.
Scrawled with her pretty script. If she wasn't a hairdresser maybe
she could have done training to be a sign writer? She giggled. It
wasn't good to be too self-proud. It didn't become her at all, but
she allowed herself the pleasure of the thought, as we all do, of
what it could be to have undertaken a totally different path in our
working sojourns.
Donning her white gown with curly frills at the neck and ankle
hems, she hummed as she dusted surfaces and polished some cups
on her little cabinet. She only had a few ornaments including
silver trays (the ones of the entertaining kind with cups, plates,
best spoons and so forth), an oaken wood carving with a clock
face arranged in it (not wound up, thus completely inaccurate for
time keeping) and some glassware. The one time she'd seen a
foundry she'd been captivated by glass, how it could be worked
hot to all kinds of bubbled and elegant contours. When it was
done just right, the glass would be etch-free and could reflect the
light in a dazzle of temporary rainbow beams. Pure loveliness!

Now, time to get to that chandelier. Her stepladder was in a linen
closet, ewww, too much dust. It took her half an hour to sweep it
out and put the dustpan away. With disgust she lifted away the
cobwebs and shuddered to think that hairy little arachnids had
been unwanted guests. She used her typical concoction of
cleaning agent and spray to ensure that wouldn't happen again.
Now finally she could lift the stepladder, venture up the stairs and
slide the bed aside slightly. Then she upped herself. She didn't
need much height and frankly didn't want her slender frame to go
tumbling off. She knew her limits and hated bruising. Besides,
that neck marking was only fading still. What a
nuisance!...polish, polish, polish. Now it seemed more the white
and lovely thing it should be. She'd had to work by candle
because there wasn't much light even with the blinds fully open to
the world. She blew out the orange flame-diamond with a gentle
whiff (her delicateness showed indeed) and tried the chandelier.
Excellent! Brighter than ever. She closed the blinds now. It felt
a bit weird keeping them open even if nobody was about below
and outside to peer in.

The home was looking immaculately clean and Andrea couldn't have been happier about it.

She went to bed. This time, the same dream occurred...but she was spared the worst. It was incredulous to think that she drifted in and out of sleep but actually woke up quite refreshed. In total she'd slept long and well.

So now things had thawed and she was working nearest the doorway at "La Upper Crust" today. Being the greeter was quite an ease this day. Gwin complimented her when the salon was empty a moment. "You really seem a blaze of merriment today Andrea, it's so good to see!"

Jenny was sipping tea by the register and Lucy was putting away some implements that helped her curl for customers. It was her true specialty, but it lent itself to high style and of course, understanding the complete opposite as well: totally straight hair-do's. Part of the trick was cutting before the curling process. Waves were something in-between and ironically Jenny couldn't measure those as well—but Andrea and Lucy could!
Andrea saw a little bag at the feet of one of the customer stools. Gwin saw it as Andrea bent at knees (correctly) to pick up the item and said "Oh! It must have been left behind...erm, Jenny, I think that was where Mrs. Hyler was sitting, wasn't it?"

Jenny agreed "it sure was, should we put it aside for next time she comes in?"

Lucy chirped to Jenny, then turning her head to finish sentence at Gwin: "Don't bother looking in the appointment book, she comes in a bit irregularly...but I know what street she lives in! Erm...Hemler...yes, that's it! Maybe we could take it there later, she'd be very relieved. Should we check there's nothing missing with it?"

Gwin the ethical: "Mmmm we'd best not do that, Ann is a kind of private person from what I can tell. Andrea it's calming down a bit, do you fancy an extra long lunch break? You've worked hard this morning. You could also see in on Ms Griffiths for that home appointment, too. I'm sure she won't mind an early call."

"Yeah you didn't take your break, Andrea! It's a good day for a walk, be our guest!" after saying it, Lucy did a silly bow.

Andrea burst a little laugh and agreed.
The bag was black and velvety. Tiny. She secured it inside her own duffel and off she trotted. Reaching Hemler might take a leisurely half-hour.

There the streets were a bit gray in tone, unlike the day sky. It was quite sunny and uplifting for the mood. As she made her way afoot to Hemler street, the scenery changed from dense urban to a more rolling sub-urban, and then she ascended the hill of the said street. Hyler's home was atop, and larger than some other homes downhill. Rusty gates gave way for her easily, even if they were above her head. The garden was thick, like a jungle almost, but one could still see through to the home. It looked governor-esque with a kind of facade, and had quite big windows.

Knocking at the front door, Andrea took a deep breath and waited only a moment before Anne's invitation "It's open, do come in! You're a bit early, but...Oh! You're from the hair salon!"

Andrea introduced herself by name with a smile and extended hand. She felt a bit meek at what Anne said next: "Ah yes you always do look so bright and skilled at your craft."

"Speaking of craft," Andrea ad libbed, "your home has a very fine kind of its own."

"Ah yes," Anne agreed, through a wrinkly smile and her soft pale pink lipsticked lips, "it does indeed and has served me so long. I can't get around to dusting it as much as I want mind, and the weekly cleaning seems to cost more and more. 'He' wouldn't like it at all if he were here just now." She said this with a nod of head at a small picture across from her window-side seat. The room had various arrays of furniture, some dusty-gray and others more colored, but none of them severe in effect, in what was a stately looking big room. "It's my late husband."

Andrea smiled again but didn't know quite what to say. "Oh," Andrea said, nearly forgetting the purpose of the arrival, "you left a bag at the salon. I'm sure you don't mind my coming by to return it to you."

Anne lifted out her hands to take it, swiftly and then carefully turning it in her hands. "I must be mindful of the energies. I was wondering where it'd gotten to. It's my more favorite bag for my craft."

Crafts again? Andrea thought. "What is you craft?"

"Readings. In fact it's very good fortune for you, young lady that you did find it and bring it here."
Seated, she opened the rope tie, the black bag's contents fell to place in her skirt lap. Then she crooked herself to lean forward and pulled the glass table at her side to the front of her. She moved the contents around and they were like colorful tiles. Cards, thick, but still cards.

Andrea gazed intently, curious and surprised by the cards. Some were blank with facedowns, but others showed the most amazing scenes, very old looking, questful, and highly symbolic. Some with numbers and so forth.

"I can tell you're not familiar with these," Anne said. I would be honored to thank you for their return, by consulting them for you. In a sense Andrea was curious about them. Anne explained quickly what they were and what she did. Andrea's eyes widened and her brows raised, to which Anne laughed.

"Your reaction is not unlike some I've seen before from new people. Don't worry, they don't bite! They can focus your feelings and I've read them many times. To the skeptic they are a useless wonder, but in fact what they do is to energise your attention and help you consider options for tomorrow, and beyond. That's how you can consider it, and you'd be very close to a good truth about them."

Andrea wasn't so much afraid but intrigued by the symbols and so on. Anne set about picking them up and giving them a shuffle. Then she shuffled even more, with speed and skill. She huddled them back into the back and used the soft clothy silk to move them some more inside. Then she shook it, turned it, flipped it upside down and more. It was more artful than a quick description might be imaged, but in the end, Andrea had no doubt the cards were so randomized that they would be beyond any memorable order, even if it were possible they had an order or flow.

"Care to see? It could help you, who knows? Or you just might forget it and go on your way without much a-do. If I may I should insist as a hostess that I give you this hospitality." Anne said that with a warm inviting smile.

After the reading Anne and Andrea spoke some more moments. Andrea asked about the cards some more and Anne went on to discuss the theories of how and where the 'craft' came about. Kings and Queens, playings, quests of life, Italian dominion in northern provinces. A beginning, just like everything had a beginning. Egypt? That was another speculation. The mystique was there, but Anne in a sense considered it all natural and whilst she was part of the mystique by very way of her 'craft,' she was so relaxed about it all and quite earthy by appearance, manner and more. Perhaps that was to remove some misconceptions? Her age? It wasn't really certain and Andrea ended up leaving later without much more thought on it.
The cards had been laid out in a kind of cross fashion for the reading and Anne had spoken out the cards and their significance, then told Andrea it was a general view of her before, now, and 'later.'

At the mention of Swords, it jolted Andrea. Her mind got a bit distracted in the quietness of the room. Anne's voice sounded focused and monotone. Just a trickle of water nearby was the only breech of the silence. Swords. "Did someone say Zord?" Andrea thought in her mind.

"Yes, Swords!" Anne said, paused, then went on, looking into Andrea's eyes some more now, and then gradually turned back to the cards. It seemed Andrea had thought aloud, without quite knowing it.
Anyhow, the reading ended and Andrea bid her thanks, with Anne bidding her own thanks and a wave of hoping Andrea great days ahead. They'd see each other in the salon, as Andrea put it, as she left.

Anne closed the door slowly and Andrea went along the path, past the greenery and down the hill again. Where had she previously thought of Zord, Swords, or whatever?

Then she recalled. With a frown of eyebrows and thoughtful look on her face, she made it back to the salon. Two hours and a half had passed.

Her colleagues exclaimed she'd been gone a tad longer than they thought she would be. It was okay. "I'm afraid I never got to Ms Griffiths, ever so sorry."

"You're in might lucky on that, Andrea," advised Gwin. "She wants tomorrow and Lucy is so keen to do the honours. So all's well."

Gwin, Jenny and Lucy had kept pace in the salon quite well enough and not long later it was time to close, but they were intrigued to hear of Andrea's time at Mrs. Hyler's home. Lucy had seemed most amenable to the card-reading idea as feasible or perhaps 'fascinating.' Gwin didn't pass judgment particularly and Jenny remembered seeing readers at a circus fair some years ago.

Andrea got home and closed the door with a thud. A gust was rising outside and she didn't want it in. She put on the kettle for some tea and took off her coat and boots. Then she stoked and lit the fire. It wasn't too cold, but not exactly a warm evening, either. Deuce of Swords? Two. Whatever. A flood of memories came back to her. They'd idled in her mind the afternoon, but now more intensely with the pressures of work away from her. She blew out a breath of air. Hmmm. Why, why? Just when peace was in her, all this disturbance again! After a drink and a brushing of her hair, followed by browsing some mail and papers, she came to something of a realisation. No. She didn't really find any help much from the reading and put it away from her thoughts with that. Leave card readings for people who want that. All the help in the world seemed at odds anyway. Was there even a problem? It just wasn't clear. The thoughts just got a bit murky sometimes and she just oh-so wished they could all be sorted out, compiled, filed away correctly. Kind of like a secretary might do. She giggled at the analogy. What a mindless job that would be! Saying yes-sirs to a boss in a gray box of a room, in the world of business. No way! Hair was real, common to all people of all walks and it invigorated her. Yes, it was something tangible, subtle, simple and yet allowed for much happy productivity too, with little challenges and many chances at interesting conversations. She had even worked on the hair of a government minister, proving her point of how her trade was ubiquitous to life.

Come evening, a rotten dream encroached on her sleep. She woke up just the once but it was enough to make her kind of cranky. On went the chandelier. It was some time after 2am and she decided to have some cocoa. The newspaper was on the table and she nibbled at a self-baked biscuit. Coconut. Maybe not enough this time. Or was it the butter? Oh! A new museum opening. That might be interesting to see!

Tomorrow was Friday. The very next day after that, she could go to the museum and browse the art of the really creative types. She was creative too, she had to be, but...oh, she knew what she meant to herself anyway...her creativity was fast and practical. Whereas the art makers could take time, leisure, perhaps painfully, but after long sessions of sweat and pain would produce things that she could admire and adore. Imageries! She'd loved such since a 10-year-old girl. It was like being transported to a million places with fields, castles, beautiful ladies and charming men, bridges and rivers, windmills and tulips and a hundred other things, all in the space of mere meters of wall-space.

The next day she raced through, like a child, wanting to dash her way and catapult into the weekend, even more than most workers do. She made good safe time even through the traffic.
A strange, possibly Zordant face entered her dream with words but even these couldn't dull her enthusiasm.

Now was Saturday. Visiting open day!

-Museum Visit-

The queue outside wasn't much of a queue. Andrea sighed a
moment, thinking of how not everyone appreciated the fineries in
life. She had put on some of her finest clothing: rare for her, a
silver brooch, on her neat cream white plain blouse, and soft
cyan-colored loose ankle-length skirt. She had her polished black
boots on, with their soft leather, suited to walking and comfort as
much as any other shoe one could imagine. Her knitted cardigan
coat finished off her appearance. Her light tresses of hair hung
down her shoulders and were lost behind her back. She felt good
but blended into the roaming figures.
She got her ticket and proceeded past the ticket window to the
inside. People ambled about, various older men in good blazer
coats, couples, and a mixture of ages. Even a small child, in tow
with its mother, but not really interested except in touching
everything in sight with pasty little fingers of excitement. It
seemed "mommy" was having a hard time keeping her little one
out of troubles.

After an hour of looking around, it crept towards midday. The
viewing time was over until after lunch. Andrea didn't mind, she
would venture back home to enjoy a sandwich, but at the moment
she was captivated by a pastel depiction of a rowboat under a
river. The scrawled name underneath was "Oscar Kirby," not a
name that came to her mind, although she wasn't an art critic as
such so that might not mean the visual artist was unknown. The
brushwork was rough but captured a good reality. She stared at it
with an intensity, and got to wondering if she'd ever get to
Venisey to feel the rowboat experiences spoken of in books of
old. It brought up visions of harmony in her and the bounty of
life, fine grapes, good cheeses and more.

As it were, the gallery was emptying out. An usher was moving
about the halls, his black pants and red coat with tails bobbing
around corners. Andrea was lost to the world but the usher was
making his way forward to ask her to leave for the lunch
interlude.
The trouble is, the usher was helping an old man to be guided out
the entry way, and Andrea was still looking at the Kirby work.
She was alone in the hall and realised it.

Turning to go, something didn't feel right, but then, she started to walk anyway.

After three steps she again thought something was wrong. Whooshing noises? Screeching?

Outside. Shatter.

At this point Andrea thought it best to get out of the area, and get the attention of someone. Glass had broken; the noise was distinct to her ears indeed. Men's voices were hushing but husky. She found the exit but an alarm was going now.

"Come this way madam," said the usher, holding her briskly and marching her to an office. Another usher brushed past them, running.
What he saw was only the dirty footsteps on the floor, and a missing hanging space where a painting had been.

Police were called and the ushers had Andrea down in a small curator's office. They didn't look at all friendly or bemused. Was she a witness or suspected? The two ushers were talking softly outside the door of the glassed room she sat in. She heard enough to understand that her being found had slowed down the effort to find the missing painting.

A heist.

She saw a man in three-piece suit come in, looking tired and with elegant moustache. He didn't speak to her. Two police were with him and she was taken away to a car. In just minutes she was in a dark interview room.
She was truly terrified. For a long time she was left in the room alone.
Then the officer asked her what happened, asking her about glass fragments and whom she worked for. The questions were fired like rapid volleys and she felt confused. She'd only been admiring the Kirby painting and forgotten the time. She'd heard the noise and been trying to depart.

The policeman showed no sign of believing her.

She broke down and sobbed. "What's happening to me?" she merely said with her face downcast. Her head fell into her slender arms, on the bare table.

After yet a still longer time and again hearing hushed tones outside this room, she began to feel like a marionette, unable to control her own movements and day life. The policeman who seemed to be senior confirmed she was free to go, after handing back her bag and asking for the third time her address details.

Andrea was trembling as she signed a sheet, without reading it, so she could freely go. The policeman seemed a bit surprised she hadn't looked it over.

The curator had decided in any event to repair the damages and use insurance. The police didn't mention to Andrea, but the accounts of the ushers, and the opinion of the curator, pointed to it being not quite possible that she was useful to the investigation.

Unfortunately, Andrea wasn't told of any of this. Tears still streaming her face, she went out the door, in hysterical anger almost and refused the offer of a taxi anywhere. She just pulled away from the front police station door and walked the long road back to her home.

Reaching her door, she was shaking even as she put the keys in and reached inside. Thumbling in her medicine cabinet box, she took two aspirins with cold bitter water and just sat on an easy sofa, staring into space at the opposite wall. Not even thinking. The decanter was on a table just beyond her reach. She stretched out and un-topped it. The whiff was strong, but she imbibed, and shook her head at the immediate fuzz that came over her entire body.
Very quickly, her chest was heaving softly and her breathing slowed.

In depths of dreamy scape, a cloak was falling on her. Red and black. Or black, with red crimson in-linings. Over her, then adjusted to cover even her head. She was screaming voicelessly with her mouth as arms projected onto her, tight, stifling her air with vice-grip on her throat.

Seconds passed. More seconds. She was choking to vomit and feeling her skin turn red then blue. Her arms and legs could barely move. She couldn't struggle. Only by going limp could she find solace this time and find acceptance of the grim dark enveloping.

Then with sudden vent of intake, her eyes awakened wide. It was after midnight and she couldn't stop shaking. It was warm in the home but she was icy cold, teeth shattering, thoughts all unfinished in her brain.

She knew the man. This murderous man could not be allowed to keep doing this. That cape, it was his, and she was sure it was the key to identifying him.

Andrea pranced upstairs quickly to her bedroom. In a drawer, she found her scrapbook and a pencil. She drew an outline, then facial features. Letting herself forget the caped man's appearance was unthinkable, not an option.

With the scrapbook pad in her string handbag, Andrea set out to the car. With a shock, a man touched her arm, to which she spun around instantly.

"Ms Levison?" I'm Lieutenant Compton of the Air Force. Can we arrange a time to speak with you? Preferably soon."

He was speaking of himself but alongside him was a black car, window down and another officer it seemed, who was identified as a Sergeant. This second one stepped out of the car, but then reached back in to pull out a corded phone of some radio kind. "I take it you're going to the salon? We can arrange to phone ahead and explain you'll be delayed." The Lieutenant said this and flashed out his identity card-book from his coat pocket. Andrea didn't like any of it and insisted on seeing the police, despite their not being her favorite people recently.

The Lieutenant sighed and made a call first to the salon and then to the police station. The sergeant remained steady through all of this. A police car arrived promptly within 20 minutes of waiting. The sergeant and lieutenant spoke to the black uniformed police officer, who then spoke to Andrea. Then he returned to the airforce men for a further few moments. Finally he came back to Andrea and reported that "Ms Levison, it is a routine manner of community safety by what I can make of it. Their ID is satisfactory and they are liaising with the intelligence bureau. I've suggested they interview you on a park bench down the street, in plain sight of the general public. I'm afraid I have to get moving but at least this way they can be on their way and so can you, without much more fuss. Government business." He said the last two words with a whiff of stifled contempt. He was sympathising with her, in fact.

So it was agreed and the policeman escorted all three of them to a park bench, right near a green field. In the distance were some children playing a ball game.

The police officer left, with the sound of crunching leaves under his black police-issue boots.

The air force sergeant sat very stiffly to the left, looking all around and then to the distance, focused. His gun in holster was unmistakeable, as was his starched uniform without a single crease, and patent shiny dark laceup boots. He was the epitome of concentration, as though memorising all that was happening by sight and sound. The lieutenant was more a relaxed figure, at her right, half turned in body and talking to her, wearing officer cap and with a blazer showing various medals. He had a notepad and pen at the ready, everything official looking.

Andrea almost giggled at the seriousness of the intelligence liaison. Men in hush-hush work, looking at the slightest ruffles in the street as cloak and dagger moments of truth. She stifled it into a cough, but it seemed Mr Compton the Lieutenant had noticed. He cleared his throat with annoyance of a sort and spoke with husky throat.

"I trust the police man made it clear enough. We are from Air force intelligence. We'll keep this all simple. We want to understand, hear what you've been through lately and sort out what implications it might have. Things like this may have importance for security or may not."

She nodded with a look of innocence and curiosity. He went on.

"I understand you have spent some time in the mountain forest and..."

"What?" She interrupted, meekly. "Am I being spied on? Am I the subject of some sort of investigation? Whatever the for? Have I committed an offence?"

"Please be at ease, Ms Levison" interjected the Sergeant, the first time he spoke and the only time, in fact.

The lieutenant looked carefully at his collegiate attendant and then shifted glance back to Andrea. "Erm, that is to say this is just a conversation. Discussion, if you like. I apologise it is a bit formal and I must keep notes of any information that is relevant. You're not under suspicion, it's the events of late which are bothering, not yourself."

She nodded again.

He raised eyebrows and unfolded sheets from his pocket. Some were newspaper clippings and other documents sealed as military. He showed them plainly, that is to say, not trying to conceal

anything, and brushed them against his leg in a sweep, as though to find his next words.
"Ms Levison,"

She wanted to say "most people call me Andrea," but she hesitated as she felt nervous and also wanted to get on with her day. How would she explain this to the salon shop? Could she? Was it permitted?

"Ms Levison," he repeated, "if I may go on," (he'd noted her change of countenance and obvious mental distraction), "...fire brigade reports, police commercial theft report, hospital records... without concerning yourself by the fact we have these, might I say the government is puzzled as to how all these things happen to one woman individual in such a brevity of time. Do you see where my logic is going?"

"Yes of course, I do indeed." "I suppose I haven't felt very well." Andrea suggested.

"Notwithstanding that," he went on, "I did in fact hear mention of a psychiatrist that peroused your medical files of late. Needless to say no details were given but it was alluded you should just be taking it more easy. Resting, no less. Personally I thought it was all irrelevant, you seem quite the balanced person to me and I'm much more interested in the facts. Tell me about your life, your job briefly please, just for the record."

She hesitated but did so. What was there to say? She had a simple life, from home to workplace.

He nodded at her descriptions. "You certainly aren't living in such a way as to induce odd behavior or excessive personal stress. Not to my military mind, anyway" He emphasised 'military.'
"Are you married? Closely connected to parents?"

She shook her head to both. "Not unless you count crazy dreams of the former." She subconsciously used her other hand to cover the ring.

He twitched his mouth and moustache.

"I read the police report about the art heist. I couldn't really make sense of it, nor do I think you are connected to it, past being there, by chance."
"You wear a ring, I see."

Found out, she felt like a child for a moment, then said "well, ...yes. It's a treasure to me."

He found it unremarkable, evidently and pressed on with other subject matters.

"Ms Levison, you seem to have an unlucky knack for being in trouble. Strange fires, strange injuries, a museum heist. Occupationally we begin to notice a pattern." The liaison counted off on his finger. He was scrawling on a pad. He was smart in his blue aerial uniform but not so menacing. Nothing like the police had been.
He impressed on her the notion of whether she had seen any strange men, criminal types or anything. She could only reply that she hadn't and it didn't feel like a lie. Even considering the thieves of the museum, for in fact, she'd never laid eyes on them as they, if they'd been there, had vanished before in fact anyone had a chance to eyeball them.

"Very well. I see nothing more to discuss here. Sergeant!" spoke the lieutenant and they both turned to move away briskly, before the one Compton said "Thanking you for cooperation, Good day, Madam."

The two of them left. The notetaking had seemed minimal. She got to her car alone, declining their offer to accompany her back up the street. At work, there was nothing a-fuss. She confided in Lucy that the men had been investigating, which seemed mostly about the fire and the museum theft.
Her colleagues were sympathetic and Gwin was her usual self. Jovial a little more in fact, than ever.

When Andrea later got home, she had a telephone call. It was the man named Compton, the Lieutenant, again. They spoke for some moments. He had some more questions and asked how her day had been. Some formalities dropped for a moment and he informed her that he would be writing up the file as a series of unfortunate coincidences, and nothing more. He apologised for the earlier disruption to her day.   Apparently a copy of the interview and report would go to the police station as well, as an 'incidence.' Andrea surmised that her insisting on police assistance may have ruffled feathers inter-departmentally, although as the matter at hand was being dismissed as unimportant, there seemed to be no serious consequence in this. Indeed, there wouldn't be, although, without knowing it, the event of having a 'civilian' authority intervene actually brought the investigation to a much quicker conclusion than it otherwise would have.

The airforce lost interest in Andrea. She would never come to know that she'd been tailed by agents for more than a week. Now they were called back to other cases.
That was the nature of intelligence gathering. Some trails would go cold or indeed become utterly useless.

As the Lieutenant was back in his base office passing a file to his sergeant to put in a cabinet, he pondered this thought a long moment. Then he got back to his cup of tea, nonplussed.
His sergeant, for his own part, had been diligent about following up all the intercepts. The "listening" department had trawled through a lot of information to 'notice' that Andrea was centre to the recent events although it had, in his own mind, always been guesswork to somehow link up the information into a feasible pattern of work by any kind of 'mastermind' with a plan at heart. It was all too sketchy and even random, but he'd done his job and his pay was his monthly reward for duty. That's what mattered in his mind, anyway.

Andrea for her part went to bed thinking over how the authorities had thought it all so important. She had seen the document from the police station. The same officer she'd seen at the scene handed it to her. He alluded in confidence to her that the airforce department had thought
her completely insignificant. They'd found her to be almost childishly innocent and hence had wondered the usefulness and even the veracity of the fire brigade's suggestion that were it not for lack of evidence, they'd have considered the fire to be the work of a devious individual.

Andrea had to laugh at it, in a sense. Was it all the words of bruised officials hurt by having their time wasted on a trivial case and an ordinary citizen?

-Gate-

Andrea had decided. She would take a walk. It was her Saturday
and it was glorious tepid calm: sun, but not overpowering, which
never suited her soft pale skin anyway. Her hair trussing down
her back, she had on a pale dress with pink and pastel lime green
patches and her black soft leather riding boots. Her brown ones
didn't work so with the dress. After the car ride up, she got to the
forest entry again. Yes she would go up and it wasn't a fuss. She
didn't even bear it much consideration. She was tired of the
heavy thinking, frankly. She wanted to look around the trees, the
hilltop, the rocks even. She needed nature, if only to clear her
head. Andrea had the ring on her finger as always, but today had
her short white gloves on. The brush was dense and she didn't
fancy scratches. It was also a way to keep the ring under watch.
Yes, she had thought over that fateful fire, and no, she wouldn't
be asking Lucy or anybody to come along with her up the mount
this or any future time soon.
This was her thing, and hers alone. Analysts and analysis could
go all stay well at bay, as far as she was concerned. She had a
backpack with some lunch packed and her all-weather anorak
inside, with some water, a pot and some tea. She'd make a calm
time of it. She had torches as well, but wasn't planning on being
here too late anyway.

Up she climbed, across the paths and non-paths. Not all of it was
marked unless one counted the random twigs, branches, mulches
and changes of grounds. Empty gaps were forming as she got
higher, but there was a lot of tree cover, even if very much
charred looking still since that conflagration. She could see little
shoots in low limbs of trees. Life always returned swiftly, she
noted mentally. Flora and fauna alike.

Through the density of trees, she stopped a moment to get
bearing. She noticed a clearing to her left. Yes, she could
remember the main way now.
She ate some bread from her pack and made a small fire to boil
some tea. Very old-style camping. Quaint, she thought, and
smiled. It was so peaceful. Middle of day and not a care in the
world. Her little secret grove atop it all, she mentally considered.
A calm settled on her and she felt focused. She spotted ants

scurrying a slow-walk up a tree nearby. Foremost though, she was resolute to make sense, take it all in stride and just...not think too much. She damped out the fire to cool it and packed away her cup, pot and tea, brushed over some leaves and found soil to throw over the space. She waited a short time until the hissing and smoke cleared altogether. There! No way a fire would start this time! She had to take her gloves off for a while but she put them back on now. Mind it didn't matter much: the ring remained a cold dull, boring red—just like the air force man would have seen it.

She walked across, perhaps north westerly (although it was hard to tell and she hadn't a compass). Confident after previous walks despite the immensity of the area and the remoteness, she was moving upwards and that in itself counted. It told her she was heading correctly.
Stones. Moss on them, grays, greens, limes. Lots of trees still but shorter. Yes this was it! She took a breath and look around, stopped her feet from advance. She took in the scene, willed to be in the place very strongly. Sky above clear. Not too many a cloud. She scratched the side of her chin from an itch and brushed back her hair. A little sweat beaded on her fringe of hairs, so she pushed them away. Her gloves had a dull warm in their leathers but they'd stay on. She didn't want to risk bites, besides the other matters of concern lingering in her back of mind. She scampered around the stones, leading to the great rock. At least she'd found it. The first time or two it hadn't been apparent.
It was dark and lighter grays. Old, musty, whatever one might think appropriate for a huge rock. Or more, maybe a rocky-hill almost. It was quite big. She wondered about trying to crawl on to the head of it, but then her eyes caught the sight of a stone path, at her periphery. The scene made sense with all her recollections, dreams. That which she had tried forgetting, refused such beseeching.
Really, this was partly all about confirming she wasn't going mad in herself. Good and cathartic, really. So she told herself.
She also thought over how good it was to have her dress today. It kept her cool and the loose material gave her good freedom of movement. Her under-leggings and boots gave her the sense of not leaving anything untoward to chances. A moment she calmed her breathing and listened. Nullity all round.

She stepped down the stones a little, reaching them. A little slippery. Was there a treacle of water flow from somewhere? She couldn't hear anything except the crunch of leaves when she'd step or turn herself. Mostly every thing had a crisp, total dryness to it. Far from Hilleton, a feeling of being removed from all, come to think of it—that was how the place just seemed to be. The stillness was so magnetic. No wonder hikers loved their hobby. Homebodies just couldn't understand the call to be in nature. The only pity might have been that there were no birds or majestic creatures to see here. That is, if one walked in search of that. Or was that the thing that observers did? They weren't the same as hikers, were they? Maybe she was offending sensitivities of partitioned pastime pursuits with her mental meanderings.

Turning her head aslant, she awoke herself to the moment again, turned and then got above the stones again. She walked around the rock to see and notice more. Andrea just wanted to understand more. Fearlessness was in her and a want of discovery. Walking around the opposite side of the great rock, the air chilled. She was in shadow of denser trees again. She couldn't see the sky much as she moved now, but that didn't mean anything had changed. So she didn't think twice to go back. She kept on, and the ground remained high and steady. The rock didn't edge to lower grounds at all; she'd left the lower approaches visibly off in distance now. Her pack felt a bit heavy at this point and she rested it to the ground a moment. The formation of the rock in front was changed kind of, and there was a tight gap. Was it important? She felt like the atmosphere around her was charged and even more silent than before. There was a grayness and a kind of watery mist that hung in the air. She couldn't hear anything but maybe there was a spring, or fall? She stepped between the gaps in the rock and was startled to see open fields! Panoramically she smiled and gaped open her mouth! She turned on her toes, and realised that in all of 360 degrees it was the same vision. Wait...no...hadn't she been near a rock...what...was this? Her mind was lulled and carried on gentle airs and silver clouded reassurances...

Advancing gently, just a stack of hay and crumpled grounds were about her. She was in a field and could see a road track ahead. A horse and cart way off in distance beyond. She had walked some way, unable to stop. Behind her, far back in distance now were a series of low peaks. Something hilly was nearer too. It was a little hazy and gray. Had time jumped so much?!

Andrea moved on. Coming to her senses now, she wanted to understand where she was, what to do, and how this all fitted. If she could speak to someone, it would help immensely.
Not knowing how deserted the regions were, she picked up her dress-tails and ran towards the roadway and the cart. It was far but she had to try!
As it were, she couldn't make it. She fell on uneven cobbles of ground and subsequently decided to catch what was left of her pride and sit herself down. Her clothing was a little dusted now. Amazing how it had seemed to age. Then again, it was so dusty around her. She breathed heavily and got herself back to a steady heartbeat.
Looking a-left, she saw a barn, cottage, or something like that. Familiar? She supposed she'd seen cottages and the like before, yes, just like Bridgette's retreat! Perfectly logical.
 She'd have to cut through the field and proceeded to do so.
The ground was muddy in places and just a little damp in others. Not a farmer herself but she could see it was prime land, could feel it, in fact. This appeared to be wheat all around her and stretching very far in fact!

As she got nearer to the barn, she thought over carefully her direction of heading, events up to the cart-chase, the stones. Yes, she had to try and keep track.
Where was all this? It did look peculiarly like her dreams were unfolding before her eyes. Her night mind's eye hadn't lied, it seemed. Frowning in concentration, she let out a "yeah" of confirmation to herself. She bent down and plucked up a handful of dirt to let it sprinkle through her gloved fingers.
This was most interesting. She was very much in control of things. That seemed importantly good, all if and of itself, as it were.

An old man saw her coming, and tapped his wife on the back.
They'd been lifting hay. A cow was mooing not far off.
"Dairyists?" Andrea thought.
They smiled and she was leaving the field, to open brow grounds and squashed tufts and runs of wild lawny grasses. There were

tools and implements scattered around. "Nothing mechanical" Andrea whispered to herself, as she approached.

Andrea didn't know it but her hair was a mess. Dairy and bread maker farmers, she thought further.

Later she would recall she hadn't found a voice to speak, but her stomach beckoned her hungry, so the old woman's guiding hand on her back was eagerly accepted, indeed, there was no other choice about.

Hence the woman sat her down and gave her a plate of food. It was later evening. They helped her out of her boots and gloves. They didn't say much but were guiding and caring. Lonely? Perhaps, but certainly with a lot of work to do.

The man went to polish a wheel with a cloth. The woman lit a fire. It was cooling even though afternoon was only late. Night would be some time off, surely.

Both of them looked withered but remarkably strong. The man's hands were wrinkled but he was barely bent at all. She guessed his age at around sixty.

She drifted off to sleep. Somehow woozy. The ring was glistening and the man carried her to hay in the barn. Away from the cottage. The woman, his wife, watched and then set to pouring some water. She re-lit a candle for some light. Night was falling now as hours passed.

Andrea's ring hand was laid to her side and her body stretched out. The old couple had no space inside, so barn and moonlight through the hole in the roof would be her bed. Her gloves and boots were placed delicately one pace away from her. The room was clear except a horse grunting and airing to itself as it munched through a tray the woman had just placed there in its stable.

Starlight seeped through and the ring glowed. Auspice or omen?

Andrea awoke early but caught the dawn. It was red but then softened. Blues appeared and mists lifted. She remembered mists. Her dress had a side pocket and she thought to take out a pencil and paper she kept there. The pencil was small but would do the job. She jotted down textual points. A little concerned then, she eyed her own hand, glowing from the ring a little less but still noticeable. It did feel chilly this morning, so she cast her head around and saw quickly her boots and gloves.

Wearing these she picked up again her paper and placed it away with the pencil. The old two, her hosts she supposed, were already outside working as always.

Andrea collected dried hay (or was it wheat?) and bundled it all up. The space of a morning's work. Then she took bread, a sip of water, and went for a wander. The two didn't pay attention to her going. It was time to look back at where she'd come from.

Something like a fog had lifted from her. Piecing things together over the morning's work, she was sure it was the gloves. She pulled them down and looked at the ring a moment, stopping in her tracks a-mid-field. It was dull again, having lost almost all lustre and sheerness of worth. Pulling the glove back over, she walked off, and then into a prance. She could see the way. The roadway, hills, mounts. It was coming into plain view.
She was sure there was some significance to this and she was not going to be afraid—well, except for the dirtiness of her garments now.
Her lungs felt good and the air felt so clean here. It was as though more oxygen pumped through her than ever before.

Reaching the hilled area, there was a thick overlay, tufts of grass had all combined but then been yellowed and browned by a strong sun. Mosses were here too, but subtle signs showed her rock. Dirt bumps at the ground edged upwards. It was something like an uneven trail, like primitive steps.
Familiar?
She rounded it, but then went to the right, thinking of bearings.
Yes, up the other way, was more correct, wait! No, this way had something more definite, it looked like the washings over of leaves, branches and pebbles. Yet it was reaching up. Fresh and new.

She balanced herself against the mount, the rock, grassy covered or not. It was still what it was in reality. No uncertainty. She would understand it. It felt natural and linking. She pursed out her hands to keep steady, shifted her weight of legs and came back the left way. East? Maybe some orienteering person would chastise her to get the lingo correct on that one.
Yes hmmm. As she moved up, it felt right, the surfaces of these makeshift steps. They needed a bit of improving. It was only

seconds of work up but her mind locked on the thought that although it was rather a warm day, she had no sweat on her at all. Her dress was a mess too, not just with dirt but with torn parts. Her feet ached a bit too...but now she was again seeing an overcast surroundings and it dizzied her head a bit. Yet she felt her way upward, forward. Blackness in shadow of trees. This time she lost a footing, but caught herself. She huddled with the rocks so as to not lose sight or way a-more. What little sight only glistened off the rocks with moss, imperfections, grays now bearing more than the previous grassy yellows and greens.

She looked and rested down on the dusty ground. Trees. They hadn't been near her a moment ago.

She thought and breathed deeply, slowly. She patted dust off the lap of her dress and found her pocket. The paper was messed but still legible.

Sanity prevailed her. This was some kind of a path. So close to everything. Elucidation made her wonder about the connectedness of it all. Myriads of thoughts pored into her and across her mindscape. Many more than even usual for her. The pain, the hurts to her body, the Zordants, even those, the ship, the fielded place (what else to call it), this stony area, the open patch between trees, and familiar Hilleton.

What had those aliens to do with it all? What had they not to do with it all, rather? There must be more to this. Not for weeks had anything seemed any more clearer.

The ring, the ring. Rubesque channels of mystery. It couldn't seem anything less. Oh, she felt a bit hungry, but she burned to find more logical conclusions if she could. What was better than self-reflection? More than a thousand offers of advice from even helpful friends, she thought. This was her lifelong observation really.

Her stomach growled. It was a growing distraction. Thinking of her pack, she lost focus and concentration of the thought. She looked around, moved about and found it. At least the water was good. She threw the other food contents away, just to be sure. She buried them under soil and leaves to feel better about the disposal.

It was hot here. She took off her gloves, and then thought it cautious then and there to take off the ring. It was cold and she was not in the slightest concerned. She wrapped it inside one of the gloves and placed it all in her pack. She also placed the paper

and short pencil in with it. Her pocket was now free and she felt a
sense of flexibility. Non-encumbrance, he he. Just as she did like
it mostly to be. Andrea knew she must stink right now with
perspiration. Although this was a mountainous area. Smells
abounded, surely! Maybe not favored by trekkers, but it was as
good an excuse as any.
Down she went hastily, found her car and found again the
comforts of home.

-Birthdays-

Andrea lay seated in a good chair and wondered if everything was indeed making sense. What arcane knowledge was invading her rather usual life?
She opened the card. It had been slipped under her door, a postal delivery. It was an invitation to a birthday function.
"Ah!" Andrea thought as she read, "I remember Aimee, the American yes! I wonder how she is doing? Does she still miss home sometimes? It should be good to see her again."

She dialled the number and advised she would certainly be attending. An Erica, who she didn't know, was keeping the lists. "We think 30 or more will be there on the day. It will be quite a celebration!"

Andrea thought a while then had some evening dinner. She fell asleep in chair and then later awoke to the deep of night and crawled up to the bedroom to have a fuller nap.

The birthday was literally two days later. It had been holed over so as to fall on the nigh of the weekend. She parked some distance off and walked the street to the largish home. It was 4.30 approximately in the afternoon. Just as had been suggested, she had arrived promptly so as celebrations could swing to action from early.
In the next half-hour or more, people came in rather rapidly and so the numbers swelled. Including garden space it seemed more like 40 people rather than 30. Perhaps estimations hadn't thought of partners and some children in tow, even discounting for some apologies and absences. There was a lot of singing and copious amounts of cake, punch and decorations galore.
Andrea had put on a good white dress and there were several charming men and women alike. There was a lot of chatter. She had greeted Aimee but then lost her to some other American accented relatives (she guessed this) and well, there were other school associates she remembered, so it was all okay.
The nibbles of cake, dip, dry biscuits were all good, as were some marvelous cheeses.
When however a Robert, who she couldn't quite remember from superior school, handed her a tall tumbler refill of drink, she

accepted it and the chatter went on. Andrea was speaking with two women. There was Grace, who was still short but very vivacious, and Altea, who had wedded just a few years ago to a banker, named Adam.

After maybe 15 or 20 minutes, Andrea felt sick and had to excuse herself from the conversation, now joined by John and the same Robert as before. There was a lot of noise and now some speeches going on, with cheers of hooray and so on. Popcorn was all across the floor as Andrea went to find the bathroom. Robert went to see if she was okay and as she emerged moments later, she was red and very dizzy. Robert helped her to a lying sofa. It was the type that pulled out to be a resting cot.
He damped her head to take away some sweat and found some water for her to drink. Andrea was barely able to know where or what she was doing.
Pulling at her clothes was helping her to feel less overheated, but her modesty was being compromised.
Some others stumbled by outside the door and Robert turned his attention that way. Andrea pulled up the covers although she was already too warm. She wanted to just sleep, or dull the pain somehow, ice, anything. She could barely speak. Her head was giving her horrid dreams and delusions, ideas of the place of fields, the great rock above the forest hill and more. It was all muddled up and she began to imagine Robert was her lover.
Her eyelids closed and her arms were moving up as though to reach out.

With a startle, she shot up! She sat upright and arms were pulling her out. "It's okay Andrea, it's me Aimee. Don't worry, we'll just get you to somewhere you can rest."
There wasn't so much noise now. One could assume the party had died down. Guests had in fact departed. Michael, Aimee's husband, used his sturdy arms to take Andrea's arm over his shoulder. Aimee straightened Andrea's garments. Aimee gulped in guilt and glanced at Michael. He was lifting Andrea outside to a verandah cot. After an hour or so had passed, Andrea was given tea.

Andrea felt angry. She felt like a woman who'd wasted herself. In the dreams, which of course nobody else knew about, she had divorced from an evil man.

"That Robert! That man!" was what she said all of a sudden.

"He's gone Andrea." Aimee began. "I'm so sorry the celebrations kind of got out of control.
Another guest left sick too. Maybe there was something not good in the servings."

"Or the drink." Michael said this, matter-of-factly.

Both of them helped to take Andrea home. Aimee drove Andrea's car and Michael followed in his own car.
After more fussing and making sure Andrea was okay, they pieced together what had happened and figured out that something wasn't right in the drink that Andrea had consumed. It was the only theory. Only moments had passed in the closed room and Andrea's garments were torn. "Robert" had been found inebriated and misbehaving himself. He'd been seen away by police.
What was more a problem was making sure Andrea was fine now, as Aimee put it.

"Is there anyone we can call for you here?" Michael thoughtfully asked. He was tall and trustworthy.

"No. I'll be fine, it's okay. "

"Any thing at all, please call us," said Michael.
Aimee seemed guilty and eager to be on her way, whereas Michael was steady and looking at Andrea with concern.

"I shall indeed, thank you both. I just need sleep I guess."

With that, the two left and Andrea shut the door. She hobbled back to her chair and living space, not so firm on feet and with a shooting headache still seering through her. She looked across at a room mirror and saw her dress stretched and ripped. It was disgusting. Robert, the place of fields...it seemed interlinked.
"I'm fed up of feeling like I'm mad!" Andrea thought to herself.
She frowned and looked at her hands, shivering a bit in her lap.
The ring wasn't there. "That's right," she recalled, "I thought to take it off."

This was remarkable. Certainly nothing could blame this one on the ring. She had been right to retain it. Dreams were invasive lately, but this was not a rubesque matter at all. She pulled herself up the stairs and found the box with the ring in safekeeping. She put it on and not long after actually felt better. A strange yet welcoming warmth glowed across her, calming yet so subtle, even subliminal.

Maybe it was psychological comfort (she'd heard this notion somewhere), but anyway, time was doing its healing if nothing else and the ring, even two hours later, wasn't an ounce of harm at all.

She found centre in thoughts again and felt calm. It was again very late. She seemed to think her clarity of times was lately always when it was time for bed, as though days just kept sweeping away from her. Grrr, how annoying!

Against her normal judgment, she resolved to stay up and think it all through. "I'll sleep after some things are more straight." She wanted to live through the dream, almost burn her mind to recall and fix the ideas and thoughts. According to the dream, she'd been miserably married. Just a vessel of stability. Cleaning and acting the part. Her supposed husband had never even touched her or glanced at her fully. Was she a trophy merely? It just burned her up to think of the neglectful abuse of it.

When had this been? No, had it been at all?   Reality was what? The other place?

"Oh, I want to believe in marriage, I want to, I want to, I really do!" Andrea thought it desperately and called it out to the room.

All this dreadful mess. Why were all these horrid things intersecting her life? Dreams, from alcoholic spiking or who knows where else? What was going on?

Yet she felt strong, fine, still young for a woman!

Her fear and dread, confusion and disdain turned to anger at Aimee. If it hadn't been for the birthday event she could have been quietly going about her routines!

She called the line. She would do something she'd never done before. Berate her former school associate. She'd never told anyone off so directly before.

The line dialled and dialled but never connected.

Later Andrea would come to be grateful that the call had never happened.

She scolded herself later for the temper of the moment. It was most unbecoming.
She cut up the dress. Then threw it away. A favorite it may've once been, but now it marked itself with memories she didn't want. It was symbolically releasing herself just a little. It seemed like she was doing something.

Andrea then changed all her clothes. She put on a towel and went to hand scrubbing her under wears. Then she bathed.
She put on music, soft, classical.
She chopped up vegetables and then switched on radio news. Everything was soothing. She called Gwin and Jenny. With Jenny she was even able to laugh and forget troubles a while.
She hadn't realised the time. 7am. She had slept, interspersed.
Yet her body was fighting back after the earlier green tea and she had surging energy.
After some controlled breathing, just like one of her old health books said, she was able to calm down and have another short snooze.

At 10 am she woke again but for once didn't feel unhappy about being up late. It had been quite a past 24 hours and anything could be excused.
Centering herself was all that really mattered! She smelt the perfume of the air. She'd wafted on some herself to feel pampered today. She placed a lime on the windowsill too, to give some fragrance. Dusting could wait for later now.

It was Saturday and she did some shopping. Totally mundane, totally a grace warranted for the soul.

Sunday was good too, a restful time. She'd met a hairdressing customer the day before but now was merely her time away from work, stuff, people, whatever!

She read the morning newspaper including a feature on an aristocratic family. Usually that was speculative information but it was entertaining reading as always.
She shook her head quickly. Imagine the life of the journalists who do such articles! It had nothing of the honor of being a news bulletin front-page reporter!
Easy enough to say.

Andrea got time off from the salon.

She'd had a call from Dr Jack Crystal's office. It was another session, a catch-up basically.
After a half-hour in his consultation room (again with aide Ms Leah at the ready in the corner on her seat, note-taking).

It seemed apparent, and simple as Crystal put it.

"The divorce and the other matters are all part of a complex, sophisticated dream. It is one of confusions and intricate, amazing layering. It's no wonder at times you've not seen the difference between everyday and dreaming, Ms. Levison. Don't worry though, vivid dreams are not a cause for concern."

Andrea crossed her legs and frowned in thought. The doctor went on.

"It seems unclear how you acquired that ring or how it connects to your vivid dreaming, though I think, it might be best to put aside that finger adornment some more, maybe put it in a drawer. With time you'll think of it less. It should not be the focal point of your life, do you see? Who do you think should be the focal point of your life, hmm?"

"Me?" Andrea asked, questioningly.

"That's right! Just you. Simple, old you. The "you" you've always known. You live in Hilleton, your name is Andrea, you colorise hair. These things are your rock, your foundation!"

When the session ended she took a bus home. She hadn't used her car today. She wanted to break routines a little.
At home she ironed some garments and the ring was in a box upstairs in her drawer by the bed.

Andrea thought the doctor's points over.

Doing some more cleaning, dusting, she couldn't decide on it. She had already done things like putting the ring out of sight and so on. To her it didn't seem it would change much and she felt better these days anyway. Andrea had wanted to open up and say more to the doctor about going back and seeing the place of fields (she now playfully called it the Elysian, something garnered from Greek mythologies).
It hadn't seemed appropriate to elaborate and she felt he wouldn't really listen. His diagnosis was complete now and he was no doubts resolute about it. Doctors generally were.

Whatever else, the ring was a stupendous, glorious item and still had a story to tell, or a contribution to make. How really had she come upon it? It was a privilege to be opened up to a new channel of life. A private world her own? Hmmm, well there were the Zordants, perhaps the only link, the only arbitrators...or barriers? Either they were that, silent observers, or connective facilitators. This felt like a frontier of science, elucidation. OH, it was stretching things, it was theorising. Yet it touched on naive to shun them away as nonexistent. In all, Andrea was quite the thinker. She knew this herself. Hurdling through all the chores and activities of mundane life, she still had space (somehow) for abstractions, fanciful ideas, factual, all. How she crammed her head with it all would have puzzled even an Einstein! Although she wasn't a focused genius and certainly not a fourth-level mathematician.

No, she was just Andrea, and proud of it. Just Andrea was apt: she did things her way and if things would get to be too much, she'd rather just be alone to re-energize.

The world was nice but always had its drawbacks. Did anyone not see this? A fallen child here, break-in there, lost running race some place else. In all fields there could be triumphs only standing along with immense setbacks and sadness after sadness.

She got up, dropped her cleaning gloves and went upstairs. Open drawer, emptied box, ring on table. The ring. Good to know it's safe. It was a testament that she wasn't mad. The thread connecting things, as she fancied to explain it.

If a person were looking in on Andrea at this point, they would see how she was gazing down at it, turning it, taking it off, putting it in her small palm and letting it capture various points of light from the ceiling glow.
Now they say the seventh "P" of marketing is physical evidence. The ring is surely such a thing, as far as Andrea seemed to be thinking (little did she know it quite that way, however). Extending, could an Eighth "P" of marketing be Power? Such overwhelming impact, that one cannot ignore? It seemed apt for the rubesque that Andrea held. Undeniable. Who could wallow in refutation? It was proof pudding. This wheat-germ of an idea found its basis in her at all mental levels. Fanciful divorce dreams aside, the ring and stranger aliens were true, and she was going to take on this reality as she felt it right! Take the reins of potential?

She had to think all of this and well, frankly the doctor's contribution to her day hadn't helped. Whether he meant to aid or not was irrelevant. It was tiring, all this advice. Who wants advice? Or do we want it just so we can reflect back to our own decisions? Is that what persons do?

"You're getting too reflective and losing track now Andrea!" she told herself voicelessly.
Pursing her lips, "I know," she whispered to the air of the room.

The divorce might be dreamy or reflect something of a previous life or...another life. Poignant? Elysian? She was not an analyst with irrefutable physical evidence, but the facts, feelings, the holistics of it all added up flawlessly. She would try to find out, or mightn't have to: Andrea knew she'd be in the Elysian again, the place of fields. Perhaps the information would simply come to her. Divorce, the cloaked man, whether they were connected, the farm, the ring, even the alien Zordants. The return would happen.

Whilst young, she was quite mature enough of mind to know something though: Often life was a subtle mirth. Finding answers didn't always mean finding peaceful rest or anything. Closure. She giggled. It was quite the word, something that seemed to be mentioned in a journal she'd read at the doctor waiting room at Crystal's. She'd heard it by radio on a program too.
Not a cynic: she just knew that whatever cosmically went on, or whatever voided in a cosmos that wasn't actually doing anything, life simply did its thing.
Whatever that was. The quest to answer questions eh? It drove everything. Filling gaps. A bit like stomachs!
Did someone once say if we solved it all, we'd all be incredibly redundant and bored?
She put the kettle on and discarded all the mental ping-pong.
"Green tea will quip the nerve feelings," she jibed.

-Elysian Purity-

The weekend had arrived and Andrea was up early and down the
road at a market. She bought some fresh lemons and was back
home busy in the kitchen.
The radio was on, she was humming a tune, and had met Gwin
while she was out.
"Are lemons really that good for freshening the air, Andrea?"

"They can't be beaten, Gwinnie! Unless you prefer garlics, of
course!"
That got them both laughing as they disengaged to their
respective days and homes.

It was a good day, everything was fine and normal.
She cooked a lemon pie. She had a moment's thought about Dr
Crystal's notions again and well, it seemed to parcel everything up
neatly, such an encapsulation.
This was good and she could rest herself. So much anguish lifted
from her.
Humorously (or absurdly), she found a new use for the ring:
cracking open cooking eggs! Maybe the original owners of the
rubesque might cringe, but with a slight tap it would open up eggs
with a neat line so they could literally be "peeled" open. No
mess, quite incredible. She had the blinds in the kitchen partly
drawn. The ring was cold but she didn't want it to warm up too
much on the gem surface, just to be sure. The only fires burning
would be her stove! This was the idea, of course, assuming the
ring really had made flames that firey day. None could say
acertain.

Driving in the car, she visited Lucy. Besides anything else of
random nature, it was a chance to see if anyone else thought her
cake creation was any good. The latter was wearing her almost
trademark red dress, albeit with woolly slippers of home as
opposed to stylish street footwear.

"Stick to coloring" Lucy said...and then burst out laughing. "Got
you!"
For a while they chatted about nothing in particular in quiet tones.
The TV blazed a drama show that they bode little to no attention.

"Well, I'll be off, Luce...but oh do you want help with the dishes?"

"No need," smiled Lucy.

Home to relax and the new crisp morning saw Andrea shivering as she pulled the covers. She had her nightgown on and it was light. The only way to sleep comfortably, but now she wanted something on her feet. Slipper shoes? Under the bed. On they went and she found her brush and sat by the mirror doing her long strands of hair. Indeed her crown of hair had grown rather long. She took the time to bristle it out and curl it into braids and then joined all these together. Adorable for me! She thought this privately in mind.
She sizzled eggs for breakfast and squeezed a fresh lemon. Un-pipping, she drank down the juice with some added water with honey and creatively chopped up the orange flesh into edible pieces and took it with oats and some chilled milk.

Although everything was settled in her mind, she could confuse herself if she got to thinking too hard. So she didn't. She read, took a drive, came back, cleaned up, and thought of the new week awaiting and her work friends. She'd see them soon. Her everyday life really was getting to be a holiday in itself. "Really, why bother with the hard thinking. Accept and embrace," she told herself. She held out her arms and hugged herself against the cold. Putting on a coat felt much better. It was evening.

Come the new week, She drove in to work and was greeted by Jenny. Monday Morning. Colder than even the weekend had been, but passably okay. Nobody else had arrived yet, but in some minutes Judith, Mark and Gwin all arrived together. Everything was smiley and good mooded. An excellent sign? Yes!
Lucy rushed in a bit late.

"Did you walk, Lucy?" Andrea asked. Apparently so. How keen.

"I want to keep in tone," said Lucy, as she set up for the day.

"You hardly need any effort to keep well! I thought I was the main imaginer around here!"

That and the next day were quite routine. Things were busy both days and Aimee had even come in for a style. Andrea had felt tense the moment she came in but it evaporated moments later in her mind. Letting things move on was better than remembering things that had been no good.

As they closed for the day, it was looking rainy and so Jenny sped off on her bike. Gwin left as well and Andrea was doing a final sweep of the floor as Lucy went about making sure all items were turned off and stored, polished and clean-looking. She fared well too, and Andrea noticed the light on, out the back.
She ducked her head in and said a goodbye wish to Judith, who was looking over some receipts, it seemed.

"Yes have a nice time, Andrea. Good job today. You're looking as bright as ever. Go and enjoy your evening."

Indeed Andrea would.
She drove down the main stretch but turned off the other way, to the forest where lay the hilly mount.

As though magnetized, Andrea was lulled back to the greenery and wanted to have a little walk. There was a party of folks coming home from a forest trek. They were packing up gear. Andrea felt a funny sense of ownership about the area these days. She asked:
"Good trekking weather for you? Whichever way do you go among the trees?"

An older gentleman explained that they used compasses. "We take a long path, mainly circling around. There's more green, unlike the top, which we understand is still charred and black. It's so dense at the top anyway and there's nothing much to see, unless you want to find yourself lost! Are you a hiker yourself?"

She said occasionally, to his question. He nodded and packed away some things. He drove away presumably to his home.
The others were going too and Andrea was walking around the general area then lost herself in some trees.

"If Dr Crystal is right," she told herself as she walked over branches and thistles, "Maybe I can persuade myself that it's all just nothing. Fancy? Maybe it's just a field of some sorts, a farm precinct. I've looked over maps many times but maybe this forest just connects differently and the maps don't have enough detail."

She was mentally grasping for logical explanations.
At the top, the stones were there, as was the great rock. The clearing of forest before it too. The grounds were greening but trunks were very charred, mixed with white, brown. Life was coming back. Dirt and carbon were everywhere on the ground. Ashes blown partly away to browns and yellows of soil. There weren't many leaves except crumpled masses. Her boots had again come in handy and this time she had faded denims on. When damp, there was still the threat of unknowns crawling around, or so she thought at least. Leeches weren't a nice possibility and now she realised with a shock that she had no salt jar with her.
Extra care needed now—and she mentally chastised herself just so.

Around the rock, huddled again and shaded by trees, mist covered. She stopped and stepped back. It vaguely cleared but now her eyes were misted.
Undeterred and wanting explanations for it all, Andrea pressed on.

Music!

She could hear soft music. Carnival like. Fanciful and happy. She could see stalls and some kind of caravan a bit closer. Andrea marched to it with a smile. It didn't look menacing. She could see faces and figures, some short of stature. No doubt children?

A man was pouring some kind of liquor or fluid from one bowl to another. He was using a huge ladle and had a moustache and old looking clothes were on his back. Grubby whites and then a sleeveless overcoat of black and red and other colors too.
"A free drink, missy? Compliments of the fair!"

She was about to decline his offer as she walked by, but he insisted and thrust it her way. He took some himself and used his arm to wipe his lips. "Ahh. It never ceases to do me a world of good."

He grinned with these words of utterance.
She took some in the proffered cup and thanked him. Moving on, she looked around at the sands here. It was quite a large ground and she could still see herself in a field, but the field was simply being eclipsed by this array of tents and now animals behind curtains and in containings behind wooden holding bars.

"Don't carnivals use metal bars for animals? Where's the main arena?" She thought to herself.
Unfortunately her legs were getting heavy. She would need to rest but there was nowhere to sit.

She stopped a short man rushing by, who had a whip in his hand. He barely stopped and told her he was too busy for such a "trifle."

She was coughing and felt heavy in her temple now. What was going on? Why did she feel like this. Had an hour passed?
Andrea stumbled around, until she fell face down. She dragged herself some steps forward and came out from the carnival. Her mind was abuzz with senselessness and the music faded to imperceptible. She just wanted to sleep and do nothing more.

After a long time, she awoke. She was in a field with flattened grasses and crops of grain. Her headache was awful. Her clothes were intact, well not ripped, but with holes, torn and gray-grubby. Her boots were missing. She stood up with some effort, confused and angry.
"How can I go about bare footed?" She frowned.
She turned around and looked down a glance. What? She noticed cart tracks. Had someone dragged her here? How many miles? Why? What purpose?

She scratched her head and brushed back her front-hair strands. A wind blew softly. It was noisy, but in fact everything else was quiet and silent. There was a horrible deafly silence.

So she ran, feeling crisp nature under foot every hurried step. Luckily nothing sharp found her exposed feet on the soils and planted surfaces.

Her eyes were foggy and she was running haphazardly. Then she saw the cart trail again but it stopped abruptly. "No help here," she thought.

The ring on her finger was pulsing a blinding red and felt hot. Feeling this, she looked down and touched it with her other hand. Something murmured. She felt fuzzy and thought, or imagined, she had heard something.

Shaking her head violently, she put her ring hand in her pocket and walked on. Vowing to use logic for this one, she looked about, walked a lot and eventually saw on the horizon some hills. In some corner of her mind she equated this with a pathway home.

As she kept walking, she was undisturbed but had a lot of time to feel hungry, tired, thirsty and to think. She even had to dare to take water from a pond on the ground. Deciding she already was blazed with headache, it made sense. Scooping up the water, she had used both hands and didn't even care to avoid submersing the ring. After quenching herself, she noted in passing that the ring was cold again and gone an almost dark crimson-purple. The water tasted good, dull, as pure as one could imagine in any normal instance.

Andrea didn't really notice that the water puddle she had now walked beyond was glittering with a beautiful sparkle as it had never shone before.

Although dazed and confused, she finally upward there was found the stone steps and she worked her way around the rock then through the dark space to the new light of Hilleton. Oh, what a beautiful dull scene it was to her tired eyes!
Andrea could feel they were bloodshot. Early evening still beckoned so she literally dashed down the hill to her car, swaying a little but mentally pressing herself to focus hard. She was oblivious to the dangers of leaches and anything else that could cut or hurt the feet. As it was, she found a leech. Disgustingly it

was on her ankle. She pulled it off with some difficulty, shivered with a shake of her head in distastefulness and then drove home. It was hard barefooted.

Andrea wondered if she'd had a trance or who-knows. It had not been pleasant.
She was tired of all the confusion. Medical advice really wasn't helping. It had worsened things. What in the world was that carnival about? And why oh why had she been so silly as to accept a drink yet again from someone?
She remembered the Doctor had advised her a kind of pill. She'd tried one and felt nice, the whole weekend. Be that as it were, she'd thrown the rest away.

It occurred to her that she might have been drugged again. She hated the memory and the association again with Aimee, but of course it was unrelated. It was unfair to have the relation spring to her consciousness but also what was more unfair was having to live all of this!
No more therapy sessions with Crystal. No way. No pills either! It didn't take an expert to realise that the drugs were dangerous. No more accepting cups. That too was a no-no!

Still, was the carnival a mirage? Certainly not her ill feeling before, though. She trusted her judgments and feelings, her sensory abilities just like any other person would.
She had said it before, but even now, more than ever, she felt it: She would face the truth of it all. Counseling wasn't the answer, it was standing up to take on all the experiences and move from there!
How she had managed to drive home is anybody's guess. The roads had been busy with peak hours still under way. Anyhow, she'd successfully dodged and weaved her way through passing vehicles to the serenity of domicilium all her own again.

She called Lucy and felt a bit silly about it. She told her some of what had happened but held back some details, keeping it more conjectural and 'dreamy.' Just to be sure.
"Andrea your life and mind are certainly more filled with grand drama than mine! Excluding music! Don't you want to just chill out with me with some records playing?"
The thought was nice.

"We'll have to do just such a session. You're right."

"I'm going to meet my mother for lunch, dear friend. We'll talk again soon."

"Or at the salon!" quipped Andrea.
It was good it had remained a light hearted chat. She didn't want her sanity being read by anyone again, not even innocuously by a friend!
The conversation did her good and got her thinking accidentally on another thought. Was she another woman in the other time, in the place of fields? Was she connected to the Elysian as another 'self?' Who was the real her? Again she'd noticed nearly no time had passed when she was leaving the forest. This just wasn't possible and it stretched her thinking of just about everything. She wasn't a scientist. She was just her own self, a thinker like anyone else could be and do.

Certainly no expert or person in establishment would believe her anyway. The theories and practice of it all was up to her. Did it matter?

What had the ring done too? The odd feelings of warmth and the noise, buzz? Did the ring work everywhere?

Throwing caution against the winds, she decidedly went again tomorrow without any ring at all. She went before work and came out abruptly from the forest rock's darker side.

There goes that thought of rubesque transport abandoned! The ring wasn't actually needed to get to the place. Was it? What had she proven? What was she dealing with here? Forces so powerful? Part of her? Insider her?
One thing was sure; the recollection that the water had been so sweet in the tiny pond and literally saved her life after the ill feelings and hours of walking.
Uneventfully she ventured to familiar Hilleton.

At night, she ate well. She felt so hungry, then slept peacefully in her bed. The surroundings of home were a blissful solace again and here she was Andrea, not some other woman and not some other place. Perhaps the Zordants had more to tell her. There! She wasn't afraid to think of them now.

-Art Collector-

As it was, Andrea didn't have to seek out Zordant words. They
came to her. With her physical body lying there motionless and
her breathing chest rising steadily up and down, in slow rhythm,
she dreamt.
The first Zordant, looking familiar, whispered to her. He is by
her bedside. She awakens, but thinks it is only the continuation
of the dream.
Standing tall and erect as always, with grayed features shadowed
by the night sky and only a tinge of moon glow from outside, he
spoke to her through whitened cloth and still countenance.
"Andrea...Andrea..." this was said was some difficulty of
pronunciation, but then elongated for emphasis and correctness.
"An-Dree-Yaa."
He went on, "We have come to warn you of what we see."
Her eyes blinked and she nodded quietly. She was up on elbows
above her pillow now. It was soporific state, still in dreamy
consciousness only. No fear came to her.
"Your beautiful annulus is wanted by a prominent man. He has
not got virtue in him at all and he trades his golds for mixed
colors on boards, what you call 'paintings.' "

"What..." she said slowly and yawned. She was awakening but
felt stillness. Her eyes were a little foggy and her eyelids were
heavy. A gust of wind blew against the blinds and the moon
seemed to grow larger than ever in silky strands of white rays.
Her face was aglow, as was the Zordants. Behind the first one was
the second aide, but he was utterly unmoving except for a tiny
motion of mist from where his mouth would be. As always
though it was hard to tell, for the Zordants didn't exactly speak,
but more threw 'thoughts' at her. It was all so dreamily real. Or
really dreamy.

"An dree yaa." He sensed her meanderings of mind energy.
"Please listen on."
An image struck her mind of a broad shouldered man in
splendored surroundings. She couldn't see great details except
timbers and ornaments.

"This is the one, you must not hold him in trust. Take caution with the ring. It is your link to us. We hope you remember as before. Always do we watch your safety from afar."

The two wafted away towards the door in shuffling movements. Her body was frozen, unable to move as though magnetically stopped. Andrea couldn't see it, but her clock was also not moving.

"Wait!" she managed to gasp, stretching her vocal chords against the strain of the magnetics.
The second Zordant turned and looked at her. He had a kind of covering on his head and spoke this time but with the same 'voice' as the first.

He projected softly to her. "?"

He only laid the un-worded question, waiting for her to say words. Myriad ideas poured through her cranial matter. She couldn't figure where to begin, but tried.

"What is the ring? What is the other place? What connection have I? What do you want? Why do I know you? Where is my life."

The torrent was sporadic and she knew it wouldn't be easy for even a professor to answer six questions at once in what seemed like limited time.
The Zordants turned in simultaneity and crossed to the window side now. The gust of wind from moments before was tunnelling outwards now, a complete change of direction.

"We shall leave you to your soporific peace now. We are friends. You and 'we' have shared information and we still learn together. Ours is not the way to know everything forward from this moment." She knew he meant they and her, when he said "ours."

He pressed on, as they seemed to fade through the window and away. "The ring has strong pulse. It fits you only, as your ventures will certainly show you. Keep it well." He spoke faster, whilst fading. The words were thoughts and they processed like precise arrows in her mind. None missed the target.

"Your landed reality is more than you see. There is much more. Yours is the privilege to see more. We can learn more together, of the place you say is 'fields.' "

He had gone.
Cold chills filled the air and then a warmth. The rubesque on her finger burned with brilliant glow and amazing heat, but not burning to the flesh.
She slept peacefully two more hours, then woke, remembering all. She noted some things down, briefly. She folded the paper up and put it away in her notebook in the bed cabinet.

At work, an elegant man came in asking for Andrea by name. He explained his boss wanted a home visit for hair styling and had requested her from recommendations.

The shock was the car waiting outside, black and long. For the sake of good business, Andrea went, promising to be back in an hour. She said this at the man and he agreed it wasn't going to be a problem.
After a brief drive to the other side of town, the driver and her arrived at an estate she hadn't seen from her recalls. Not that she was in this area much actually. It seemed rather exclusive. Inside the large home, something of a mansion, she met a Reginald, who was a suave large businessman, with a stern look in his eyes and immaculate appearance.

"Pardon my methods madam, but as you may observe I won't actually require a hair consultation, but the distraction was necessary to have you attend here."

Andrea didn't know what to say, but wanted to have matters finished with. The driver assistant stood by the door, alert and waiting on his boss, the master Reginald.
She saw about the room much ornateness. The room was as much a study, office as well as a display room. Timbers, polished and many artistic things lay about.

Then Andrea realised what was in one corner. The lost painting.

"I see where your eyes are focused, Andrea. I won't leave you wondering, I'm a man not fond of wasting precious time." She figured he might be around fifty.

His hair was a little gray, but greased blacker and slicked back from his forehead.

"Basically I'm a collector of distinguished works as is easy for you to see. I acquired the piece, to put it simply. I acquire many things, but most of all is something profoundly less material: information."

She was puzzled as to how this fitted into her ordinary existence. "I don't feel comfortable being here." Andrea said, scratching her neck nervously. She felt vulnerable with just her day blouse and work skirt on. She still had her cutting apron on, too.

"The ring on your finger." He pronounced suddenly.

"I don't want you to take it discourteously, but I do want to buy it." He picked up a phone and spoke for a moment, then rested the phone a moment, pausing and proceeded to say to Andrea: "my broker will fetch an excellent fee for the painting. I'm prepared to sell it, and proffer the proceeds to you."

"For this heirloom old ring?" Andrea said, thinking quickly and holding her hand up to the air. She was standing quite apart from him in the large room.

She was centre, the driver at the door and the master at the other end behind his huge oaken desk and the curtains half drawn open behind him.

"I have my connections, private, official and of course the press." He picked up the newspaper as he spoke this.

"So, come now Ms Andrea, let's not play games." He wrote a figure, clicked fingers, and handed it to his driver attendant as the latter rushed to his heel, then finally it was given to her.

Andrea was shocked at the immensity of the money this meant.

He looked at her, waiting and asked his broker to hold on a moment more. He cupped his hand over the speaker of the phone.

"Think, woman!"

She did and said nothing.

He put down the phone, ending the call after whispering
something she couldn't hear.
He used both hands to raise himself from the table and then
walked around, hands behind his back in the aristocratic way, like
a man poised in thoughts.

"I'd hoped it wouldn't come to this. I have other rings." He
pointed to a cabinet with sparkling gems.
"That's not the point though. I collect, Andrea, and yours is
special. Come now, flaming blazes in a treescape? It must be
something of a focusing stone. If I don't get it, on these quite
generous terms alone, I will simply expose you to all the outlets I
have access to."

Fearing this and her own delicate small life, she relented finally
with a sag of her shoulders and downcast head.

Around a week later, the man is dismayed. He'd taken pains to
grease his smallest finger to be able to adorn it: then proceeded to
wear the ring for days and yet it remained totally lifeless to him.
He'd tried laboratory tests and even thrown it down in disgust,
then picked it back up, pressed on and worn it day in, day out,
even to his retirement each night to sleep forty winks.

"My employer would like to consult with you again, though this
time I am sure you will be quite satisfied with the dealings."
Hence Andrea was again recalled to him for a "touch up" of his
hairline. Again she went along, but only at the driver's urgings
and her boss Mark's peering into the room to ask if everything
was going fine. She wanted this to be over and was hoping to
bargain for her ring back. All week the Zordants' words in that
dream real had bothered her. She didn't bother to think where
dream or reality collided or crossed each other any more. It was
all a continuum of the real.

So Reginald told her, in his office "keep it, the deposit and the
ring! I've had the most horrendous headaches and nightmares!
How ever do you stand this thing! He threw it, causing it to
bounce off his desk, and across the room to fall to the ground.

The servant driver rushed to pick it up, wrap it in an embroidered handkerchief and place it in her hands. He led her out.

On the way out, Andrea noticed the man's hat stand and was surprised, as she left his mansion again. He had a cape, black with red. His steel gray eyes at both meetings now recalled in her mind, and it struck her that this was related to the attacker in those wretched nightmares she'd had of being attacked.
Andrea decided to cancel the cheque she received, deposit and main fund both. For indeed ill-gotten money could be vile, as the adages of old truly tell.

The businessman called an editor. He wasn't true to his word. In rage he betrays Andrea with spite and pith. Yet the editor remembered being scorned a long time ago, many years a-back. Now he saw opportunity:
Police begin to peer into the life of the businessman. Editors always had police contacts, truth be told. It was and had always been a mutual benefit effect for leads on stories and catching the crooks. Everybody won out.

As it happened, a bank trace showed monies written in cheque, but one, to a Ms A. Levison, struck no more than a glance of temporary attention: For a second entry showed it being returned, uncashed. The officer of the law knew this effectively disclaimed ownership for whoever the recipient was, this "Levison."

Clearly it was A. Levison's lucky day. Nobody wanted to be connected to this shady man.

After some time, Reginald quietly skipped from town and country on an uncomfortable sea ride.

Skipping the law, he didn't escape for long.

Art fraud was unusually high risk.
The editor, a journalist with much experience, got first-rate photos of the nabbing and subsequent sentencing. It was amazing where tip-offs led, and humorous to think that the informant had become front and centre target suspect.

-Alissa-

She was walking. It was beautifully sunny, everywhere, all around. Her body's chest was rising and falling one moment, then pacing the next.
A long dusty trail was before Andrea. It was so familiar. The stony steps weren't in her memory so much. The rubesque was glistening brightly, happily as she walked along, swinging her arms with freedom. Her pale yellow dress almost camouflaged into the background of the sun and the wheat stalks all around her and the smell was sweet in the air.

Oh, the farmstead! The barn too. Shimmering too, some hours later, she was labouring in field. Life was good, normal. Nobody was around her but that seemed okay, 'perfectly normal' as Andrea felt it, more than said it. A crisp breeze blew over her a moment and helped to cool her skin. The afternoon sun was long as she worked with the shifting fork, making bales. Sheep were bleating some way off to the West.

Andrea had advanced her way to the edge of the long field. Sweet home was a way off but the day still had some strength in it, as did her muscles. She felt glistened with rays, tanning her skin and it felt good. Brawn was building on her biceps and triceps. Mmwa! She was in peak, she felt it. Everything was flowing, sensible and nothing else crept into her mind. This is true life. Is it? Yes, yes.
She tried to think of yesterday on a whim, but it was blank. Oh well, ignorance is bliss. Now where did that thought beckon from? She'd learnt so much. Corn. Buttered. Oh it was a sweet combination, fresh from the crackling fire and rotisserie turn. That would be dinner and some dough. Not for a while though, she had to take forth the burst of all the day's harvest offered. Her sleeves were rolled up. Her blouse was ripped a bit, but tied at the centre, exposing her mid-centre. Her skirt swayed as she worked, heaving, lifting. Confidence was her king.

"Who could that be?" she wondered, her ear pricking her attention, to which she looked up, gazing and seeing a woman enlarging from the distance.

She wanted a name, but none came to her. It was a brunette, quite attractive. Women noticed this about each other, for it was par for the course in all circumstances. She had her chin up and had a purpose to her stride. Her clothes were black and deep green and she was wearing a sun hat which softened her look, making her seem more friendly as she swayed forward.

The woman stopped near to Andrea and was talking. At first Andrea was too caught in taking it all in, the essence and look of the woman. Alissa? Who's Alissa?
She thought and the woman was waiting for her to reply.

"Are you Lucy?" She thought to add, "from the salon?" but then stopped herself, mouth still open, not knowing what significance the salon had to the present situation.

"What's a salon?" said the woman and Andrea was caught surprised too, and just shrugged.

The woman spoke of the land's lord and the great expanses and asked Andrea was she a countrywoman, and what house of family she bore from.
Alissa took Andrea with first, suspicion then almost deemed her a simpleton.
"Can you not ascertain yourself? Yet you work the field, why?"

"Fielder."

"I beg your pardonings?" said the woman back.

"Andrea the Fielder, that is indeed me."

"Yes yes of course."

"Do come though," the woman continued with a curt nod and pointing with her left arm and hand, "wouldn't you like to see some of my blueberries and a nicer place? It's such a lovely day and you've worked long, it seems."

"Are you familiar with the forest?" Andrea asked.

Alissa was taken aback by the left of field questioning.
"Bah...what? Oh, there are bush lands and forests, but I shan't think of them much. I like open plains much the more. I like to know the expanse around me is void and see things before me, do you not yourself?"

"Why do you worry for such things? Is it not safe in your regions?" Andrea asked, although why her mind expanded like this on such things, she felt struggled to know, even if it seemed in another sense natural.

"May haps you don't have experience with the Lady's households. I served them a whiles. Yet you do have the grace of one who could do well."
Alissa said this while looking Andrea up and down quite brazenly, taking in all her slender feminine features.

It made Andrea angry and then blush.

The woman just snuffed as though it were trifle to be so self-conscious. She laughed and said "Begging sorry, you take me too seriously. I shall leave you but bid we meet again, or if you prefer the offer is still available to you to see my place."

Andrea felt recovered in modesty and understanding. She felt a subtle memory and clarity. Hilleton....a torrent of thoughts, feelings, wonderings.
In all of two minutes, as Alissa stood there, Andrea was putting down her implement softly and rubbing as a caress at her ring. She felt radiance and warm feelings tingle her and saw all of her life. Both lives, but more Hilleton. Putting together logic, she would recover herself. Alissa was smiling and waiting, picking at invisible loose threads and some straws on her gown.
"Yes I shall be along with you. You are kind for your offer. Is it afar?" Andrea loved the surrounds and would learn more. This place was sweet. She didn't think of the Zordants and didn't want Hilleton for now. She could stay here as by will and it was inviting. It had purpose she couldn't explain fully.

So the two of them went off, hand in hand, giggling as they started to skip and prance. As two girls, although both were more like thirty.

Andrea thought of blueberries and smiled in delight at such a little pleasure. They were friends already.

As it were to be, Alissa felt occasion to tell of losing a child just after his birth. Andrea informed Alissa that the latter's 'region' is Elysian as she knew it. She spoke of Hilleton but Alissa could only understand it as some far-off land, despite Andrea's trying to explain it some more. Alissa feared the forest and mountain so much that it seemed hopeless to suggest they could both venture that way to see the path to Hilleton or anywhere else for that matter. Further pressing, Alissa revealed her husband was a lumberman and died doing his craft—hence her illogical-otherwise fear.

The thatched homestead was quaint and cosy, not so large. Yet the plantation stretched far with a tinge of blues and greens, leaves and rounds. Alissa had literally run through it laughing merrily, with Andrea in quick step behind. "Do run faster than that, Andrea!" So said Alissa with her quick lilted voice. The accents were careful and not like any Andrea could place, because this whole place, this Elysian, seemed to have such perfect speakers, well, when speaking did occur, as now. What about the older couple? Parental figures, so caring...he mind was drifting and now she observed Alissa on a cut log stump, chest heaving, regaining her breath. Her clothing was a little damp with perspiration, too. The woman's skin was quite pale, to the sight. Andrea took a seating too, but there was none, so she sat down on a patch of clean ground, knees bent, legs to one side of her. The two of them both looked around and took back breath to a steadier pace, each.

"Are you all but alone here?" Andrea offered to break the silence, as Alissa began looking on her.

Sullenly, this cast a gray cloud on the moment of Alissa's face. "Not always so," she sighed to Andrea. "My husband was here with me and he worked the land as much as I, or even more, and after some years of being together, our happiness was almost complete..." she trailed off, raising her eyebrows and looking skywards.
Andrea sensed her meaning and pointed at her belly.

"Yes," Alissa said, "you take me correctly." She went on, shifting on the log, her back arching a little lower. "I was the proudest of women, Andrea. Another beating heart inside mine and I knew it would be a boy child." "Enluke was taking on more to the fields, tending leaves and things, talking to the freepickers, and more."

"Enluke?" Andrea interrupted a moment, then regretted it, her face and body stopping, for Alissa wasn't looking at all comfortable talking these subjects.

"It's okay. Enluke, it was my husband's name. He was a dearie, ever sweet. What more could I want but he and the young?" She shivered and her eyes began to water.

Andrea came to her side and shouldered her with arms, then turned front-on to hug her. Alissa cried some tears slowly.

Andrea felt no inclination to say anything but to hold and comfort her newfound friend. The fields all around were very calm, as though the air itself was listening.

Alissa went on voluntarily. "I carried this child right to the end and felt the pain then the beauty of seeing his little face, beaming. Hours later he was coughing up blood. Lots and lots. I was inside and didn't want to disturb Enluke in the field. It wouldn't stop though. So at last in desperation I called out to him and he came very quickly, hearing my distress. We tried herbs, cloths, anything we could imagine to do. We knew nothing really and none of it made sense. Ikuln...the name I gave my son...Ikuln just seemed to whiten with the minutes passing. He was hot then went colder. I was fussing but Enluke got me to slow down, to not smother or try too hard."

"What about a doctor?" Andrea exclaimed?

"What's that?" Alissa asked. She didn't understand at all, it seemed. After explanations of sorts from Andrea: "Some people use the herb, but there isn't much here and nobody truly knows, Andrea. I don't think I know what this doctor tribe could have done either."
Andrea was a-gasp and her mind racing to see through the implications of it. A world without any medicine at all?

Alissa blinked nonchalantly through red-ringed eyes at Andrea, seeing the latter concentrating her mind. Alissa thought her absent or daydreaming and asked so.

"Oh I'm so sorry Alissa, no, not at all. I was just thinking of what happened to you."

"Ikuln faded in some time. I couldn't stop crying and Enluke became very silent. The pain, anger, sadness was all mixed on his face. Andrea, our gleaming son was with us just a fragment of time but he was a beaming joy in our hearts and then taken from us. It was without any reason. Our beautiful, perfect boy gone. Yet it was not all."

"Not?" said Andrea, pleading the question, for she was perplexed and intrigued to learn more of her new friend.

"Enluke took no more to the field. Ikuln was laid to permanent rest and the people from afar left us to mourn. That is the way. All say it necessary to purify beginnings."
Andrea watched Alissa turn her gaze away and pick at her cloth, removing fragments of lint, straightening herself and then pushing back her own hair.
She went on. "Andrea, the disasters stayed with us. Everything changed, everything. Nobody picked. Fruits rotted then stopped growing at all. Enluke took up new work with axe, lumbering in forests. I know he needed the time of solitude and he came back faithfully every evening." I needed time too but I still felt lonely. We could not bear again to try for another child, it seemed wrong, to me."

"Such many things have happened to you in such drastic ways, that it makes me feel my own life has been like a perfect charm," Andrea proffered in verbal return.

Alissa smiled faintly, "you may say that and I thank you for your thoughtfulness, friend from far. I'm getting a bit tired, maybe we can go inside and I can share with you some fused essence of tea?"
So they both got up.

"I am at a wonder that you have done so far then to restore the plantation here, my new friend. It is impressive," Andrea said as they took the steps to go inside to a simple room with carved chairs and table with heavy woven spreads of cloth on it. Candles lay at the corners of the room on wooden shelvings and wood placements. The roof, made literally of finely interwoven twigs, was thick but allowed in light, keeping the place in soft illumination. Andrea felt it was late afternoon now.

Alissa had made fire, boiled and then poured out the teas. The waters had a greenish tinge from the leaves and she added a hint of bluish drops to each mug that Andrea understood to be sourced from berries and jarred in tiny increments.

Seeing her observing this, "these are ripened a long time in sun and more tart, less sweet than the normal fruit. You will find it pleasant but easy, you need not but relax for it keeps you alert but calm" she offered in explanation.

She took her own cup and then Andrea followed, cautiously, then smilingly assented to a more generous swallowing of the warm liquor.

"It wasn't so hard in the end." Alissa began to speak again, while turning her cup in both her hands in a thoughtful way. Her composure had returned, belying her tears just a short space ago outside.

Adding: "After Ikuln and some time, the field and all the berry plants renewed themselves." She straightened as if to strengthen her steel of determination. "When Enluke departed me forever, I got to tending and restoring the field and sure enough, the freepickers returned with time. It was very fortunate for I myself was in dire times, almost without any means or food."

Andrea could see her pains to say this, yet then her release, as though weights came off her shoulders. Alissa slumped her shoulders down slowly and shook her hair, taking a long breath. "Good, my friend" thought Andrea, yet she did not say it, or inquire directly about Enluke and what Alissa had meant about this part of the story recalled.

"This land has its way, Andrea. It puzzles me that you know not of it so much, yet I know you told me you are from far." Alissa was studying Andrea with quite an eye of judgment.

Feeling self conscious, Andrea did more the talking now at this time. "You're right and it's what I can explain more. What is this land called though?" "In relation to mine, how can I address here?"

"It is the land, Andrea. The lands. What other is there? It is all far, and surely yours is connecting to here."

"Elysian. Fields." Andrea said these two words. "It is how I have called it, and it can be for the mean time.

Alissa nodded with a genuine smile. "Perhaps, as you will it."

Andrea plucked courage to go on after taking the last of her tea and setting it down on the table. She placed her hands at her lap and composed her elegance but relaxed her words to be fluid but soft as was her befitting character of norm.
"My 'land' is Hilleton. It doesn't seem so far, but it means going back, oh south I suppose, through the wheat fields and towards the stones, forest, mountains. Do you know of which way I mean? Beyond where we met?"

"I do know the direction yes Andrea, but I have not seen it in detail."

Andrea and Alissa spent considerable time, both on this day and the next.

In the new daytime, Alissa went about her day, in what seemed a routine. In the distance some free pickers were working away, coming and going, but never spaced much together. They did not huddle and nor found much to say but simple hello's or grmphs of words and checking the produce. Alissa had explained it was like this though, so Andrea thought nought of it, as she walked the lengths of fields a little while, with the sun warming her marvellously. Both women had consumed a quick breakfast with fresh milk supplied by a freepicker the day before. Supplied? Delivered, rather, with beaming delight and again, not many words, just "to your kindness, madams." The man had blue clothes, a little after the fashion of dungarees, or pull-up trousers with straps for the shoulders.

Alissa worked on, Andrea helped, then took another break, eating some berries at her fancy. It all seemed amazing, the more she perceived of how far the expanse of the growing plantations of berry bushes was, so neat, none too tall, all like bristling soldiers. As if by miracle did these grounds grow blueberries from the branches. The crops had never failed, but rather, kept weighing down more and more with each year.

Many a village delighted on their supply from Alissa's farm. As a modern twist of mind, it occurred to Andrea strange to think that nobody would threaten Alissa, for she aboded all alone. Alissa showed the answer though, for peoples literally came and went throughout the next day, picking and basketing off some of the fruited goods. They would leave baskets of things they didn't need for Alissa, and so strangely, everything balanced and nobody felt any burden so much at all. "Barter" was the verbal that came to contemplation.

When Andrea was a little distance from Alissa, who had taken a nap after running frolicking through the fields in the afternoon, she got to walking in long grass and wondering. Out loud she spoke to the wind "What place really is this, that the earth is so unlimited in bounty, how can this be?" Yet her mind was also taken to other realities of the place, the places, all the places of this place of places: it was a dusty, huge place, with many grasses and fields, far off mountains and things beyond all hope of eye's sight. The place just teemed with enormity and yet one thing it seemed, was the tiny presence of people.
"Where are the people?" She thought again, and spoke. Catching herself with a gasp, she put her finger to her lips and cautioned herself to be careful talking so aloud.

By the following evening Andrea had told Alissa of many things, trying to embellish on what Hilleton was like, what it stood for, how she herself had lived there. Alissa tried to understand but many times had a vacant stare. Andrea pressed on for the sake of her friend and taught many a thing, resorting to many figures drawn with her hands, using shapes drawn in dirt or analogies to objects around them. The immensity of people was totally foreign to Alissa's understanding in particular. Finally, Andrea had the thought pop into her mind, after quite a lot of deliberating with Alissa, that perhaps her friend could be guided to come with her to see Hilleton.

"That I could not do, absolutely never." This unequivocal rejection stunned Andrea with its harsh register. Alissa's voice and mood darkened. Andrea realised this was a sensitive emotional ground in Alissa's mind but not knowing why, she just decided to diplomatically ask what the reason was, whether local law or not.

"There is not a binding, not a 'rule' against it. Except for me. I did not finish telling you before. It's where my husband died."

The next day Andrea left. Conversation between them had ceased.

A further day after though, Alissa saw Andrea again and once more the old couple Andrea "lived" with waved her off with not much of any word, but with the meaning clear, that she was a 'child, free' to go with their blessing. Andrea sensed it, very vividly. Placid, wonderful people, who were so timeless and patient.

"I'm sorry, Andrea." Alissa quipped as they walked and got back in her homestead by the blooming berries once more. "The pain just came back to me. I needed space again. Forgive me."

"Oh I do! Do not worry at all. We have shared much and it is delightful knowing your company." Andrea meant it, too.

"Enluke died after learning a new craft so well. He provided well and his timbers were carted far for the building works. I found him, sadly."
She sighed and cried again, softer. Andrea held her again. "It was so horrible. I've been marked ever since and could only vow to myself to never be near that dreaded set of stone and forest, mountain and hilly peaks! I cursed the uneven lands and came back to what felt wholesome. This," she waved around, now standing and looking out the door with her hands spanning out from her sides. "This expanse, this golden, grand plain. It is the love of me, it is all. It is clear, far, wide. Whereas, the forests are such an anathema. Andrea, do not think me craven. The deepest

problem is that Enluke was not the only one to lose his life there in those spaces."

On this end point, the two women could not so much feel commonality any more. They drifted quickly a little from each other's estimation. Why? For Alissa wanted to forewarn Andrea about the stones, the forest, those places from very which Andrea had emerged. No matter how they spoke to each other, and Andrea learning that two people lost to a landscape would be more natural causes than any thing other, the superstition made a rift between them.
Andrea was much a spiritual person, or entertaining at least of things beyond the understanding of the material and scientific, but it seemed the bond was broken for the two women. The divide was too much. Andrea could not see the bad in a pathway she'd taken, and why beggingly Alissa would implore her not to ever venture there again.

In the end, Andrea drifted back to the old couple, taking the long walk to the yellow fields she knew. It was her, her place, her love. Perhaps each had their land love.

Now who was that lady? Hadn't Alissa served someone? What a pity, now it seemed there were barriers between them.

With a pain, and feeling like she was lifting up from a tunnel, Andrea stirred.

She was in Hilleton, in her room and she didn't like it at all.
The home was far too warm, and she was perspiring. She stripped off the bedclothes and took off garments. She began to cool and found the fireplace with embers still burning.
Downstairs it was even warmer. Luckily, no danger, just ash and smell, lots of charcoal. Andrea sighed.
With some effort she swept, cleaned, and then cleansed herself in the bath. She still felt frazzled, annoyed.

She had been in Elysian! She knew it, she knew it! She'd actually noticed blueberry stains near her lips as she looked into the mirror. Yet she could remember nothing of the forest path, the stone, the rocks, trekking the fields. How did she connect?

She thought hard until her head literally hurt. What was the point? Of telling anyone? She was tired of being felt mad, special, anything other.

With effort she dried, dressed, found bearings and realised the time, day, moment. It was evening and it felt like the day had been robbed from her.

Andrea brushed her hair to pretty curls by the mirror in her upstairs room. She smiled, a fainter one than normal. So much had occurred. Her skin was a little more tanned, refined. Good. Not that she wanted to be vain, of course. Alissa came into her mind but only briefly, some wistful thoughts. The ring sat cold on the top of the dresser drawers.

The next day she went to work and had an excellent salad meal during her break. She bought it from a nearby shop. Normally she'd bring her own meagre amount of food but today, she felt as ravenous as a horse and certainly didn't want plain old grains.

-Stung-

Andrea had bade Lucy and the others farewell, after a busy day.
It seemed there was a professionals conference in town and so
passing trade had picked up, particularly in the early afternoon.
Not that this was a problem! The minutes and hours flew by,
although mostly with plain old cutting, simple styles for men.
College cuts were certainly the order of popularity today.
It was a pity, not a single coloring job to challenge her true
calling.

After pulling up her humble automobile and getting inside her
hallway, she took off her coat, damp from the moist air outside
and just stared. Nope, nothing much to see here but she needed to
unfocus her mind from the day. Hmmm, things looked a bit
dusty, and so she literally took her bag upstairs, adjusted her hair
a moment and then went back down to boil some spirali, simmer
some tomatoes (fresh of course from the community garden) and
then head back down. She dusted around the sparing items of the
hallway and then followed herself up to other rooms,
unconsciously. Dinner was ready by adorable aromas and then
she sat down to think among gulps of the sustenance.

The next day Andrea couldn't remember much, she'd slept so
soundly. She put on a transistor radio and listened to broadcasts.
Polishing her nails and putting on a good blouse, this was going
to be another average Wednesday. The foot mirror could flip
horizontally on its hinge and had intricate loops and golden curls
for the frame. It was grand for taking the mind off all and sundry.
The face was though, not thinking...which was something of a
new skill, almost. All of yesterday she hadn't worn the ring and
didn't even notice it gone. Today she forgot it as well. Was that a
good?

At nightfall, she found herself breaking a baguette of bread and
adding pepper to her cheese. It certainly made for a strong taste,
although not unlikeably. The butter glued it altogether thinly.
With a plain glass of water it might have made for a comical
status of sheer poverty but today it was all Andrea felt the desire
for. The day's lunch had been hurried but heavier.

It was hard getting to sleep. She hummed a few songs and read.
Still nothing. Some stretches and exercises, then a long bath with
some good soap. Her skin gleamed with sleekness and her legs
would have impressed an observer, if there'd been any. Andrea
found her modesty again, de-robing in her room and putting on a
white night gown. Her hair was dried thoroughly by now after a
little effort.
Finally she felt sleep overtaking her eyelids and she barely lay
down on the bed, not even connecting with the pillow square-on.

The brilliant yellow fields adorned her vision-field. She walked.
Nobody was there at the homestead but that was okay. She felt
herself ready and back in a good place. Home. Setting about to
hoe the soils and walk the grounds, she checked stems and tied up
bunches. She went as far as the fields could and to the dusty road,
marking the edge in one direction. What were these perimeters
like? It seemed nobly right to understand all the lengths and
breadth of her place, here so sweet, with the lovely old couple.
Words weren't needed from them, she rationalized, for their
kindness was like a shining in their faces every time. Maybe
they'd gone to a town or for some trip.

She noticed some reeds, growing on a watery edge of the great
endless fields. Not a tracker herself, but it seemed somebody had
bent them all over carelessly.
Grasses were large in this section. She'd walked a way, but hadn't
any sense of the time passing. Did time pass her much? What
was she asking for?

She bent down to touch the reeds, which had been bent, twisted,
fashioned, almost marking some kind of brief trail. She could
smell a staleness in the air and then happened to glimpse wood
and a wheel.
Whoosh! A sudden heavy club was slicing, cutting, swaying
through reeds and there was a grunt. A scowl, and a brawny man
in torn animal skins appeared in face, looming high and black
brown with filthy covering. Down came a swift strike to her
back, knocking Andrea's breath away, winding her. She fell to
knee then to ground and her tanned hands were out in front of her.
In less than a millisecond she thought about the fact that she
didn't have anything in her hands to defend with, that they felt
bare...but then an inhuman roar made her gasp, open mouthed and

scramble hands and legs to try and get out of the way. Struggling and swaying through leaves, dirt, mud water, the man was tearing down on her fast. He lost momentum with the club crashing to the ground, missing her by precious little. Trying to heave it out, he somehow let go and was mere moments behind her. She had moved westward, not far from the twisted carriage that assumedly was his travel craft and he lifted a piece of wood.

What on earth was going on? She thought this in a rapid moment but more the terror and need for flight erupted into her brain, taking away any further higher reasoning.
Hot, psyched up, she staggered and pelted away, struggling against her skirt which caught on a plant and ripped, just as the behemoth of a man swung wood timber at her, bang, swing, bang. Dropping her. Yet the last bang wasn't landed on her as a pain. Instead, she lay still, shivering, almost surrendering herself to the end, her breathing faster than her thumping heart, as blood dripped from her temples alarmingly. A hiss somewhere told a story. A hiss, of a watery serpent.
The savage man, this husking brigand, had disturbed a reptilian of primitive exemplary power.

Cutting its skin, it recoiled and lashed out for defence. Stinging him sharply, he clutched at his ankle in pain and fell flatly down, with an "urgh!" squeal. The snake loomed up on its end-tail, hideous brown savior-menace, foul and large. The man scampered, wasting energy and scrawling with arms and legs, then beating with patting hands at his ankle, thinking it would dull the swirling circles of pain that spiralled through him louder and louder. He stopped then, breathed shallow and finally lay silent.
Unfortunately, his thrashings had alarmed the snake, which smelt blood and feared still more onslaught. It lay back down to earth, it's natural sounding board, and heard breathing. Andrea's. It circled a slither over the piece of timber intending to murder her, and connected with her clothing, lose on her. She tried to pull back from her revolt, but it was too late. The natural instinct to recoil herself in alarm and give a muted cry was enough to make the serpent bite down again through the clothes.
Was it a tear? How much did it penetrate? Stirrings in her brain clouded worse than before. No signals could get through and consciousness seemed to be drowning. Fading from her. Stung.

Throbbing welts of pain well over her. In her head, Medicine insight pulsated to her front of mind: that the venom dose would be almost nothing, after what the brigand received.

The serpent for its part, job done, lost interest any further and submerged to hydrological depths, scant ripples in the water line marking its former presence.

Sick, absent minded, stirring weakly, she found herself crawling. Almost hysterical one moment and delirious the next. There was a dark cave and she escaped the burning mid afternoon sun. Or was it mid afternoon? She felt herself dying. How on earth she was pulling herself, it was hard to tell on later reflections. Blood caked on her forehead and torn sheets of grotesque filth were covering her body in a symbolic display of harlotry. It was the most unbecoming thing but totally outside her domain to do anything about.

Hours passed but it all seemed a blur. Her tongue was hard and dry, a weight in her mouth giving so much dread.
The darkness of this cave, where ever it was and the cold, were charms that gave her the only solace possible.

No better place to die could there be.

-Recuperating Again-

 Light. Daybreak. Sound. Trembling of body, almost tumbling
down a path. Forest again. Questions. Doctor stunned at her
raggedness. A week in recovery. Then shock at the calendar
date. Have things shifted back? What in the world is this? How
could only one day have passed since her time in Crystal's therapy
practice chamber?!

Myers, Morvan (virologist), Crystal...now Stanley. This doctor
took notes down on everything. The previous hand bite and
difficult recovery concerned him greatly, and now this ankle entry
point for possible serpents venom was extraordinarily alarming.

"Miss Levison, you're lucky to be with us at all. Are you much a
keen forest trekker? Is there someone to take good care of you at
the moment? Best take up some other hobby instead, in any
event. Wilderness doesn't seem to like you, quite frankly." He
said it with all professional courtesy and a hint of dry wit to
lighten the moment. Truly a pragmatist he deemed her quite
sound of mind and scribbled nothing to the contrary. Anyone
could suffer a string of bad luck.
"You're a strong one though, I'll say that. Wherever did you find
that amazing finger annulus piece?" He glanced at the ring a
mere moment, but then a nurse took his attention and he rushed to
another room before he had the chance to lift her hand for a closer
quizzical inspection.

The slip at her feet, on the cot she lay in, was brushed up by a
blonde haired attendant nurse. He had orange, deep-tanned skin.
"You're release form is counter-signed. The doctor's happy with
your progress now, so you're free to go," he said quickly, a smile
carrying on his beaming young face. Women nurses were
laughing in a distant corridor and a cleaner's actions were just
outside the doorway to the room. All was sparkle white and in tip
top ship-shape as could be expected for an infirmary of the day.
The nurse looked like a seaside swimmer as she lay studying his
face a moment with her now wide-open eyes.
He then suddenly clipped the form and clipboard together, placed
them against his chest in both arms, turned on heels and rapidly

scurried off to whatever next errand might have awaited his attention.

"Obviously a professional, that one," she casually thought to herself, and lightly scratched her left temple.

Looking around the room and then at herself, she stood up. She loved her hospital garment in the reflection of the functional plain mirror. Her blouse was on a corner chair and was a complete mess, by contrast. She knew why. She believed. The dirt and ripped seams were telling her, all very very real.

Blood trinkled down her leg. She had no pad. Such an elegant organized girl she'd always been. This wasn't the normal Andrea. What would her mother have said to see her in this state of affairs! Now she was ashamed, self disgusted. She dabbed a cloth carefully on it all, then set about her general appearance. Adjust this, fix that. Yeah. An improvement already. No more smugness in protective white walled accommodation. Hospital dreariness was setting in. Time to depart, assuredly and let behind all the thoughts by just keeping busy with the usual 'stuff.'

Lucy, Jenny and Gwin set about cleaning and then more cleaning. It wasn't a good week particularly. There were customers, but just not enough.

Mark and Judith hadn't been around lately but this was only holding back the inevitable reviews and questions as to why business was slow. It had happened before though, in unexplained cycles of trading.

"Do you think me mad?" Andrea asked Gwin, in earshot of Lucy. Gwin was looking over some sheets behind the counter and on the verge of deciding to send Lucy home early. The conversations were flowing in the room, idle chitchat, then Andrea relating how her life was going, and so forth.

"Come now Andrea, of course not!" Gwin busied herself as always, dismissing more conversation.

Lucy for her own part just smiled and kept on with polishing stock and trade items on the chairs and desks. She did end up going home, having actually asked Gwin before the latter had the chance to mouth it out.

Earlier that day Andrea had asked Lucy the same question and things had been more congenial. Lucy was a good listener lately and Andrea appreciated it very much.
"Call you later Andrea!" she said as she left the workplace.

Andrea realised she'd asked the same question twice in the day. Sighing, she realised that nobody could really understand things.

On the telephone that evening, she tried opening up to an interested Lucy, but some things were just hard to explain in a sensible way and she held some details back.
Friendships only went so far, it seemed, in this life. There were nobody to truly trust and confide in. Andrea felt solitary, more than ever. She hypothesized she was waking up in the night to go and see Elysian. Sleepwalk likely, or that her mind was suppressing the link from this world to the other. Kind of partitioning. As good an explanation as any!

The week went by with no unusual events at all, excepting Andrea's thirst for tea and just staring at the ceiling each evening, thinking and doing still more thinking.

-Circle of Lights-

Andrea heard a report of odd lights on the horizon. She thus decided to go out to take an evening walk down the main street, as did other people at what was a warmer time of year. After all, who knows what other nice sights and sounds could greet her curiosity.

"Those horizons lights are definitely coming from up there," she thought.
She was browsing little stalls as were many other citizens, when the realization was clear, that the said lights were coming from the hill, the mount. Glowing large.
She heard a child muttering of the lights being "bigger than they were before" and it got her wondering.

Taking her car, she headed up, but the road was blocked with temporary gating, fencing.
"Very sorry madam, this roadway is closed," said an officer in full dress uniform, including white gloves such as traffic direction police would use.
As he spoke, her eyes spotted some groups of people and camera equipment with news reporter vans.

"Whatever the for?" she innocently inquired from her car window. The man stood on the road paving just near her vehicle door, as was the custom.

"Some falling star possibly, Madam" she was told. "Best go home, there will be bulletins to follow, but we don't know it's safe yet. Could be debris or further falls."

Andrea drove back as per instruction but then coming round a curve realised that somehow the streams of officials were in the wrong area. The light was actually reflecting many ways, but stronger in front of her.
Failing to see a reason to not proceed, she parked and went upwards. She had a torch and good hiking boots (kept in the car now) and sturdy trousers, instead of her more usual choice of skirt.

Although it took time, this seemed like familiar trail grounds to her. She was not afraid. The ring was with her, after all. It glowed an orangey color, in mixed interest it seemed.

Long before, she had concluded it was emotionally tuned. The stone and path loomed in front of her. Nobody was near, no more wails and chattering. The town was far below but she did not look back.

The lights were in a circle, obviously an intelligent arrangement. The air was swirling and there was a humming. They sensations in the air, blew Andrea's hair around. Her attention was directed to a large block, something else. The lights and mists were guarded by trees and could be investigated later, she rationalized. What was this block? She looked at it and thought there was some kind of opening. This was besides where a path was more cut through.

Idly thinking and questioning if this was some kind of forest fire management trail or something else, she looked further. Beyond trees, there was the stone formation after the path and she found a cave. The cave she already knew and where she had refuged? It was hard to tell and she hadn't seen it from this side. Goodness, time and distances were a bit hazy, even for her familiarity with this area. The torch flashlight was good as was the trail, but still it was hard to mentally count and she had no wrist-piece, unfortunately. Perhaps her bearings were out. Wait, she'd known a cave from Elysian, not from this region. Hmmm.

Summoning curiosity and trust in herself and the ring, she stepped in and through...wow, this looks so different, but familiar....yet what is this....

Her confidence dropped like a dead weight. A chill at her spine brought her to shiver. She turned back, hearing a night owl and walked briskly back down to her car, and to the mundane of Hilleton.

What had the circle of lights meant? Was it intended to draw attention? Her attention or everyone's?

The news story wasn't broadcast until the next morning. "Sky anomaly" seemed a non-explanation, but apparently the lights were now gone. That night Andrea saw no evidence of them against the celestial background. Somehow, the air had felt electric up there and given her that strong shiver, in that moment in the cave in particular. Dread made her very uncertain. Her ring was an odd pseudo-green color for most of the day. It was weekend, and she had to replenish groceries for her kitchen. Necessities did not wait for intrigues to be played out.

When she returned home, packed groceries away and relaxed, she happened to be upstairs in her room and re-placed the ring on her finger. It was now its deep swirling red color again. With a pleasing sensation across her body, it warmed her smile. A flash in her imagination reminded her of the strange circle. She thought of the Zordants and wondered if it could be them. If it was, what were they doing? Where-to did they depart?

The cave provided her with something still more mysterious to ponder.

One reporter, Mr Draffey, had ventured at the mountain site and noticed traces of a remarkable fluid. The trail led to and from a distance, greatly away from the authorities. Nobody had listened to his story though. He had, during daytime after the lights incident, tried to follow the trail. He had found a stony formation and what appeared to be a shallow cave. Finding nothing of note, he left and shrugged off further thoughts. The day vaporized the fluids away.

As the car of Mr Draffey came down back into town, so Andrea was coming up. The cars passed without recognition, of course, for they knew not of each other for any reason. Andrea found roughly the spot she had stopped at before. Thinking better for it, she went on to find where the roadblock had been. Nothing. Her curiosity was killed. An odd smell permeated her as she started the car up and doubled back on her journey. She went to where she imagined it would lead up to the light circle and indeed, she was correct. Her march up, in the strong sun, proved correct, after some trouble initially finding the trail.
Was she going mad? A smell somehow here too? She shook her head and dismissed it.

Getting back home she took the car for inspection.
"Hello," said the broad shouldered man, overalls on and grease everywhere. His smile seemed genuine. "Car trouble?"

"An odd odor. Can you check it over for problems, leaks et cetera?"

"That I can. Leave it with me and come back in an hour."

"Yes I shall, thank you already!" she smiled.

"No leaks madam, your car is perfectly fine. I really don't need to charge you, but you can have my business card." So the man had said and handed her the information. She noted his name as "Saint-John Fortley," partly for its unusualness.

Departing, she went home to rest. Andrea thought over all this. Had the authorities seen something? What? A landing? She thought one thing: Nobody would say much and no doubt nobody had pieced together any explanation. Might it or not be the Zordants anyway? Surely falling stars were relatively possible. Although these coincidences seemed a bit weird to her.

Time passed as ever it does with Andrea feeling more a calming in her days now, getting better and better. Her last occasion in Elysian had been okay, she told herself and breathed easy at night. The immensity of it all was her reality and she was warmed to it all now. The extraordinary became the norm. It brought her back to being an apprentice cutter in a sense. Some experience and then things mellowed in the ensuing years until that sense of comfortable knowing crept over one. So she recalled.

She flicked through quite an appropriate book she had. Dostoyevsky. Yeah. Nothing real, but all permitted. In her case, she'd bent this philosophy a little. It's all real! It's her real. Or her REEL. If time was a tape being played out, that is to say. Oh, this was getting fanciful yet conveniently it laid everything into place, like utensils and plates on a good dining tablecloth. It helped to find perspective and inner peace. She smiled. Even Buddhist leaning? She wasn't, but the eclectics had appealed to "them" and it did to her too. Them. Don't think about it further. Just keep it at 'them' for today. Yes. Are those alien ones the cause of the mind drifts? Are they also the cause of that other world? Was it their making? Who found what? She just had to find out more. Questions lead one to need the answers, didn't they?

One niggle Andrea felt though was a creeping de ja vu, that whenever things would settle, then they would be all stirred up again. Of course a little drama in life could be a good thing...even if her life now seemed to add multiple dimensions of complexity to such a basic notion! It could all get too much, if she let it. Breathe deep, solace of sleep. "You can do it, Andrea!" she told herself. Chaos was what she could be good at handling! Even if her general life just weeks ago had been humdrum!

-Dalliance-

"Ahum ho!"
Andrea heard a cheery cry in the air. Here she was, lifting bales
in the long yellow fields. She was alone, but that was quite
pacific and not at all fearful in Elysian.

"Rather me twist these threads than being to hearing things"
muttered Andrea as she bent down, her apron neat on her and her
blue dress paled with the days in the sun. Contented as always
with the hard labors, a week had passed and she'd barely rested,
for these days the sun set so late and rose so early. She was
sinewy and more bronze than ever, fine featured and gorgeous to
the discerning man who took a while longer to look beyond what
some might see as plain featuredness.

"Ho ahum ho! M'lady, can I find a drink of cool water?" He
trotted out of grasses and paced over, now in focus with dust
clouds behind him. He had a bag at his back and all his clothes
were patches of different shades of green. It came to Andrea's
mind that in a greener place he might fade from view altogether,
in foliage camouflage.

"Who are you sir?" She asked politely, up of back and looking his
way with hands on her hips. The bales lay now at her feet,
steadied.

He was tall, strong, muscled but medium to slim. "Me?
Esmeraltin! That's who!" He bowed low and then rose to smile.
"What a beautiful sight, a working woman, more gold than the
crops them selves!"

She stared them began to smile. He was a charmer.
She took him to a water pump and filled a can. Next she created a
small fire, taking minutes to boil the water carefully before lastly
removing it, warm. "Sorry...maybe it should cool a moment? It's
cleaner this way."

The ring literally sat in her pocket, unused. Thought of it in this
possible situation didn't register with her.

They waited and spoke. He politely explained who he was and his living.

"Forester. It's far, m'lady but this world is not all fields as some may have imagined." She'd already explained her "province" was far. Again it was the only way to describe it without getting blank stares. Alissa had been hard enough to swing around to any further understanding and that had taken considerable time to achieve.

This was a man of action and the world. He may not perceive more than his practical life had shown him day to day. However, he did seem wise and all, from what she could tell. Perhaps he was forty?

"It's been many rises for me," he nodded, almost answering her unspoken question. It occurred to Andrea that years weren't really measured here. Time was...less important.

She poured water, it being finally cool enough. She brushed drips of water on her apron and felt a bump. She remembered the ring, blushed, put her hand away and looked at him to register he hadn't known anything astray, and thought of how in a bit of privacy the ring could have cleaned the water with no heat at all. These several things were in a mere heartbeat or two, no more. Unperturbed, he spoke onward. "M'lady, may I beg your name? Or is that not right?"

"Andrea!" she interjected as he still finished. She smiled and perked up her neck and head. He nodded politely and raised his cup in thanks.

"Oh, coolness, I truly needed that. It's been days. Foresting takes me very far. Sometimes, as you see, I get adventurous and go some more."

He snickered. "Truth is, I can also find myself lost. I have a group of men, but in some rush I headed off another way and now, here I am. What chance to meet you eh?"

They spoke a long time, with mirth, comfort and laughter. He insisted to sleep in his knapsack, very far from her hut.

The next day they worked together, and chatted. Near the end of the day, she brushed his leg by accident. Begging sorrow, he said not to worry.

As they walked back to the barn, he guided her hand to his own well-worn "mit."

The next day, they shared kisses and felt happiness watching the stars and moon as night fell. It was a simple, fragrant, soft and gentle closeness they felt.

They were innocent companions, with common points and sweet, open hearts.

Things remained respectfully aloof for them on the whole and they no more than shared one more kiss.

By the eighth day stationed with her, the fields were well worked and he had told her by campfire that he must be off soon.

He apologized profusely, but as he'd already mentioned earlier, he had to help his men in gathering the forest mosses, which were rare and so prized for cooking pots especially by some farm folk but most of all by the household of the Lady who serves.

She thought a moment and offered to be with him, but he shook his head.

After a long moment with both silent, he took her hand, then put it down and pulled his own hand back to look into her eyes straight by the fire blaze light.

"The problem is Andrea, that I also defend the forest reaches from the marauder tree people. They live there, and would ravage the forest to extinction if not kept in check."

He described them a bit more today.

"If they are such savages," Andrea begged to ask, "why are they not done away with entirely or moved somewhere further and safe?"

"Oh we don't mean to eradicate them, mind, but just keep them down! Their right to exist can't be questioned. Is it so different in your far-province?" he asked this innocently.

So it was that he set off and Andrea shed some tears. It meant something to her but then she had her life, her solitude, her beauty of living here and he might well return. In another place, just as many other women had known, men had to venture off, if thus called in life and women had to go on. She wasn't even sure the depths of what could be and neither of them was so ready for romantic liaisons, even if the beginning of it was, like a gentle butterfly, in them, somehow, impossibly yet probably.

He left her a green cloth, to think of him. She found it as she woke up from a wonderful slumber and walked outside. It was at the doorstep and she knew he'd departed and no doubt wandered far all night. It was the way he'd described his calling of life was. Did things turn, or did all fellows stay set in a way?
She pondered then snapped back to present matters. She kicked up dust as she ran inside again to clean and change.

The A-hum Ho man. She laughed. She looked up and bellowed laughter. He was pleasant and funny, witty, good natured and charming. Rugged. Dazzling in life experience and sweet. Esmeraltin. With pencil and the note in her other pocket, she wrote it. Not wanting anything to be a trouble to remember! No telling what mishaps might shape her tomorrows, if yesterdays were any guideline!!! She laughed at that too and went about the day's work as always.

She didn't know it, but Alissa was at the same time going about her routine, but in the blue field, unlike Andrea's yellow.

-Jeweler-

Andrea was drawn back to Hilleton and not so much by choice.
She looked at the ring, but it defied description. At a distance it
appears to have gold filaments twirling in dragon-like dazzles on
the reddened face, yet when held close to the eye it just clouded
over. Elusive opacity, one might say. She pulled the ring off and
took it to the town jeweler (Mr. Mirkson). "What have you got
here? Yes certainly I can look at its history, clarity, opacity,
facets, carats. For a small price, it's fine."

"You mainly make money by buying, I take it?" she asked.

He assented and she was handed a small document with number,
his signature and the annotation of "jewellery analysis" described
on it.

He couldn't get to it for a few days. Other important business
clients were onto him and there were bridal rings to prepare, melt,
shape.
When he did, he was surprised. "I can't even scratch it or dent it"
he thinks out loud. What rarity is this...hmmm.

Andrea went on with her work. She called in once but he said to
give it another day or two. He had some files and wanted to look
into possible international profiles, which Andrea thought must be
a fascinating enough exercise for him. "Oh it is indeed." She
heard him smiling through the phone as he said this.

She missed it so terribly for the days it was off being assessed. In
fact, she began to feel encroaching paranoia at someone else
having it. Apparently it had no price. Not priceless, just
impossible to quantify at all. It seemed impermeable, as a
diamond, but it couldn't at least normally be with its ruby shading.
That was the jeweler's only conviction.

Andrea went home and had some tea on her favorite chair,
looking at the simple painting and her room. The curtains were
open to the outside world. Street.

In the next few days Andrea went on with work and so forth. The ring? She put out of mind the jeweler's surprises and simply used it carelessly as a mere door knocker, in defiant deference to dull daytime. Maybe she was psychologically grounding herself, bringing back a reality to a crazy existence she was finding her predicament to be. Late youth and strength, coming wisdom on her shoulders and yet all this? How to encapsulate. She increasingly spent time thinking. It felt like being some kind of theoretician, a lab worker maybe or an astronomer at long hours of doing nothing except mental gymnastics and synaptic conjectures. Not that this wasn't appealing somehow. She smiled. Yet creativity of another sort was her trichological delight anyway. It had been hard in her earlier formative years, but she'd taken to salon work and actually not looked back. Stable, forging ahead, building on things she could do and not testing the water of the 'unknown' too hard.

Hmph! Now unknowns of all kinds were around her, creeping in, yet still she was able to mostly find context and sort it through. Was there a prize for mental self-grounding? What a pity to not be so.

-Colonists-

It had all been planned precisely, over long deliberations.
Lighting speed mental corridors and fire-lines of brain waves.
Like two hives combining, there was homogeneity and
heterogeneity that synchronized in a dance all their own, swaying
and so. Now over, came the physical, spatial becoming of it. So
many dimensions now reduced to just the corporeal. Oh, there
was time too, in its relative, mental and absolute senses, but the
space sense was most critical for the steering and supplanting of
security to their bodies and new abodes. This they knew.

The craft had landed. This Hilleton. Not so much primitive but
vastly different from their far world. Alien in every sense. This
mountain gave good cover. There was no point over-exposing
and all the lethal threats to bodily integrities. The second had
peered forward, investigated around a hilly edge. Panicked a
moment, the other two companions could not perceive this one,
until moments passed. Then their missing one reappeared as
though a ghost come to life once more.
Now more pertinently, all three marched methodically and, to the
world, silently. Yet their chatter spattered in bursts and stops,
unspoken yet thought to each other. Unisons and disharmonies
that channelled, tunnelled, but there was a pecking order. The
First Zordant was the main 'caller.'

"Call," as in to call to attention and action, end debate, keep drill
and plan. Planning, psyching. This they did. Eons of lessons
learnt hard and having been morphed into their developing
biological journeys over countless generations. First Zordant,
caller. Second, Assistant Pilot. Third, generic mediator.
Mediators did most things but also held back, to simply obey. It
was this way. Such few numbers now...a pain-like sadness could
overwhelm, yet focus was so important. The First impelled this
counter-zap to his two and also calmed himself, or rather, re-
steeled himself to task.

The Zordants moved smoothly and swiftly. The air was thinned
and they needed equipment. Time tests and more. The second
was having odd disruptions to body integrity and breathing
mechanisms. They thought in unison and no words were said.

This place was desolate. It could be built upon. Surviving and thriving were smeared into each other in their hurried actions.

It wasn't to be. Time moved against them.

For now, the assistant pilot was dying and a craven local was too close.
Being seen had not been in the plan. A will, a mind, not close at all, was clear and was not abiding them. The craven one was stoppable by their will, but this other mind had taken them by surprise. Literally dropping tools, they had only one thing to fall back on: fleeing, that arcane, ancient instinct to evade. Losing strength, it seemed miscalculations had been on them.

Time speeded up for them and they would need recuperation after evacuation. Lights and mists, silently departed, but in haste left fluids.
So few left. Such sorrow and lack of maintained order. Regroup was the ultimate, the prime necessity. Zordant one to Zordant three ordained it.

Leaping through the portal bridge, Hilleton beckoned and they stomped pacedly to craft and away. Debriefings and repercussions were already assessed and being debated. The biggest punishment though was simply the loss. Loss was hard, impossible. Or it should have been, by their code, the creed to betterment and survival that was their all. Now back to dreaded roaming.
Yet a question: Had they taken back Assistant Pilot?

-At home, Peace-

This time, in serene slumber, Andrea drifted. Further and further, she breached the gap between dream and wake. It is a heightened state of somnambulance which she could not perceive at all. As if levitating, she fell by the stones and jarred her head. Awakening, she was overcome by shadow, dizzy and shivering at the cold chill of the middle dark night-time.

It happened again, she evaded barriers of space and time, to find herself in the other place. Warm fields with bristling wheat, identical to the mental dream wanderings just moments ago, are painted in the third dimension before her senses. Walking alone she ups a fork and goes to raking, sweeping, moving earth matter, this hay, that weed. Day after day the old farmer couple smile to have her there, for she is as their daughter now. It dawned on her they were mostly mute, though if voluntarily, it was not to say.

The ring glowed as she did not even know it could. She barely noticed it, however. Yet the warm across her body was reassuring, settling, true enough. An observer would do well to ask, is the ring mightier here? The waves of calm emanate from her and it. Impossible to pinpoint who is doing it, Andrea accepts it. Her mind even dares to love it and the old farm couple smile a hint, in unison to her thinking. A separate part of her mind, subtle logic, seated calmly within, is awake. It is a second channel, quiet, small...it is "seeing." It is not the dominant actor in her mind, but it reviews, draws on what it sees and something like this. This subtle channel sees the glory of the rubesque that calmly stretches out psychic waves. Yet she has not the scientific know-how to relay these thoughts right, or communicate them. She just knows it. The dominant and the second are still one. She is not mad, is not "split." In some other place, she knows people would use such a label. Yet she had always rallied against this small-minded perspective. The mind can talk to itself. Self-talk, the other place calls it, does it not? Bah, this 'other place', claiming some once-primacy, is a fading. Andrea quickly casts back to her present predicament. How to bundle the bale of hay at her feet. This is her daily task in a daily job that is right, that is her. It is all that matters. It is, therefore it is and she thinks just as it is. This was a good self-evidence.

If the wind itself were speaking, it were luring, reassuring in this bounteous, fertile land.

"What an irritating thing!" Andrea said out loud.

"What might that be?"
It was Alissa, the second speaker.
She smiled at Andrea. "I have a bucket of berries for you. Don't worry, I can't stay." Andrea had gone to pat down her dress and invite Alissa to sit and break bread and sip tea.

"Have you been working here hard as can? I've been to see the Lady myself."

"Oh?"

"I volunteered a time."

Andrea wondered about the blueberry field. "Who cared for your plantation?"

"Oh. Nobody. Somebody. All bodies. The free pickers. It's okay Andrea, really!"

Things just work. Yes. Andrea caught on and smiled. She knew, she sensed it, she felt and lived it. Just little disruptions to her thinking order and pace. That 'other place' that need not much more mentioning.

Alissa left, seemingly to urgently do something or meet someone. She turned and had a backpack on with basket, Andrea noticed. Picking herself with the free ones, it seemed logical to say. Andrea brushed wheat crops with her hands, in a wide turn. She smelt the air and went to her hut, with a prance in her step and not a care in the world. The rubesque was enlivening her with a lovely tingle even as she concentrated on it, all while humming, then whistling as she reached the barn and homestead quickly. She'd covered quite a distance in no time at all, barely a moment passing! It seemed it, but maybe not accurately. Bah, what a care!

By quite early evening, she wanted rest. A snooze, and to feel it with the warmth of day to help her. The old couple were around. The man had strolled up and was mending a water trough and instrument for releasing water. The old woman had baked. Glorious smell! They all ate.

It delayed her rest, but not the matter! They went on, working, the man tilling and he woman off somewhere else. All perfect and well. He'd nodded and said hello.

"All be so, child." The old woman had said this as she swept and came in circle near to where Andrea was.
Andrea thought a moment. "My oh my." They had never said much, it almost seemed amazing. The ring glowed. She dropped the thought, remembered her sleepiness through hazy eyes and walked to the barn.
Hay! Hooray!!

On soft hay bed, Andrea dreamed so real an actuality. She lived in twin. Another one of her, living life in modernity, while she was "here?"

It's so confusing, her head pulses with extreme headache pain. She fights it hard and madly searches for the last breadcrumbs she had to eat the day before. Eating some with vigorous speed, she keeps on thinking, working through the pain, trying to break it. Her eyes hurt and are heavy, bloodshot.

She looked haggard in hair but did not know it. No river to check her reflection in yet. Hmmm. No. She was only here. The dream was wrong. It was as though time stopped. Shaking out the thoughts, she blocked the problems and felt waves of calm return. Her mind rewarding her with clarity, will, strength, presence. Focusing, she got up.
What was it all? Dreams didn't mean much did they?
It was vivid, so vivid, pumping in the blood of her temples. She couldn't shake it. She ate a crumb, took water from a pale around the corner. Even worked the field. Waved to the old couple who were together, chatting odd words and still ambling with their endless duties hither and thither.
Nothing shook it. She wrote on her scrap of paper. Notes, notes, brief but sharp.

There was the caped murderer. Black cape, crimson red-lined.
She would know him on sight, and murder him first. This felt
itself in her mind. Not a thought, but a feeling that grew by itself.
"Oh come now, Andrea" she told herself. Dreams don't grow in
wake! She'd read that some place afore. She rubbed her hand.
The ring hand. It felt soothing and the ring glowed, yet with
slightness. Imperceptibly it seemed to twinkle. Dazzler that it
was. It grew darker as she looked on.

She decided to take a walk to clear things. This land was
beautiful, surely such a place of peace could not harbor
undercurrents of unrest?

-Murder-

Like a sudden gust, the scene was highly tangible.

A brown clothed man, atop mottled brown/white horse, with
black leathers. Blue fields to one side, green grassy meadows the
other. He saw her: walking.

Mind on fire, ruthless, he charged. His black cape, with red inner
lining, unfurled and flapped in the wind of his wake. His steed
spurred on unquestioningly.
Short seconds only pass and his is upon her. With a cane he
lashes down, and takes a turn too sharp. Yet he doesn't fall. He
clips off the beast, catching himself and stumbling heavy but firm.

Andrea is alarmed and shocked. Her head struggles with survival
and the flash of mental musings from her last night's sleep. Help!
She runs, but the heavy footfalls of true leather boots tramp along
and catch her easily. He has leather gloves, and a brown glove
mask covering his face with only slits for nose, eyes, mouth. His
moustachioed mouth sweats heavily and he utters no words. He
backslaps her and she evades, but he keeps coming. He reaches
out to strangle and her arms are waving around. Andrea defends
herself. Swiftness of panic helps as the ring glows blazing hot.
Stunned, she tries to un-seat it from digit. He is on the ground
after a surprise kick from her to his mid-section sends him
momentarily down and a little away. Water splashes from wetted
ground. His steed is neighing violently and swirling about. He
seems not to care except to whistle it back. The horse thunders
forward and he reaches for its reins. Using these to pick his own
heavy weight back up, he then next second in unbroken motion
smacks its rump and urges it with a "yah!" to go for her. The
horse flares nostrils and comes at her.

In terror, she falls and has an ankle trampled, but then the horse
spits the air uncertainly as his master, the caped man strides next
to him. He grunts low, and the horse grunts in accord. He bends
downward punching at her, but she rolls. The horse turns,
blocking its master by accident a moment and with water, mud
and grass throwing chaos at her eyes, Andrea lies low, eyes
flaring about, then hears the trots splashing steps near her. In

madness she stretches out, ring hand and connects. The ring
knuckle scrapes and the horse bellows in heightened pain and
downs to the ground. Whinnying like a new foal and flapping
grasses and waters, this but-moment-only alarmed the horseman a
split second. He yields forward, reaches and lifts her with one
strong arm and crushes down to bear on her throat. His other free
hand, the left, winds her intestinal tract to near breaking as a
pugilist. At his back, he has some kind of shield-square tied in an
x-cross. Life is fading from her fast and he throws her
mercilessly down to the yucky ground.

He looks at his horse and sees blood seeping. This angers him
incredibly. He unties his back shield and pulls a sword from his
horses leather side pack.
Imagining he is a knight to battle, he peers through sweat at her
and lunges. She is up and stumbling backwards. The sword just
brushes her, touching the dress before burying itself in ground.
Mud sucks it in and as he pulls it won't so easily lift, so he
decides to use the shield only, as a kind of ram bludgeon. He
swings, swings, she is half-running, half falling with her wounds.
Somehow, she grasps one side of the shield and as he tries to
yank it from her, he slips on unfirm surfaces. His horse screams
yet more and the confusion is in the air.

Time slows.

Andrea can barely breathe. He is heaving. Insanity only
prevailed. The sky itself seemed to darken and boggy fogs were
near to their footings. Rocks, mists, slight breaches to the
otherwise uniform green highgrass surrounds. Clouds passed
over and the air itself seemed to cry alarms and injustices.

Was the horse dying?

She felt sickened and dreadful, her hair messed and some torn
from her scalp. Would he stay down? He seemed so strong. Yet
now she had seized the shield and whipped forward with the ring
again. He swung a confused punch which nearly shattered her
palm and wrist. Bones jarring but the ring just managed to
scratch him. He pulled away and yanked his body back a little on
the ground. His boots and heavy leathers weighing him, now his

cape caught on heavy weeds mixed with mud, water, grass, dead wood sticks.

She wanted away, but also wanted revenge.
Angers not in her ever before, suddenly bubbled out. She upped and looked over him, kicking his shin to take the advantage. She threw herself onto him, with shield first, so it lunged like a plate onto his chest. It only barely crushed him and he glared burning hate through eyes at her. He tried to free his arms underneath and then decided to brute-force them both up. He pushed and she flew in the air, then causing her felling to earth.

He got up and bolted forward, not bothering to wait for her to rise. He was lifting, dragging the shield despite his lowering energies. Fighting in marsh was tiring. On her again, the same turf, he thrust the shield, quarter-corner, intending to rip her torso open with malice and a final assault to mortal end. She could only duck and roll, but this meant it connected to her spine and stung like a million bees. It nearly immobilised her.
If not for the electric power downing and then re-lighting from ring to her body, back and forth, surely it would have been her end. This was becoming a blood bath.

He dribbled blood and foamed saliva at the ends of his mouth. His fist was bloodied.
She was face down. This time, he stopped inexplicably. He saw her bloods rising and then ajar, saw her hand and the rubesque. Quizzing his brain, he lifted her seemingly lifeless arm and stared down at it. Wrenching, crunching, pulling he tried to tear it off. Slipping fingers, both arms now, everything was too greased. He patted his hands and arms down on his own clothes but no good. He couldn't grip and couldn't lift it off. It dazzled and made him en-tranced.

Withdrawing a little, he sat to take breath, ignoring the waters, grass, discomfort. He gingerly pulled out a cloth, perhaps a kerchief and wrapped it slowly over his blood-dried hand. Cursing he glared at her.
With difficulty he heaved her over, so she faced up. Her eyes were white, the irises rolled up into her forehead. This happened to give him the opinion she was gone from the world of living. Her shallow wisps of breath were undetectable.

Hands over her roughly, he found a paper in a pocket seam of her dress. Touching her fleshily and without morality, he grunted approval. Sickening all this water! His thoughts were simple, tarnished, a mixed up warrior of no purpose. Left to rot, but nobody would know, not this wench or any body other, for the matter.

He wiped his face with filthy water.
Again the ring glowed. It actually struck his eye, capturing a shadow and then bend of light from the sun above. This annoyed him, causing him to squint.
Avowing to try again, he used both hands to pluck, pull, wrest, twist, turn until finally, he had wrested the ring off her finger, and with the moving of clouds, it blazed like the sun.

He gathered himself, dripping wet and all, muddied clothes and stood tall in triumph. An unexpected prize of the fight, he conjectured and convinced himself. So tired and hunger gathering, but he swallowed, licked at his own cheek and willed these away. Years of discipline could do that. Perhaps the horse could serve one last purpose and then he could gain another by stealth of night as 'afore.

The shield lay rudely next to her. Instrument of death. Or? She stirred just a little. Sharp stings bit at her, but she pulled the shield to slide up atop her own breasts.

He heard the sway of water and grass and looked down at her from his mere foot-stride away. Surprised, then enraged, he decided to make this wench really feel final pain now! Twisting his arm, to clench his fist and align the ring right, he would crudely thrust it down. He aimed at her eyes, to maximize the injury and shock. Wry smile, her tool against her, he envisaged.

Yet: with the shield atop her, the ring had without warning charged up and now a red flare of laser emission poured down at infinite speed. Unfortunately it was turning on its owner, but then, no, the burning energy pulsed straight back, a perfect reflection, killing him dead that shocking instant.

Murdered by his own murderous intent.

In a blackened crisp, his sickening corpse lay there, charred completely, and the ring harmlessly bounced off his greasy finger and down onto grass blades on the ground. His foot was atop her leg, the only part of him to touch her as he went down to the ground deceased.

With trepidation she found purposeful mind returning and plucked up the ring. It could kill, but that was more observation than any more. It was hers. Raw power. The break of peace, the conflict, was over.

So many emotions hit her.
She was sobbing and pained so badly. She crawled just a few body-lengths to a drier spot. With the ring back on her finger, she could only pray and will it to aid her. Her body dried in the blistering sun. Droplets of rain fell, a light sprinkle after some short hours of her laying there. It seemed to cool and clean. Her breathing slowed and her pulse rate declined. This was not good.

Sanguinal sugar energy in her was nearly void.

The last thought she mustered, after seeing events of her life appearing then petering away, was to summon her small finger to rub gently on the ring. It was gold, green, black, tunnelling colors. Although she would not actually see it.

-Rescue-

At her word, they kept their word. Rigged in gas breathing
apparatus and with heavy packs, silvery suits on top of their
normal silvery suits, they hid behind forest tree grove-lines. They
sat and were calling. Going deeper into Elysian was an
unnecessary risk. With technical know-how, they willed with
minds a traveler to draw near to them and they communicated
wants and worries. His mind became distilled with their urgings
and he saw them not, although they sat right in front of his
cowering countenance. This wandering man would retrieve her
body carefully on his shoulder. He was slender but sinewy of
muscle. Remotely willed, he ventured out. Burning in his front
of mind was Andrea's identifying features.

Finding her bedraggled, he looked about mindlessly. The
Zordants were straining to control him from so far. The hum of
their electrical equipment beat in tune with their bodies, seeping
up to their powered minds as though there were no physical
breakage. Linked. Curiously strange it was, to a squirrel foraging
nuts wide-eyed in a high loft tree with drizzled piny brief leaves
that towered to the scorching charged sun. Airflows were low,
the second Zordant warned to the first. Splitting his thoughts, he
took the mental 'nod' from the other and then re-focused on the
wanderer.
The wanderer found the horse and took a blanket cloak. Yes, do
that. The Zordants urged him and suppressed the man's desire of
body to take rest break.

When the man finally came, the Zordants snapped to action,
putting Andrea on the tray table. Very surgically and white it
appeared, totally out of place in this unscientific world-sphere.
Taking Andrea's lead, they thought of it by the name Elysian, but
only for cataloguing convenience. This would all be in the
chronolog another day. Dangerously low, they found the stone
steps and then the cave ducking-place. Dragging her through, one
at front, the other at rear, their air nearly expired as they pulled
off masks in haste on the Hilleton side. Dark night embraced
them in greeting. Cool air and moony sky's crescent, caressed on
a background of stars they knew too well.

Behind them, in the other world, the wanderer was forgotten and had dropped dead. Sacrificed to the greater promise, his energy depleted.

Word was word, quest was quest. Still learning and searching a way from plan to fruition, the alliance of Andrea and they was too important to disrupt or chance to fail. She would live by the power of their all-equipment. The laboratory on-board the craft waited humming at a stir. Antimaterial nucleic crystal foundations, powers that no other world could understand, were fuelling without skip of beat, as always.

The large craft had immense empty space inside. It was order, solitude, almost an island of size and sanctuary indeed. Totally sterile and programatically controlled.
Silvers and whites adorned the stark undecorated interiors, only broken by halls, doors and the rare portal allowing a view out. Everything could glow. On their entry, everything did, in welcome.

In the smaller lab room, their miracle work paid off. Her spine renewed, wounds fading with their spectral gear and warming radiation-makers. A special gas impelled her to breathe. They studied the ring over and over. Commune had them agree the ring's inner energy had been the only salve keeping her mental processes in gear at all.

The craft was away. They all had the knowledge, but it still stirred them raw that their assistant pilot was not here. Lost. No. Gone, that was the word for it. Beyond ever their repair-surgical-energy-turning skill. The loss burned their super-charged minds nearly out of control, even if emotive threads were not so much a threat to their neutral logics.

Up and soaring, stars blazing past with the craft's total speed, it was not long to bear. A mere hour passed, no more, and Andrea was strong enough to arise from the table, a-gasp and surprised as the day they had first met.

"Your mind will clear in moments." the first Zordant advised. He slowly plunged a yellow chemical from an injector and vial, into her torso side. She was too queasy to shake a protest. Her head

fell back but then a minute later she was up again. The Zordants were still. The second had scanned some electronic panels on a portable console he now put back on his utility-style belt.
"You are privileged to see more things. In a sense we are learning together," the second Zordant shot the thought at her.

Andrea didn't want to resist. Depths of her were open mentally and they were allowing a mid-depth of their own minds, in free offer. Better than the shallow normal they gave access to, anyway.
The first was memorising and considering properties of her ring. That they had once held it in custody and yet only now, with its gifted new owner, did it offer up any glimpse of its other possibilities. It did not compute easily true, for what was a cross-cosmic communicator and nothing more. It was a mineral, that while curious, had never supplied anything other to them in the way of utility.

Now the view outside changed as they crossed the horizon from blackness of space to blueness of a world. Down they bent in craft and the vessel swayed a little as they dipped, then surged in new speed. Only gradually did they orbit down and stop curving. They hovered the surface and would not actually make landfall.

 Towering ferns marked the terraced gateway to Diafernia. This was the home of the forge-lab of the rubesque ring. Enclosed in an enormous dome, on a dusty planet of low air. The lone Zordant showed it to her, the second having left for another part of the craft altogether. It was explained the other number of Zordants were away, forging a new planetary home. Their 'war' was with the elements themselves. This he described to her. Again he mentioned how 'privileged' she was.
Apparently none other of her kind knew anything of them. She was the first they'd approached from her world. Others had since been tried but none had been much use, all apparently dismissing the Zordants or simply having nothing to 'contribute' with informational focus.

She nodded to them and looked on at the open rectangular viewing portal/screen.

The Zordant also described her body's injuries and briefly how she'd been restored. He left out some details and only gave the vague thought to her that nothing more was needed known or could be known. She took this to mean things beyond understanding.

The second came forward and gave her a drink. He went to open her jaw with his hand but the first raised his hand and nodded to glare in regard at him. Instead, the second found custom in his mind and then correctly offered her to take the drink from his hand. It was cool clear water and refreshed Andrea.

Andrea happened to spark a curiosity and probed a little at the first Zordant, in mind. He stopped her and the ring only blued in color a moment, then greened. Under-swirls of red came back up like something bouncing out of deep water, as a ball might float back to surface. The second Zordant noticed it and urged his fellow Zordant.
Andrea spoke out "I do not understand why I'm here, why I have this, and what you want! And why was I attacked?"

For but a moment, one of the Zordants, the lesser, had a picture in mind that Andrea saw, of a caped fiend just as her attacker had been, yet doubt as to his motivations. The "suggestion" of a lord's guardian hopped from his thought to her, but then instantly seemed to withdraw as though a rug had pulled from under someone's feet.
The caller focused mentally on her. "We must return you, there is not more time."
His mind was strong and rained calm around the borders of her thoughts. No escape. Still convalescing, she didn't have all energies or coherences in her anyway.

"I need rest" she said breathlessly and fell forward, caught by the unready second Zordant, who laid her down on the floor. The square of floor below her rose to be a table, elevated by a single middle stand base on the underside.

They left, consulted each other away.

The craft swung round hard. In annoyance they strode to her home world. They had none. None yet. The second would do the heavy lifting to her home.

She would be in her bed, and their rescue done. Problem averted and observations, trials, searches through calculable possibilities would go on, as they must for the cause of the Zordant all-ones.

-Reality Check-

Andrea was again back in Hilleton.
On waking, for a moment everything was puzzling. With a shake
of the head then, she set about doing things and was going out the
front door, to perchance find a letter waiting. "Bridgette!" she
exclaimed. She took some minutes to open and read it.
 "Terribly sorry, I've been so busy as always, keeping on top of
things up here, and battling a fever for a few days as well. What
have you been up to?"

Andrea made two calls. She asked for a later start at the salon.
Mark said "done!" without hesitation. Things were cool and
quiet, or "just might be" as he put it.

Then she called Bridgette.
"Hi Bridge! It's me, Andrea. Thanks for writing! I'm glad to
catch you by the telephone, too."

"Aren't you just! You know me, out, about, busier than a bee
most of the time. How are things down south for you?"

Andrea gave a courteous reply without over-burdening detail.
Bridgette was a great listener, wonderful old friend, but too many
details might fluster her simply because of her busy life there in
accommodation work.
They talked a while and Andrea promised to post a return letter to
Bridgette.

The next day Andrea didn't work at all, so she sipped tea by the
upstairs window, in her bedroom and wrote.
This was a chance to tell Bridgette more, express her feelings and
describe her 'vacation.' In a big sense this toning down word was
unfair, most of all to Andrea, because honestly, more than
Hilleton and even the bizarre Diafernia that slowly recalled to
mind, she knew that her heart was more in Elysian these days. It
was bold, new, undiscovered, glorious, big. Sure it had dangers,
but the potency of the rubesque was like her shield and only, if
only, she could unpeel it like an onion: then she would be better
able to wield it for good, for herself, for others too and make right

and glorious of her own life. It was crazy to think, yet it seemed a new vocation.

She even wrote of the ring. Perhaps describing its powers or potentials wasn't easy to do or even soundly advised, so she left some information scant. Bridgette would read it all and move on. Seeing Bridgette again, embracing as two adult women, would be very nice. She hoped to get up north there now and thought of it a little.
"Considering a bit more, Maybe even Elysian isn't everything."

Thinking on: "It seems the one thing I can't do is bring others with me."
Before being blocked, she had read in the Zordant's mind that even the deceased Zordant's appearance had uplifted and improved back from Elysian, slowly, before he perished.
Why was she immune? Did anybody know? The Zordants had also intuited that they couldn't survive in Elysian. Was it all hers for the experiencing only?

Putting it to the test, she asked Lucy to come back to the mountain with her.

It was fruitless; Lucy didn't want to fear another injury up there. Judith became an unexpected ally though: She herself had wanted to see the wreckage of the burnt forest and the place where the press media had spoken of the strange lights.
So that afternoon they set up the hill in Judith's car. Andrea didn't know her that well. She was the Salon owner with Mark. More a payroll master than anything like a friend.

Anyhow they made the most of it and were getting on fine.
After quite a trek with Andrea's encouragement, Judith was getting a little tired. They sat down but Andrea spied the stone and steps not so much further, at a guess (through trees). Judith was probably 10 to 15 years older, but it was impolite to ask such a thing. Andrea had been observing her walk-partner but then looked away.
They each sipped a canister of water they both separately had (at Judith's insistence). The sun had perhaps two hours left in it.

"We'd best get back. I'm going to make dinner for Mark. He wants to play at the golf course tomorrow after taking the burden today of the money and paperwork."

Talking shop wasn't something much of Andrea's interest but she nodded, then said "look! I know this area from before. Oh please let me show you the great view beyond this grove and this large stone!"

So they went. Yet whether first by the steps, or by the cave, it seemed Andrea could peer through to the plains, forest and golden fields (with keen eye) but Judith simply could not.

"I don't see anything special, just dense countryside and fog. Your eye is keener than mine, Andrea. Yet all the same I do not see a reason to venture deeper on."

She could only agree.

With an inaudible sigh they both went home.

It did confirm what Andrea suspected though. It only made sense that the ring might be connected to all this strangeness more and more. How many properties and possibilities could be attributed to it?
How many energies could a tiny item possibly hold? She had scars and injuries to prove it was all current, relevant, truthful--yet it was only for her?! Or, at most, only for someone who could bare to wear the ring at least a time without the headaches claimed by that ignoble business man Reginald from afore. Nightmares indeed! Oh, she'd had some but overcome all that. It made her tingle with pride in a sense.

She thought and then now was sitting at home again, having farewelled Judith. She dried her hair in the bathroom and combed it thoroughly. Now touch-dry, she pulled it back and tied it into a ponytail. She felt sweet and womanly, glad to be alive. Yet missing something, missing the old couple, the free pickers, Alissa and all whatever more, for it was all-enthralling in that beauteous immense landscape. The magnetic pull on her heart was strong.

-By Her We Serve-

Her life was now going back and forth. Though this time, Andrea was totally in control. She was up in the mountain, inspecting the great stone and path. Then the cave. It didn't make sense and yet sure enough, she had no problems going through the "gateway" herself. Why didn't it work for anyone else?
She felt calm. The ring was on but she had gloves on. It was warm but she didn't feel the heat that much generally. She had long pants on, good hiking boots, and a cooling white blouse top. It made sense to also look at things from the other side (so to speak). She took to the cave and had a crawl through.

A young girl was prancing around the field when she trounced through, motioned down path and got close to the yellow areas.

"Helloooooo" she called out to the girl.
They met, with the girl short of breath, huffing and puffing. Her blond hair was in two braids.

"Are you ready for the Lady? You look very smart."

It was explained to Andrea that the "Lady" passed through areas to find more to do service.

The lady who serves all… "She is our servant" said the short freckled girl, "so we in turn serve her." It is how it is, she admonished, quizzically. "You must know this already! Did you forget? Does the word travel so slow? Are you from so far?" She frowned at Andrea with childish uncertainty and a feeble attempt at wise judgment.

"The lady who serves all?" thought Andrea. The girl wandered from view, lost to other passing propositions of her playful head.

Little does Andrea come to realise all of this yet. After all, who would know what to believe from a girl? She bore to mind books she had perused in libraries about children and psychology. Sighing, it was all a bit much and learned, but basically in many senses little girls and boys strode a view of things which was half reality and half imagination, but all geared to fun and play.

Nobody knew exactly when the Lady would arrive. Andrea got to wondering. She'd asked the old couple about it. She'd even visited Alissa to try and understand some more, and a picker named Mickle.
He'd known a lot, in roundabout manner, though made it clear when he was done talking and only wanted to do his usual labours.

Then later that day, as Andrea also helped pick not far from Mickle and Alissa as well as others, a galloping trot of horses pulled in.

A sturdy and proud woman, shrouded in fine linens, was in Andrea's shadow with attendants. She was aided down and looked at the rows of pickers, villagers, peoples gathered.
They all stood in respect and waited for her. An absolute answer.

  When Andrea could finally see the "lady" as her procession drew near, including many horses and carts in tow, she thought she was seeing double.
The resemblance is truly astonishing for the woman is just like her, but with jet-black hair and a single white streak, where her widow's peak lay high at her forehead. Yet nobody else could notice the eerie familiarity, of the Lady's movements and face.

Nevertheless it made Andrea very afraid. Afraid? Or perhaps self-conscious, that she would dare to be like this 'royalty.' All bowed very low for the lady. No title or name did she have but simply as it was, the Lady who Serves All...

Andrea trembled and waited. What would these people, more her brethren yet still opening to her, think? Could she trust nobody else would notice their almost twinship of features?

-Will you serve me?-

Deliberations and hushed discussions went on. Some people
began to stir, move, go back to tasks but none strayed truly too
far.
The eye of the Lady was hawking down on everyone, looking all
around with dark thought and clear, judgmental leadership.

Then, it was finally the time of calling. Citizens appeared at the
road from all of nowhere, even more so than before.

   The Lady did her choosing. She walked along the crowd,
swaying and looming in her tall frame, then reached nearer.
Andrea is looked upon, but as a cloud passes over, glinting her
tresses a little darker, the Lady sees her almost as an image of
herself. The Lady who Serves, matched by this outlander she had
hardly remembered from before? What?!
   It betrayed the lady, it was effrontery. Yet mostly it gave her a
shudder, unlocking memories.
In a moment of still more silence and dread, Andrea was trying to
glean emotions and what was happening. What did it mean to
serve anyway?

Snapping, the Lady Who Serves spoke, uttering: "Bah! This one
is no good at all. On to the next!"

A woman was led. She curtseyed and followed without any
impulse otherwise. The crowd stepped away, the procession went
on and all went to duties with out missing a breath.

Straining at her mind was a thought from a book of her homeland.
Mass hypnosis?

-Meeting-

   Alissa visits Andrea with a solid stare in her eyes. She is alive,
but bewitched of purpose. She guides and urges Andrea to 'attend
the Lady who serves all."

After three nights of endless walking, on a stony throne, in a
forested fortress, Andrea emulates Alissa, in kneeling. The ring
glows with alarm even through Andrea's gloved hand. A strange
magnetism bows her head low, without her own bidding it
wilfully. Then snap up, her head is lifted to see the Lady seeing
almost through her, with ashen icy eyes.

"I know of the murder," she boldens. "And your almost-death.
The knowledge came to me. All does, always." Lifting hands,
which twinkled with strange gems, rings, and stringy metals
attaching down around her palm and wrists, she towered over
Andrea and stood tall. She moved forward to be directly over
Andrea.
The ring energised Andrea and she felt a surge in her, urging her
to impulse. Andrea though, feared the moment.

The Lady hesitated a moment, feeling the very sameness and
raised her left eyebrow erect. Searching, searching. Then with a
swift shake of hair, the lady continued. She peered.

The pain to Andrea was a jolt, then it echoed away like waves
fanning out on a pond, after a pebble is thrown in. Andrea gasped
in shock! The lady was seeing into her. Peering.

Silence for some minutes stood as shimmers of sweaty beads fell
from both women. The lady took backwards steps, keeping
focused on Andrea and then others, attendants and Alissa herself.
"Aliss-sar who is charmed and has served, of the blue field, you
have earnt the finish of this task."

Her pronunciation of Alissa's name was noted by Andrea, who
felt something lift off her, a weight, somehow. The air thinned
and sun seemed brighter now all around. She looked at Alissa,
who was on the ground, had fallen, but now was stirring with

arms and picking herself back up. The Lady was again on her throne.

There was no bowing. Not a thing. Alissa turned to go, and went to take Andrea's hand, to urge her away. The lady interjected "You are at ease. I know you acted in justified manner." Alissa's mouth gaped open, but the Lady cut the air with her Lapis Lazuli covered hands. "I say it, you-from-far. I deem you have served. All do serve in their proper time."

Andrea's mouth opened as though to speak. She couldn't, the Lady hushed her with a shoosh and a finger at her own mouth, the meaning obvious. She shuffled like lightning, forward, and lent over to Andrea's ear so no others could hear: "I know you are like me. The others don't see it, but I see all. You are from outer lands I gather assume. Be you to remember your place and my honors of grace extended to you so kindly."
Then, she was tall again, stepping back, sliding down to her seat of power.

Both Andrea and Alissa left slowly and then took greater pace. Andrea's ring softened to stillness. She had the strange feeling come over her that the Lady had wanted them to go so she could meet somebody else, in deference to a higher power still, but it seemed difficult to decipher the meaning, or fact from postulation.
On a third night of transit again, both women were back at the blueberry plantation. Neither of them had talked much. Andrea chose to sleep on some hay outside, suddenly so tired, just as Alissa went in with parting words of "some things are not so easy to teach. Better to feel them, friend."
Alissa had avoided saying "my friend," and this clipping got Andrea wondering as she drifted off.

At early dawn, Andrea did not feel the desire to disturb Alissa at all, and simply went to the yellow fields and her elderly parental ones of this world. She set about tying bales again. Thought after thought came and went. All the immensity of things took so much time to gather into a logical solidity in her. "Aliss-sar..." she thought out loud.
It was her determination to not forget a thing, although she needn't worry. She remembered everything explicitly these days.

She unconsciously put her hand to the ring finger, feeling it through the glove. She thought and thought a moment. Again it seemed everything was more powerful here, even her mind.

-Reflections of the Lady-

The Lady who serves shook off the impressions that came from
Andrea. It was too much to believe. She went into the recesses
and touched the icy stone. Feelings and ideas poured into her.
Her presumed-late husband still spoke here. Was he gone? Or
just far away making treaty? Her attending servants were
watchful of their words and indeed, like the great many, they did
not speak much counsel in the main. However she couldn't avoid
hearing the rumors that the icy stone was the chamber holding her
husband. Sometimes she even believed it herself, but a fear and a
blackout of memories wouldn't let her probe further. Imposing
into the minds of others was her reaching-out power, and yet the
same thing could never work on herself. A leopard cannot reach
out and attack itself, or paint on more spots.

It was simply true that she ruled. She knew it. So long had it
been so. Always? It seemed. It was weighty but correct. As
things should be.

Where was her husband? She could not hate. It was not a page in
her mental repertoire. She was stern and ruthless in maintaining,
preserving. The land must be preserved as is. Inside her this bore
true, so true, truer than anything else. Only her husband's love
could temper her to regard anything else. Now he was gone,
things all merged to the one point of ongoing pain and numbing
that through ritual, rightness, rule and seeing through the
timetable of servings. It wasn't really a timetable, but rather
simply her own incredulous will. She would see it, then call it.
Out to find the ones or, if too inwardly focused a day, the serving
attendants, then those who currently served her in all, would be
emissaries out. Whatever it took, but with a steady hand. Not
that anybody resisted anyway. Her will had a way of gently
spirally out, a lull in the wind, a whisper to all those working and
being about.
Yet there were limits. This outlander had shown it. It seemed
more apparent. Yet promises were promises and realities meant
diplomacies. People served different ways, yet in the great
endless chain of things, all the serving made a sense.
The shining light of the icy chamber and room didn't make so
much sense, but then, what was a cosmos of total sense? No,

mystery was the advent of more to do and that willed men and women on, which led to order and a purpose which was her calling at the top.

Yet woman she was and her husband had been mirth, wit and mostly the measure of order and noble-hood. In other senses the grandeur had been more theatrical, with appointed peoples acting at counsel. It was all showy and but a muse, although her husband gave it all life, every time. The fields didn't cease, all found place and more. HIS sense of the stronger will was more subtle than hers.

Yet far away, far off, even captained afar from shores, he was willed to venture and extend the blessings, the might and order of all they had. He had gone and he was not the lesser to be obeyed. Equal yet a boorish brute, but in romantic high gesture. Others wouldn't and couldn't see it. She took a moment to caress her own hair. She lifted off the veil and diadems and lets braids swim out. She shook her hair and gazed into the staring-glass at her self. That woman! It led her to feel brought down. Yet she summoned energies and recoiled to her upright posture. Even a twin-like one, all new and about, here then and next vanishing, was not a thing. What had happened at the calling with Aliss-sar? Was it the doing of the outlander? What the matter, nothing had changed. So she consoled herself.

Somebody called. She was not omnipotent, so she hastened to re-dress herself in radiant elegance to set all a-right, then pulled open a decanter to take her lime fluid essence. It cooled and was her favorite essence of field fruits.

To the other chamber she went back to the business of state.

-Called-

Esmeraltin had returned from a campaign in the forests with his
men. He was again alone, this time not randomly wandering, but
going with intent. He wanted to see Andrea again, that was the
hope.

He didn't make it past the blue fields.
A soft horn was blowing and a scruffy attendant on horse stopped
by him. A plaque under his arm, with gleaming gem, said it all.
Emissary.
"You are Esmeraltin" he bellowed defiantly. "You are called to
serve."

Esmeraltin ignored and continued to walk away. Then, the air
shimmered and his vision dimmed a little. Things appeared to
gray. Far at the other end of the blue fields, Alissa felt it too.
Time of calling.

There was no resistance to it. Resistance didn't come into play.
So his shoulders slumped. He went. With the rider he sat and to
the chambers, the buildings, the immensity, the place which was
home and dwelling of the Lady Who Serves. Now he would
serve her, serve the land.

A part of him was a little smarter than all the simple call of it. He
was more conscious than most. This could likely be a long
calling.

The Lady bore down on him, when he was inside, oiled, greased,
his new clothes white and loose on him. He glistened, he stood
tall, looking back at her with puzzled regard. He neither resisted
nor relented. He just charmed. She actually for but a moment
smiled back. Then she laughed and cast back her head, then
shook herself back. Other attendants around exchanged glances
but then held privileged silence as they were respected to do.
Accommodating, she called him to a rear room where only one
attendant guarded, with pillow in arm and robes at hand, head half
turned down but back very straight. This guard had on gold and
green robes and was a permanent, in the hold of those called to
serve. He was in fact, born to serve. Very high honor, but aloof.

In fact, he had no tongue to speak of symbolically, for his loyalty was only to the providence of the woman he served, dare he not even utter to think such a travesty of non-regal title, rather she was the Lady, one and only. He dared to swallow. All his mind open to her...but he need not worry, she was abuzz with the man at hand to her presence.

She stood, he kneeled to her will.

Strangely, he rose again, and Ilvic, her attendant, thought it his finality of duty to tear limb from limb to defend his Lady, something he had dreaded should never happen but might, for he was guardian as much as any other duty urged on him. Yet she smiled and took the man's hand.

"You are deemed of good skin," and for a time, she thought-projected at him. He nodded. "Come consort, your role has been assured. Do entertain to stand at my side, and Ilvic shall measure, for the clothier can then come to find your garb for the righting of binding."

This meant she would advise with him and be the nearest any would be to equal.
He knew about the husband. He couldn't take such posting but instead, as a consort would, he would be her assistant of special ranking. No doubt as others she had felt and seen him with her far-seeing, for quite some time. His wanderings and services in the forests were at times beyond her scan, but the nature of his work and his own adventurous spirit would always have eventuated to bring him back close enough to her mind's eye. Nobody really knew the lengths. It was all too much. As if spellbound, all simply did as they did and thinking was perilously low or weaved away in other things, for such was the shimmer in the water, the contentment, the natural order of all that was "Elysian" as Andrea had called it. The opening of his mind, courtesy of her "outlander" self, was intriguing to him, but scant not all. He had loved her but now this would fade even more than time had already conceived to do.
Yet he would not cry or wonder for other lives, because another part of his mind knew he was what he was because it simply was the summary of him and he was contented, too. Did things ever truly change?

Andrea soon knew. Alissa came to tell her one day in the field. An exchange of ground wheat and extracted blueberries had been good but jinxed by the downturning of this news.

Andrea felt like a spectator to a play. She had felt for the man, he was amazing and insightful. He was her "Jon." She giggled at the dream that was so long ago now. Yet she had already known things had moved away, their spirits had drifted by different destinies, even if a little bit of her had dreamed and ached for more, like a single vapor of steam from a large hot spring of a watery lake. It was nothing but insubstantial scintillating touch, like a cat stroking its tail past the leg of the master who is a-slumber and barely able to notice it.

She harbors resentment to losing her Esmeraltin and yet feels unpowered. The thought of him was what counted, truly. She curled a hair of her head without thought of it.

Unconcern overtook her after some minutes of vacant staring. Alissa left her to be, she knew how Andrea was and well, could relate to it. The things of life even in a paradise were not always so happy. Yet beauty of solidified mind always returned. This was the thing about the world she knew and loved as nothing else. Andrea now had this pumping through her veins too, this was evident, and, no doubt logically right and good. Things always turned and resolved. Alissa smiled at her own counsel and went back to her home with a swing of hip and feeling womanly intent in her stride. Blue essence and a pie would do herself some good!

Andrea strolled home. Her purpose in working the field again feels the encompassing of what she is.

Yet as she comes to terms with the losses of feelings, things oddly unfolded.

Away, away, a man from the field of battle, Endamene, the true husband of the Lady who Serves, appears on the scene only two weeks later.

The astonishment of it reeked through all the chambers and walls of the Lady. Delight, bewilderment, more. Not many saw it, but those that did would be calmed and forget it anyway. Will carried so much weight from her castings. Her dear Endamene, her

husband! Yet he was ripped, torn, wasting of skin and will. He is dying of wounds from fighting in battle and the Lady mourns him.
A mere twenty-four hours with him was something so brutal. Esmeraltin and even Ilvic were dismissed with filthy glare from her presence. She wanted alone this time.

Forty-eight hours later, not having eaten, Ilvic dared to wander in. He was not shunned. He aggrieved in worry for his Lady. He tried to perceive but had not all of it in him. He did remember Endamene but husband-and-wife matters were not in his life-course.

He was ordered to release Esmeraltin from the outer chambers where that one was teaching. So it was done.

Esmeraltin walked out. His mind erupted clear, but empty. Confused. Fourteen nights with the Lady had defined him already. Now, he would wander again. His men, his men. Teeming back into him was the only thing that made sense; his original duty. Out of directional rectitude, he went to see Andrea anyway. Plans were plans. Now he could at least look upon her and talk with her. Another goodbye and with reason, more things learnt and a thank to her.

He let her know that he had been released but no longer had feelings for her. Andrea, on seeing him, tried to awaken her own latent feelings and project these into Esmeraltin, but it was no good.
It had been odd seeing him in white fine robe. She had not doubted it was the Lady who granted those adornments, then humored herself to wonder how long they could last in raw forested places.

He would drift away to be a traveler far off. He could only surmise that yes, while Endamene had reunited to the Lady, that it had ended again, so he could not see how anything would amend to how it was. She had asked it but his manner of reason was unshakeable. When he asked to where she had before departed, several times, it was the end. Confusion only followed. They were both wanderers of world, or worlds.

The mood shifted and they shared tea and more talking. Sun loomed over and Andrea's ring softened in glow. She felt rays of goodness in her and he beamed again a little brighter.

After reassurances, they parted company. He was sure his travels would mean they meet again. Friendly regards were the lasting place for them and it was good to be in such.

The land had redeemed for them. So Andrea felt, so strongly.

Timidity welled up in her when they again kissed. It left questions in her, a faster heartbeat, but then the need to sleep.

She woke the next day with gentle thoughts, sweet dreams the night before but a sigh of calm and contentedness. The ring was warming and took an orange black tinge to it. Just a moment, then it swirled back to its indescribable arrays.

Meantime the Lady's grief literally darkened the land and stopped the fields. It took some days, but then there was the blackening of leaves.

Time moved by days, weeks and the land began to suffer.

Everyone was calm but losing will.

Gloom of minds only met itself with the skies.

Andrea worked harder than ever but was getting less return from the fields. Others said the same. The old couple spoke a little but went on, their hearts embedded in belief, trust, routine. They spoke of the lady who serves as one who could not fail, yet would she? Only a time, they proffered, for not a thing could be remembered in living times they'd known. Confidence was supreme inside them.

Only by an accidental tripping-over does Andrea find her next day spoilt. As it happened, the ring finger was dipped in the mud and the rubesque slid off her hand.

Frantic, she tried to find it.

Sloshing about, she did, but oddly so:

She didn't feel where it was by touch, but rather, by sensation of temperature. Radiance was surging out, out, outwards. She got up to walk and felt it under her feet. She tried other directions and it was the same sensation of heat. She ran, ran to the barn, the home, the old couple and shook the old man to tell him. He had been asleep in his chair. The old woman came in too.

They listened and smiled, nothing more. "What would it take to make you people worry to care?," this said half heartedly, not scolding.

She left them.

Nightfall came and she slept deeply.

The new morning shocked her, not only for the brilliant luminescence of the sunrise.

As her eyes told her, crops were blooming, sprinkling everywhere with aroma of new life and the buzzing bees and delights, hopping insects of hope and all the more. Rain droplets dispersed from a crescendo of puffy peacemaking cirrus clouds above. Vaporing gaps implored her to laugh and cry, jump and squeal!

The ring the ring! She wanted to prance and did. Surely it was the ring! Yet how? Always doing catch-up...for her to learn of it.

It bore true but in its own time.

The yellow field, the blue field of berries, and many others grew again. Weeks passed and things were restored like better than before.

Far off, The Lady places her beloved in the ice chamber, which seems to turn the imagined past into a strange reality, as though time is wrapping around to make the false become true.
Only in chance conversation with a free picker, whose time to serve had ended, did the news come out. Andrea learnt of this, and she was very much mystified again.

Stirred in her thoughts, was the astonishing: She was called again to stand before the Lady.

The lady learned of the ring, but then a shining stone beckoned her, and she communicated with someone unknown behind a screen. Although Andrea was not permitted inside, the shining lights reminded her of things she had forgotten.

Had someone intervened the moment? The lady forgot all about the ring, or more correctly in fact, her memory of it was displaced, she dismissed it as simply not a thing.

Andrea had come alone to the calling of the Lady and that in itself was different. No attendant, not Alissa or anyone, had approached or urged her to stand before the Lady who Serves.

The lady held her forehead as though pained, catching her thoughts better."Go. You are in your fields. Not here."

Thus in any event, amid a torrent of inexplicables, she was leaving again.

On the journey again home, Andrea discovered that all the places have restored in crop health. Thus the lands recover as though not a thing had happened at all to them.

It seemed the people might think of it on the Lady, and not she herself. Although it didn't matter. In time the Lady would be a new self, her strong self. Feeling the hairs on the back of her neck erect, Andrea knew the very next day that the Lady was peering out on the land, taking back control.

Word finally reached the Lady of the ravages and failure of crops, then the sudden about-turn. The Lady made no comment to anyone, not even offering words of advice or counsel to chosen citizens of the land. Nothing, zilch. There was no pretence of anything today. Usually there was, but then like everything else, all things were beyond definition and simply assumed, simply were so, as was always.

In the satisfaction of things simply working to harmony and good fruitage, nothing would be challenged or wondered about. There was no mental need. Even Andrea's best discernment and other-worldliness struggled to find a reason to bother.

At home, it was a struggle to shake off a headache. She took off the ring, sipped some brew of berries and green leaf, picked at her hair and then scribbled on her papery notes. She fastened them back in her deep secluded pocket and went to cleaning herself with water in a basin.

The cool of night time was beginning and it made her shiver a little.

With time, she slept and the headache faded. She woke and remembered to put back on her great rubesque.

-Bargain-

Waking from the bed of hay, Andrea felt herself bound to
mission. It just seemed right. She'd gone to sleep with the notion
and still had it now, if that was any useful confirmation.
So she set out, taking the path to the Lady's domain yet again.

"I seek the counsel of she, the Lady who Serves us" she said to
the attendant at the doorway.
The attendant was a tall man with tanned skin, white robe and
folded arms. His physique was muscular, though not overly so.

Saying "us" wasn't strictly correct but it caught the attention of
the man and actually fell in her favor.
She was granted in quickly.

"Well met, your presence raises my brow. What is it you desire?
How can you and I serve better?" Enunciated the Lady on a large,
wooden chair with arm rests, which some may perceive as a
throne.

Beautiful tapestries adorned the spaces to the sides.

"Endamene," emboldened Andrea.

The Lady quivered and perked up attention some more. She was
seated but now leaned forward. She gazed at Andrea and looked
in, but then held back. Sometimes the common way served more
finely.

"Tell."

"I know how to revive him, amazing as it may sound."

"Bah! How so?"
Furtively the Lady listened and Andrea explained.
  The lady insisted on knowing further and further detail of how it
can be accomplished and why Andrea would help.

"I stand innocent. As always I seek to know more of these regions." This was very true. After all the time and times she'd been in Elysian, she still felt a newcomer.

The Lady decided to peer, although she feared the ring, and knew Andrea had it on, under glove. She perceived enough also to know that nobody else could sustain the strange ring.
So the Lady guessed intentions in other directions. Guessing! How unbecoming. Serving was a challenge at times, these days. She felt a little older in herself and this too, was novel.

'I can't read you,' thought the Lady under her breath inwardly, 'so I shall resort to measures to soften you.'
Fear and lost understanding were the rule of the moment. This land was not one of bold frontiers into the progression of the future. It didn't surprise Andrea so much. It seemed quite typical of governance generally. The lady clapped once, but almost silently.

Thus so, Andrea was punished. Walked away by two serving attendants, Andrea had a mixed mind. In the name of resolving things, she didn't even attempt to resist.

She is locked in a room of silence and forgotten. It was cold, damp, but not frightening particularly. Her belly was full for now and she had no hurry to be anywhere. The move had puzzled her, surprised her, but then as she knew all too well, the entire land was a surprise from start to present.

Andrea grew tired of so much thinking. She called out, across particles and airs. The Lady woke and didn't like it at all. Dressing, she bid her serving ones of this month to bring her henceforth to the holding penance and solace room. Minimally secure and seated, Andrea stared out waiting.

The Lady in night robe looked in waiting for a cue. The holding room was held by the bindings of mind more than anything else. Costly security was not needed at all. Confusion between the two women, who in half shadow looked like the mirror image of each other, was stark. Neither understood the intentions of the other.

So Andrea broke the mood. "I will make bargain, search me and see for yourself."

So the Lady peered, probed.

Pale resistance paid off.

The pouring in of spirit allowed a backdoor. In a sudden electric burst, like lightning forcing down with the power of a trillion candles, purple hue glowed. The rubesque was black red violet. With the odd taste of sweet candy at her mouth, Andrea controlled it, mouth a-gasp at the very power, and she let an immense push field the air and into the mind of the towering Lady in front of her.

Through the power of the ring, Andrea pushed back against the Lady's probes and uncovered a glimpse of an otherworldly silvery figure in the Lady's past, which seems to be Zordant-like. It is only a momentary glimpse though and not much can be gleaned from it. A glint of red seared through the Lady. She stumbled backward, only catching herself on a column.

The Lady has a change of heart. The mind jostling appears to have affected her. She cannot understand all of Andrea, it is beyond her. Off guard, tired, weary, over powered by the events of the land and her husband's return only to be followed by the trickery of sudden new loss, the Lady for the first time truly relented. She steadied herself with hand and sat down on the cold cobble stones.
She breathed silently and touched her own chest as though to re-compose.
Andrea found herself mentally meandering in quiet, putting sense to what she'd "peered" into. What was the dark, yet not-dark in the Lady's heart? Something ambiguous, scarred?

Then, the concentration was broken.

"My attendants shall prepare you for journey. You won't be staying here now. Find Endamene's life again. I will be with you in caravan. The journey to where you said, shall be as you suggested. I will it!"

So it happened in agreement. Malice was not there, although it could have been. These two were equals in more ways than one. Mutual gain could work and the wisdom was there. The Lady saw the rubesque and Andrea as one, and now she knew a little more than was comfortable of the Lady's past. All vestiges of superiority had fallen.

The passage was slow, a bit agonizing for Andrea, but the Lady set the pace and things would come through. It was an experiment, admittedly but her thoughts were guarded and the two did not speak so much as others might in journeys.

At the lagoon they arrived.
Andrea waded in, without much ceremony at all.

The Lady who serves had brought at great weight the ice-blocked Endamene in covering cabinet. An attendant helped pull down the bulk but only to the water's surface edge.

Skepticism crept over some of the people serving, then evaporated at the might of the Lady's will once again. Thinking only went so far around here, around anywhere.
In the water, and with gloves removed, Andrea willed and worked. Fully immersed, the body was still and nothing happened.

Then slowly bubbles began. Circles on the surface quivered. The water clarified before the squinted eyes of all. Seconds passed to minutes and gentle peace remained, as all waited, fearing even dare breathe. Something stirred different in the watery reality.
A short time later, Endamene is miraculously revived, but remains weary of legs and arms. He is only fit to be carried. Some of the attendants, breaking respect, laughed in delight and shock, before the lady frowned looking their ways.

Task done, bargain kept, equals at uneasy peace,

Out of protocol, Andrea beckoned at the mind's edge of a helper. "Attendant! He needs nursing and feeding back to strength! Do this for your lady who serves, at once!"

In shock, the humble farmer man serving his lady did so, with a slight look for approval from his ladyship. The latter nodded almost unobservably.

Endamene was dried and placed on cot, then finally in a wagon and attached to a horse, with rider waiting patiently for instructions.

Another attendant appeared suddenly at Andrea's arm as she dried herself with a towel on the river bank.
"The Lady who serves wills that you are well and honored from this day forth."

The lady departed and thus it is clear Andrea is freed.

  The Lady steeled herself to hide the two tears falling from her eyes as she embraced and took her Endamene back for recuperation and appointed post.

-Something More-

Andrea was alone as the riders and caravan departed. She stared after them, embracing the solitude, gleefully in fact.
In pause she reflected some. Still more secrets beckoned. Did the mind-touch with the Lady motivate her, or widen her own sensing? Andrea couldn't know it exactly.

She took a deep breath and sighed.
Turning to go, Andrea spied out a shimmer on the water, which was definitely not a fish. Had she missed something? Tools, garb, items belonging to the Lady's husband?

Duty bound, she waded back in and dived under. Not being too strong a swimmer really, this would only be a precursory glance under. Water filled all her external senses and it was murky, difficult to see much further than a handspan.

Yet then, next to rocky reliefs and mosses, was something of a curiosity.
It looked alive, or something that had once lived. Shark? Whale? The color would have presupposed such ideas, but feeling and looking more, she took to shock and was then truly phased by the discovery that it was a silvery man, condemned to watery grave.

Heavily decayed, there he lay. He loomed large but despite all the ravages of what appeared to be months, the resemblance was of a Zordant, somehow.

Pulling and heaving, now her head above water, she managed to tow it with her arm upwards and across to the shallows. Hauling it up the bank was another matter.
There was some distance away some treeline and she happened to chance on vines growing there. Yanking with all her weight she tore some away and brought it back. The body had slide back under, muddied, but determined despite the instinct of repulsion, Andrea continued. The body was clean enough, the more it emerged. She tied the vine and lifted, lifted, pulled, strained.

Enough of it held to the bank that she could take a rest. Hard work indeed. Just as she was wanting to abandon the project, she

mentally checked herself. The importance of this was immense,
if she hoped to make any sense of anything.

Andrea rubbed at her ring, wanting to tell the Zordants. What
more relevant time to use the rubesque as an intended
communicator than now?

However, nothing happened despite repeated attempts. All in
vain. How could they be more far?

It mentally came to her attention that in fact she has never seen
the Zordants in this place, no contact at all to her. Yet here this
thing was, this one.

What were these strange lagoon waters? How had it reached
here, to lay resting in indignity? She shivered at a change in the
air. Or maybe it was hypothermia setting in. She really needed
warm, dry, thicker clothing.

Doing her best to cover up the body and ensure it wouldn't sink
again into the lagooned waters, she exhausted all the large leafy
matter she could and then turned for home.

Stagnating, she couldn't so much make it home.

In an irony of life, she noticed for the first time ever a horse.
Obviously tamed, it still had a leather saddle on it but it was
roaming, foraging, puffing with its lips in contentment. In a
pocket she found some dried grains. This wasn't so unusual these
days, they got in all her clothes and boots all the time. She
clapped her hands, beckoning its attention.

The horse was so tamed it actually approached and ate. With
only a cautious single stride backwards, the horse regarded her
with the decision she was not foe and there it was to be.

She tried to gather energy to clamor up on the steed, but it wasn't
going to happen. Exhaustion predicated her to do something else
and just take the reigns in support as woman and equine began to
stroll. She was half leaning on the horse for a good part of the
way, which swayed them off course this way and that.

Finding the humble abode of a picker who vaguely recognised
her, a Menthis and her family, she found abode for the night.
Strength returned while her horse had its own equivalent of a
banquet and water, tied outside. Sharing a tale with them about
the Lady, they all got on rather well, with intrigue. Andrea slept
contentedly and set off despite their offers for her to stay as long

as she wanted without feeling to be anything of a burden. The young children helped her to saddle up.

Andrea took to riding with an unsteadiness that bemused her hosts but then her memories flooded back to being a small girl and having some lessons on a school excursion. The connection of her mind didn't extend much further into Hilleton except for this necessary thread.

Instead of home, she used the peaks, forests and the path of the sun, as well as sheer guesswork and willpower, to amble her way back to the lagoon. Later that day she made it. It was okay. Time had been lost, but her four-hoofed friend could more than make up for this now she actually knew her bearings from this landmark. It was lucky to find rope for the retrieval.

The horse didn't complain about the new load, but it did mean Andrea now had to walk along side.
At the cave, she patted the horse to freedom but it hovered a moment before losing itself to follow a butterfly that randomed the brushes near by. She mouthed a thank-you to the horse and looked back on it. Its colors were blacks and browns. She wondered how many horses there could be in the world, as she'd never seen any others, except those used by the Lady who Serves. The only other horse, she could vaguely and now reluctantly recall, was that of the caped man who tried to end her life. Lurid strangeness clouded her thoughts but now, she regained her psyched-up will to pull this Zordant through the portal, the dark edges, and back to Hilleton. A mission of mercy, a return to the rightful tribe of beings.

The weight made for hard going. It felt hideous to be carrying a cadaver. Although this was no ordinary kind, and it was doubtful anyone could mistake it as human. This was important really. It was well cloth-covered and gave no particular odor to befoul the air.

Who could ever have imagined a series of events like this? Despite the physical labors, Andrea's mind surged with thoughts and unsolved riddles. Why, oh why, did she find herself hopping back and so from one world to another, when she really wanted this to end, to take control of her life and be as she wanted? Just whenever she would make progress and let go of the former, it would impose itself again. It was cruel, annoying, but then just the unfolding of who she was. She rationalized things away and it helped her coping immensely. No use crying for what has passed. Some other dimension of her liked both worlds. No point denying the veracity of the fact.

-Rightful Owners-

She didn't need to call them. It happened that she saw lights and
began to walk towards them. This time, before they uttered
anything or gave a thought to her, she declared she had something
to show them by the cave, for truly it was an impossible
proposition to drag it with her arms.
With slow walking but no apparent trepidation they followed.
She saw the Zordants visibly shudder at her discovery.
Some frantic communing with each other ensued.

They quizzed her on the find.
"Where did you find this?" And the other: "Who saw this?"

"In a body of water I chanced it." Thus doing, Andrea told as best
she could all. No thought communication went on in this
exchange. It seemed in their stress they had toned down to verbal
mouth-based communication with her.

She wanted to ask them how a Zordant could have gotten there.
She had the chance, but they again did not supply answers except
to speak of a spatial accident. Andrea feels they may not know
further.
Or was she being kind to them by so thinking?

The oddest thing was when she asked them what to do next,
pleading them with her eyes. They snapped the air with their
thought "It is not ours, it is yours, to bid with as you would
proceed."

The English was clipped and full of uncertain meanings, but she
gathered enough for they slithered away, refusing to look back.
The second was telling her mentally as a whisper. 'I have a cart
for you to take him on.'

So it seemed the problem was for her and her alone. Who did this
suit? An idea grew to reality in her head. After this encounter,
Andrea knew the body would make too much suspicion and
commotion in her modern world. So again she took it back to
Elysian and again dared to present herself to the Lady who
Serves.

Removing the cart and blanket she had added for the long journey to provide some privacy....the atmosphere was bewildering. It astonished the lady and her serving attendants. Some hissed, some gasped, some obediently did nothing much of anything.

Dismissing all the lower and more important attendants, the Lady and Andrea were alone with the once-again shrouded body. It seemed quite sterile and clean; neither of them had much fear spring to mind that it might not be a good idea to be near it.

Andrea suggested, and The Lady agreed, to place the body in the ice chamber as a monument and preservation, as the only "rightful resting place."
This wasn't the end of the interaction and the bizarre twenty-four hours (as Andrea felt it. She was now immensely tired but willing herself on). Closing the chamber firmly, an attendant finished the job and then bowed and left.

"I knew one, in fact this one."

Andrea looked at her and listened with inquiring intrigue, despite her own reddening eyes.

"The tiredness is in you, you are welcome to rest in a chambered room here. Although I'm sure you want to know more firstly."

Andrea nodded to both suggestions and smiled appreciatively.

The Lady, to Andrea's astonishment, explains that she and the silvery one had met, long ago. An explosive accident had taken place, but the 'silver one' had been revived for a time. Apparently after some days though, the inevitable weakness returned to the Zordant. In a further complication that day so long ago, a huge mountain of a man, breached the fortress perimeters. He was completely out of control.

The Lady broke her elucidation.

Andrea could imagine that in such commotion, the injured Zordant's fate was sealed. Filling the gap of understanding, someone or other had decided to place the body out of the way.

Andrea mentioned the Lagoon, but the Lady who Serves dismissed the idea, instead suggesting that a cohort of the berserk fortress invader had whisked away the body, dying or dead already.
Not much more was discussed.

Ilric came. Was he called? The Lady said, "I had expected you and you were prompt. Andreee-a will be here for the night, do find her quarters."

The trill of her speech mispronounced Andrea's name, which in fact was typical.

The next day, Andrea woke very well and ate the food already laid out. The Lady was not available but some attendants rushed to her side to guide her out, when she began to step away from her chamber. No doubt roaming around freely was not on the agenda of this large fort.
The Lady did not say, but Andrea came to wonder if the silvery man had not granted her powers of rule in Elysian, or more. The Lady, in explaining the day before, had mentioned in forceful conviction that the world had always been, in her recollection, and that a silvery one had never been known in her reckoning except that one time.

Andrea had chance to think and when outside but still near, she stopped in her tracks. She turned and asked to be back inside. Andrea wanted to set things to meaning.

The tall guard at the gate tilted his head to one side. "Why would you enter again? Nobody does such a thing."

"Well that you say, but I must insist and you shall do my bidding, for I am special to her."

He merely thought a moment then nodded. "Your risk, not mine."

"I'm very sorry, My Lady who serves us. The same outlander woman is here again, requesting, claiming she is special. If it be your will, I will insist she be gone. Truly, I can be very persuasive, such that she shall disturb you no more."

Sighing, "No, that shall not be required. Bid her come to me. That more I shall assent."

Again getting audience, after waiting an hour or more, she asked the Lady to come see Hilleton and her far-land.

"You are someone extraordinary in your serving to the land, so yes, there is merit in the idea. It has quizzed me to not have already seen your region-parts."

Thus the lady agreed, more readily believing Andrea despite lack of understanding. Arrangements were made, with many items, attendants, guards, foodstuffs. Again it was a while to reach destination, albeit easier on the people, via horses and carts, which made it much easier on leg-weary Andrea.

To a great disappointment, the Lady cannot see the stones, the path or anything. It is all veiled to her, a nothingness in the distance.
Andrea urged the Lady to step with her and trust her. It was pointless and understandably she was trying the patience of the Lady.

She reasoned politely to the ruler. "Where would your ladyship suppose am I then going? Do try to follow."
 Andrea steps through alone, back to Hilleton. She cannot know it, but across the divide, the Lady is convinced of herself that Andrea has run off or something. Dismissing any other possibility, and walking around near to where Andrea had paled away, she turns back and sets to matters of state.
 She was tired and needed rest, she told herself that was all that would remove the murky things from her mind.

There were more important things to do than one crazed woman vanishing so far from everything. It was not her responsibility to protect everyone each moment, if they should be foolish.

-Ice-

She wanted to turn back and go on with her new life in Elysian, her adopted homeland, but the scene before her stunned her senses.   Sheer white.
 A sudden gust gravitated her forward, half lifting her to keep going on.
Winds had swept through.
Andrea was lost in the forest, trying to get down to reach town and home. Not going well at all.
  Ice and snow had capped everything with a blanket, in an eerie fall that she couldn't remember in all her years, except as a young infant.
Keeping her wits and everything else out of mind, Andrea knew there wasn't much else to do in the emptiness of her surroundings.

She summoned the will to call the Zordants.

The now-second Zordant noticed the call by the hum of his instruments, which in turn whizzed a response in his mind-thoughts. He alerted the first Zordant, the commander.
Glimpsing ahead, temperature controls didn't give a lot of hope for the Hilleton woman. Although this would all go in the data logs and, she was their main contact with the planet: This was important and bonds were bonds, after all else.

Sure enough, the ring transposes light all around, as Andrea shivered against the breezes, dark, damp and white crystals around her. She was crouching down by a tree, feeling weak and peering around through frosty eyes, hoping and waiting that something would happen before she completely froze solid, unable to consider going on.

Not long passed and the bright light gathering around indicated a craft appearing. She jumped up and began to move in its direction, adrenalin coursing in her veins.
What a shame that her foot connected with a protuberance on the ground. Now she lay half trapped under a fallen tree branch on thick cover of snows.

-Approach-

  Both Zordants were walking broad spaces apart but their minds
worked in close link. Masks on, lamps in place, they screened
and also "thought" their way around, searching. Heat was
detected in one section and beyond the trees, they saw a prostrate
body. It was a false alarm, it was a small wood creature, perhaps
a rabbit. On they trudged, as silvery walkers shimmering and
shining with each flex of knee and elbow. They trounced down a
slope a little and then saw another heat point on their instruments.
Larger, they took the typical slow pace and went to investigate in
silence but with minds humming in commune, steady.

Indeed this was her. Heat and shelter were needed, the basics of
life. One took the arms and two took the legs. Nothing else to do
but get her back to the craft for immediate attention.
This time an information transmit might be more direct and
opportune. Ethics might have dictated it cruel to take such
opportunity but it was not killer, just efficient and seizing the
matter at hand.
On board and barely in the door, the two of them hooked up a
heating table and then placed the brace on her head. The gentle
swim of electric stimulation caused their patient to stir. It was
okay. Heat and soothing brain waves would lull a rest in the body
and lower the resistance to memory investigations.

A side effect was that she would awaken with the last few hours
very vague in her head. Calmness would not erase, but grease
over different events. With time it would sift through and the
neurons would re-establish differentiations, unless of course the
subject were foolish enough to intoxicate too early. The best
thing to do was let the patient rest as long as possible. The logic
applied across all species known.

She awoke, but her mind was still not clear at all.   The second
Zordant emitted a thought of concern, so the first asked her a
question.
"Tell us of this Lady. Can you mention her some more, what she
does, what her life is?"
They showed a lot of interest. Things were so blurry still, that
Andrea got the feeling she is unlearning, having her mind 'cleared'

somehow.   She went back to sleep for "her own good," as they put it, talking again with mouths in the humanistic way, rather outside their habits.

Awaking again some time later, she felt the truth of the experience of being in here, recovered and cared for in these once-in-20-year weather conditions, was awkward. The vulnerability left her stunned, but inside her, deeply she burnt with distrust and dislike of the predicament. Morally she contained herself, though. She upped from the table and left to go.
The Zordants of course knew and walked to approach her, but then a waive of the hand indicated her freeness to go and the door widened to let her alight.

It was still snowy and cold, though less windy. Her inner warmth was enough to endure now.
So as she got down and found public transport home, she was feeling more a town member of Hilleton than before.
It wouldn't occur to her that the Zordants had done more than just a heal and a chat to her. She couldn't know of their brace-investigation of her head. They had done her well, kept her alive.
It was a new day finally and some of the snow had melted, to show new sun but wilted plants in many places.

The Zordants didn't much understand Hilleton's weather patterns either. Yet it was trifle nothing but good, compared to the ravages that the "Elysian" place had done to their companion number. Other species cared for their own even beyond life, but it was not always so with their peoples. Order and reputation were important too. It was disgusting to fall from grace so awkwardly as to see a fellow traveler depraved in rotting cadaver form. Wiping hands of it was easier after the disaster of task.

With telescopic zoom they regarded Andrea as she went away. What more could be done? Deliberations had to be made. What had they learnt, was more worth it, was the quested goal any closer to the time of reaping? What was the scale of burden to return? Cool calculation and council was essential. What a pity more numbers were not here to share and engage in this mind-meeting.

The first Zordant also wanted to entertain other possibles for the future. Arming a person on this visited planet with any more knowledge or tool had to be managed carefully. The female had seemed a good choice, more than lucky indeed.

In short commune they began. Taking control, they choose to lift to the skies again for security, and for the emptiness of space to be the tapestry against which more decisions could be fermented. The computer instruments were more acute there too as were all the electro-crystals. Tools meant more mechanical minds and these aided the higher causes as could as much anything other.

The side effect of the head brace had turned things to good intent and advantage. Andrea could be trained back into her original life, where ultimately, their observations and trading in knowledge meant much more, than the other inhospitable place Elysian, which by all their reckonings (and revelations from the female) was rather backwards technologically, a problem, an aberration.
The ultimate purposes beyond this still were discussed, and were very long and complicated. Nobody could understand it, for it expanded the realms of logic of humans and ripped them apart, with new horizons of impossibility, extension, contradiction turning itself to logicality, and then further, across all scientific and cultural measures. All had to be, and lifted to purpose. Other species didn't link it all together, although of course every grouping had their own race to run, and limitations both self-imposed and externally afflicted. It was not denigration but just observation. The way, the quest, the knowledge...yes. The two Zordants bowed a nod to each other and shared a soothing thought of collective pride.

Besides, on the ethical front, everybody was gaining. Even Andrea and her people. New bounds, new experiences. The female could decide how to divulge the new possibilities, or not. To risk public view was ill advised and time wasting. For truly they were preserving themselves at cost, and the comfort of greater Zordant numbers loomed large as a goal. Cruel travesty even afflicted them, to have to stoop to wielding the strong fires of wisdom to base needs of long-term survival.

-At a Loss-

 Back in Hilleton, Andrea goes about her old quaint life but feels
disconnected from it.
Her colleagues noticed it. She'd come in, do her work, speak and
such but nothing so connected as in previous times. Of course, as
always, for them time hadn't so much passed during her periods in
Elysian. It was useless to really let them know more about it or
anything of her life outside work, which seemed not so
descriptively "private" any more, with so many key individuals
like Zordants and more. Yet things were gray, vague in her heart.
Where was she and who was she?

Regular customers came and went. Weeks went by and she
collected her wages and had some more happy relations with
Judith these days. Mark was away, out of the country visiting an
aunt of his.
All was really fine; if only it had meant something. Regularity of
life had formerly made so much sense. Without so much as
thinking it, it just didn't work the same, in her state of sapped
spirit.
What was the matter? A customer had even noticed it; with
acuity he'd asked if she had a virus passing from around the
community. It was typical, general talk.
"You don't seem yourself today." The remark shimmered in her
mind for a time.

To settle matters with her colleagues, she even went to a local
doctor. She passed with flying colors. "You're healthier than
people half your age Miss Andrea and at this rate you'll live
forever or more," quipped the physician, named Dr Whitmore. It
certainly was an uplifting appraisal, as she practically bounced
her way happy to upstairs home.

Times had moved. Perhaps everybody has that sequence in life
where things don't seem so much important or exciting any more.
Many could relate to it, so far as Andrea could tell from
conversations and even a biography or two she'd read. She leafed
through one at home, on her bookshelf. "Times and times" by
Rick Morbankcroft was as much a biography as a philosophic rant
by a former writer and essayist.

So, she got to thinking and knew enough to surmise that possibly the void of the Zordants had left her feeling no purpose anywhere. She took off the ring at times and forgot. Her finger got itchy or she wanted a bath with lots of bubbles and even if it was indestructible, it still seemed silly to have it lost in the cleansing frothy mass of water and suds. Unknowingly she was in fact detaching mindfully from all the extraordinary experiences she had lived of late.

Other times, she would wear her annulus gem again, as a mere adornment.

Days more went dreamily by and in fact, speaking of such, Andrea's dreams became so clear that she could see herself in natural senses, just as a lonely woman in a small life. That was fine, or had been fine.
What to replace it with? With any change there is a cost, right?

"Oh you are the logician today," she mused to herself. She dusted a lot and lost herself with green tea and a lot of housing work. That same day, she tried but couldn't remember so much the things she's done. There was an Elysian land, right? Her head hurt. Gaps that didn't make sense in her made it difficult to continue with much. She took a day off work on a whim and that was that.
The whole week in fact. Digging at the back of her mind was a moment's concern: How much longer would her workplace tolerate her lacklustre attendance?

She failed to report to work altogether for 10 days now and sequestered herself.
It was tiring to feel and be like this, all muddled up, lost, trying to find traces, even reading scraps of paper but still having empty threads just beyond her mental reach.
"Ergh!" She felt awful, and in an act of frustration she carelessly threw the ring into the raging fireplace that was keeping her warm on this yet-again colder than cold day.

She called Lucy and forgot worries and weighty things.

"We've missed you...well I told the others it is probably a virus weighing you down...yeah.....ah huh....when are you coming back?"

The conversation went like this.
Andrea wasn't saying much so Lucy got her laughing and helped her relax.

"Call Gwin okay? You promise? You have to say something. She'll understand! Judith too!"
She did, although Gwin wasn't home, it seemed.

Still in perkier mood, she got to clearing ashes hours later the next day, a Saturday and, she found again the rubesque. It was gleaming with a happy orange brilliance. She returned it to her finger and continued cleaning, again with only vague thinkings. She rinsed her hands with water and then thought of the diary. Yes! She had a diary! That much was important. Maybe it could un-fog her mental mess?
Her hands felt around, outreaching, overturning things, pondering where to look next.

After some searching, finally, she found it. Scraps of paper in the pockets of her torn dress were now added to it. Getting more organized, it seemed things were running more as a thread of a story, well almost. Now one could be inclined to wonder what could have been if the papers had never been there, but this is hard to say in context. Can memory be jogged?

Blowing out a candle, Andrea tucked herself into bed for a long snooze. The soft white curtains were closed. It had turned out to be a better day and she felt more merriment.
Could anyone ever know and feel what she had? Or what she would? Things were just beginning. It was true. The fields of tomorrow were broad and long. She actually smiled earlier upon looking at her own naked self. Bronzed and muscled, powered, glint of eye adventurous and witted, clear forehead, faint lines that gave even more superb definition to her and a practical trailing hairline. Yes indeed, her braids were longer and natured, crispy with little turns and curls. Statuesque was probably an understatement. It emboldened here to confidence and was quite a booster.

At night, in sleep, memories flooded in.

She woke in fright! Amazement! Dream and fact coexisted. As though her night-mind had been connecting pipes, beams, streams, possibilities, solving puzzles and gluing reams of information into coherent gems of verifiable matter. Turning, forming, magically correcting and dissolving, then reforming with greater crucibles of waxy clarity. Incredulous. Memory doors were opening.

Taking a deep breath, it gave her calm and solace in all the new-again revelations.

She literally pranced through the day, at the markets, then meeting Jenny in town, and back home. She was walking on airs and bouncing a beautiful joy.

The next night she wrote and wrote, transcribed and thought, collected more pieces to perplexing notions and thought more questions that did not make her fear, but gave her insight into her part in dreams, quests, adventures and purposes beyond what the simple mortal might.
It felt so tinglingly good to have clarity and will, will to more, again.

She let it grow, ate well, exercised herself and then a week later, set out for the day-- feeling powers surging in her, as they say, more the mental and less the physical, yet this was really saying something for such a strident and chiselled woman, only humbled by simple-trained clothing habits.

She felt wholesome and continued to work and sleep in the blessings of sweet providence.

-Seeing more-

It was time to take the action. After much planning, the Zordants
ushered their own way in to Andrea's room in the cool of deep
night.
Andrea must not know yet. In silent consideration of her resting
body beneath the sheets, and now communing rapidly to each
other, they concluded that she isn't being suppressed at all. It
seemed she was unable to resolve herself to a peace, a role, her
life-place of now. This contact was important for putting things
into context, yet at this moment, it was important to do some
more reflection in clinical conditions back on board the craft.

The next day passed and they returned to her room in the cover of
darkness. The slow heaving of her chest up and down conveyed
the correct sense of her sleep.
Only some minutes went by and they were deciding which actions
to measure up. Unknown to them, Andrea stirred very slightly
but remained in her repose, outlaid on the bed and under a sheet.
Her breathing was even. She could see them, white and shadowy
against the moonlit night. As this was not the first time seeing
her other-worldly visitors this way, she had neither anticipation
nor reservations. She studied them as they communed with each
other, locked in thoughts, forgetting her presently. Their forms
appeared larger here than on the forest top.
The windows were closed yet there the two of them were right in
front of her, beyond the foot of the bed.
From corner of her eye, Andrea tried something. She focused,
and peered into the mind of the lesser Zordant. Taken off guard,
she raised his surprise, then got a decisive response from the
other.

  "Stop this!" the main Zordant ordered.

Holding on, literally with her arms now pinning against the edges
of her bed, curiosity and determination drove her. Andrea peered
and peered, further and further down the shafting tunnel,
identifying and showing little regard for the locks and stacks of
crafted walls of mind-forces. Her ring glowed on her finger,
under the covers. Flooding with fluidity, she was driving wild,
not really knowing what it was she was even doing, but taking the

thrill and letting it pour forth, from her to the Zordant and then outreaching the pool of teary drops and gathering torrents of stormy words and visions. Blind strength drove her enchantingly as a champion.

She kept at it, until the connection is gone in a whoosh of the wind and a sway of the curtain.

The Zordants quietly expressed fear and alarm, for the first time ever. Microseconds went to seconds and then they were away. She could see into them, and although she didn't understand the language, symbols or images she had seen, she could now try to piece them together into ...something...like a jigsaw one had never trialed before.

It wasn't fair that they had walled her up, played with her, treated her to their own wits and ends. They had been kind in many ways, but not all.

This mixed nature, of friend and foe, was truly something crawling and alien. Ghostly morally ambiguous monstrosities. This was what she reckoned in her mind. It no longer seemed unapproachable to reckon so.

Alone and after some pause, she got out of bed and had to pat herself down from all the perspiration. The bed was soaked of sheet even though cold airs were in the room and the touch of the floor boards.

Squeezing a lemon and placing it in warmed water, she drank and relaxed until around 2 A.M.

If anything was a turning point, this was it. Whatever had occurred before, this was stark and monumental. She would not be a passive participant any more, not in life or psychic plane, nor intent.

Pinning her elbow to her other forearm, she sat as Le Penseur, or perhaps, 'La Penseuse.' Moonlight shone on glowing facial lines. Henceforth bolder, wiser, was she.

-Away-

The Zordants had a well equipped craft. They went into suspense, or what might be called sleep. Awakening, they went back to duties. Search, discover, analyze. Whichever way things were sifted through, there had never been any other alternative worlds presented as viable. Nothingness in the galactic surrounds.
So they used instruments to soothe themselves, and took sustenance. It seemed the female had grown outside their containing control.
Could anything be done? Were things eventuated past a point of correction? Was any return justified now? Retreating resignation loomed on them.
They cruised the emptiness and could not reach decision. It was a dangerous place to be, not being in psychic and situational control. Had they been primitives, their decisive response would have been far easier, lashing out like a cornered creature. No such luxury afford them, however. Atavistic wanderlust indeed!

-

As regards Hilleton and beyond, the Zordants vanished from all knowledge.
The forests were their own again, and signs of any craft were laid banished by foliage and damp, remoteness and airborne dusts deposited.
The world wouldn't forget and also could not, for in fact it hadn't even known at any time of them, barring Andrea.

Walking around her now familiar forest, Andrea resolved to go again. Enough facets of logic and will steered her to the sane matter of choice.
This brute of a life had been stirred up like a tornado. Everything was unsettled and she wanted to embrace anything, but also feel herself at the helm.
Andrea just couldn't bear her existing life and so decided to take refuge in the place she loved, in Elysian. Dark corridors of her unconscious would have to tackle the flood of information

gleaned from peering into the silvery one. Her front of mind already registered it would be a rather slow endeavor.

She took a grand, fallen stick from a tree and playfully used it like a walker as she casually moved into the darker grove and then faded from Hilleton's forest, to emerge in a sunny and vast plain. She made it to the yellow fields again, in the shadow of a good pace.

"Andrea! You've come back from your excursions. How nice." The old woman greeted her with a warming embrace. The old man downed his hoe, stepped closer and smiled, nodding his head.

Yes, this was home. New home, true home.

Times passed.

Her life adapted there.

She didn't long or hope for her old cold world any more. This new place's warmth was matched by the duty and will of its people.

The Lady who served was not a factor in everyday life. Those serving were called few in actual number, and the stamp on life was really about the bounty of the ground and the exchanges of drilled, devoted laboring people. Communication was low, but harmony and liberty for individual souls were high. A political or social observer might have had a field trip of a lifetime to perceive it all. Smirking, Andrea thought it wouldn't have done much, for her old world was narrow-minded to other possibilities, anyway.

She put aside the past and focused on now, now, now. It was beautiful. Nothing would take this from her.
It was as though the shutter has come down on her old life. She felt stronger, more radiant here, and with new purpose in cleaning waters and clearing fields. She joined the blueberry pickers in silence and found solace, good harmony, that words could never give. Truly a refuge, the Elysian landscapes were doing wonders to her skin, muscle, mind, and vision of life itself. Possibilities

streamed endless. Forests, plains, many colored fields, a far-off sea, mountains. This immense place would yield so much if she wanted it, in adventure and lore.

   Though most of all, it just WAS. Contentedness flowed in the air and the hearts of all.

-Hut-

Andrea's mind grew lucid. The next event would surprise her. A man of the road, back from serving the Lady, met with the old couple.

He knew them from many years ago.

Coming to know Andrea, it seemed clear to him that she deserved her own place to call home.
"The fields are vast and you can have something to call your own on these estates."

The old couple could only agree with happiness "It is true, Andrea, a great suggestion," said the old man.

So it was settled that the man, Queaves, would serve Andrea, and make her a hut. He was a skilled carpenter and arranged all the carts to deliver timbers, vines and all the necessary things to thatch the roof and make it altogether. It took months, for he worked alone, in sweat, pains and small injuries.

Over this time, Andrea still worked the fields and helped a little, but Queaves refused much help. The old man would at times offer suggestions to him and the old woman would bake pies and give them liquids of sustenance. All was harmonious and without quarrel.

Queaves came to admire Andrea very much.
One day as he was resting under a field shelter, he sat admiring her, bent down, working the wheat crops.
He upped and went to speak with her, declaring his admiration and affection.
Andrea was not altogether surprised and blushed a little. She needed time to think it over.
"I had my Esmeraltin, " she told him and the tale was long, not holding back on details.

Queaves showed respect and courtesy. He waited on Andrea's words. They had more conversations and he worked as hard as ever until the hut was ready. He showed her inside and in a sudden moment knelt to take her hand and asked her again for the chance to court her.

"Please, Queaves," she began, "you have been so kind and the old couple know it, but I have thought and thought. Esmeraltin is alive in my thoughts all the time and it does not diminish. I cannot divide myself or see things anew."

They shared a fire camp dinner and Queaves showed a little melancholy, but masked it behind his thick moustache.

"I understand you Andrea, it is noble." These were his words. Late into the night he went to camp under the stars as he always had, though first she graciously thanked him many times and kissed him on the cheek goodnight.

"Your softness is unforgettable, " he told her. She smiled and found good comfort in her own sleep, now in her own new hut. She could not forget the once-was Esmeraltin, the closest thing she'd had to actual love and tenderness in the worlds.

He departed middle of next day and Andrea only heard of it from free pickers that had come by the yellow fields.

Meanwhile, the old man of the couple, for his part, had ventured off on one of his infrequent trips.

When he returned days later, he bore news that Queaves had wedded to an eligible maid in another province. Andrea's spirit lifted, to know that he was now happy, for she truly wished him well.
As a fact, she decided to send him word of congratulations and had almost intended to go and visit him and his new wife.

"I shall visit," she told the old couple. The fields had been well tended, and whilst they always grew, now was as good a time as any for a journey out.
They bidded her on with good fortunes.

For Andrea, life just went on and on, but if someone had been keeping count, she had now been in Elysian for over 8 months.

This was long enough a time to make her truly feel it was her own homeland.

As Andrea set out to see Queaves and offer him field harvest thanks, she skipped along with purpose and merry feelings.

Stopping by Alissa's direction along the way, she came to be told the news of something very unexpected. His bliss had not lasted.

"It imports that you need to know something, Andrea, dear soul friend. Words have traveled far."

Nobody could confirm much detail but that in the wastelands of rocks and mountains, he had set out and in fact presumed to die. Rumors said suicide.

It was something unexplored as a social reality in this realm; things like this were not thought of. It was the land of bounty and contentment, if not any other description were arrived at with ease.

Her heart sank at the news. She gulped hard. "What of his new wife?," she could not help interpose.

Fatefully, guilt passed to her.

She stayed with Alissa a day and then two more. Now it only seemed appropriate to take the gifts she had brought, and lay them in the place where he had fallen. Welling up in her was the thought to console Queaves wife, yet Andrea knew her not at all and so, the notion dissipated as fast as it had arisen.

Could anyone help guide her to where he had expired? Two free pickers, friendly and well known to Alissa, actually took to the challenge. They had some information to go on.

The journey was immediate and swift. Everybody agreed that Andrea's idea was good, although she in fact recollected that she did not know how the dead were treated in this place, nor had she ever heard tale of anyone passing. The free pickers didn't seem to be drawn on the subject and she let it be. They were a male and a female, both around age 30, if any guide at all. It could be very hard to tell with these people and be assured because the land kept people very well preserved indeed.

The sight of Queaves' torn garments was enough. Leaves were scattered around, partly smearing the bodily remains. The air was thick, grim and unpleasant.
Without warning, the male free picker began to strike sticks and managed to burn a small circle of leaves. This charred the remains. The female held Andrea back with soft arm of restraint, telling her "it is cleaner this way. Your gifts can still be here, at a side."

Andrea shuddered and needed much comfort, but the female was very kind and good at providing this.

For a few days Andrea did not as much work but rather than rested in the hut, went to the barn, saw the homestead of the old couple and otherwise simply walked or stared at the sky for long moments.

Only after a solid two weeks' passing did she feel renewed and better. It had been emotionally hard. How things could turn sad, she reflected. The people she was bonding to, the community, while austere and rarely spoken, were her people more the more. It was so true.

The ring warmed her and her own views of life were strengthening against the whims and grantings of vicissitudinal existence.

-Proclaimed-

The land grew lush and prospered amazingly so.

Days went by and things were so settled and good. Andrea's heart
and mind were repaired. Living was moving, marching on and
finding the peace that good purpose brings. She felt this in
everything she did.

Then one day, it was a curiosity that the Lady Who Serves came
passing by in her horse and carriages' entourage. This time
Andrea saw it at a distance but moved in to hear of whatever the
tidings were. An attending servant blew on a horn.
"The lady is pronouncing through all the provinces. Come all to
hear of it." So he spoke with bellowing, but soft and inviting
voice. It was not threatening at all.

The Lady herself stood up and out from her closed carriage.
It was a warm day and she seemed composed but for soft mists on
her face; perhaps it was a water decanter applied liberally by the
Baric she'd heard of, another of the more privileged attendants to
directly be at the Lady's beck and call. Or it could just as well
have been Ilric, who no doubt still would serve as seemed his
unquestioned desire, apart from any decrees from time to time.

The Lady looked about with a good gaze and gleamed a smile.
The gathered peoples, not many, but here so and so, there too,
stood in quiet respect.
"Be at ease all. Must I say it to each grouping I meet this day, on
my speedy steads?"
She paused and chose words carefully.

A man in attendance, all green and with velvety garbs, that
Andrea didn't recognise, leapt out of the carriage to attend to his
Lady. He brought out a brush and dusted off her shoulders and
then turned in a small half circle to face her. He unrolled a
parchment and set it out before her, to her now outstretching
hand.

He looked to her eyes and she nodded, to which he stood aside, turned to the crowd and took a respectful single step backwards, but watching all, with eagle eyed concentration.

She began.

"In all that is of wisdom, and to those new and ancient in all these parts known, I do give greetings and await to serve you all. This is at it has always been of course, but now further tidings are important."
People stirred more easily and tried to listen.
"Blessed are those always serving. Who among you has found it a foul burden?"

Some murmurs came up. Men and women nodded, some said "Aye" and other things, for truly they knew that to serve was in fact an excellent thing.

"These things have become the norms of our land but I see a new norm. I want those to serve be ready to usher a request. That is, if they serve, there may be the chance to object or consent. This is to immediate effect. Many choose to serve and do ask me but are turned away. Others are called. Now, I would want to allay such confusion. If called, let servants say a yes or no. If requesting, let it be as is good for the all-lands and the needs thereof."

The words digested on all.
She stopped reading from the scroll and looked upon all. To Andrea she looked as well but not with any clue as to her thinking.

  The Lady Who Serves touched all the minds present with a fine simple tingle. Then her attendants gathered close and she entered her carriage, to depart with the gallop of many hooves and some unfurled dust on the path.

All the onlookers turned and went on their respective ways.

The thing was remarkable. It seemed political, an effervescent thing, as though a marking of age in the world had occurred.

Nothing challenged the way things were, or the Lady who serves. Yet now, it would surely be that people would begin to choose their serving freely or indeed object without punishment or fear.

Had all the events, the losses, the tidings since Andrea's first arrival, left an indelible mark on the world? Or was it inconsequential?

The next day was something of a noteworthy passing, if she had noticed it in fact (but did not): An entire year passes in the life of Andrea in Elysian, as she realises from the movement of the sun.

-Pulling In-

The Zordants had gone an ample time deliberating, planning, seeing ahead, pondering, plotting, you name it, they had done it. It was mechanical and logical, non-alarmist and full of conjecture and calculation. Computational aids came into it. Scientific reasoning was the greater way of course, but multi-faceting of knowledge forms was something that Andrea's kind didn't do quite so well. The only element not entered into was the religious, which to the Zordants, seemed an allegorical, submissive and moral pursuit that had in civilizations past been a founding provider of order, although for their number, it had in fact never existed. So what was there to draw upon? Was not a newborn brought into life with nothing of knowledge? Explorations from infancy led to practical descriptions of reality and sociological rules. Surely this was the main thing to do?

The first and second realised that Andrea wished to be in but one world now, and worse, she had not chosen to be in her original Hilleton. This is something they could not agree to or abide. They found reason to be alarmed, a trait that did not sit well with them. For the ring, the communer annulus with its crimson shadings, had been put to usages that were not at all intended. As a contact point it had not served so well, meaning they had to repeatedly return to watch over and interact with Andrea, whether by distant regard or direct interaction. It had been a mild disaster, only outdone by the loss of their assistant pilot and his desecration. What they could not bear to even think though, was "the one of the lake" that Andrea had dragged back. It would remain unexplained, un-thought.

Back to the point, it would be essential to use their minds, great seats of influence and skill that they were, to bring Andrea back. To negotiate and convince her of a better path was vital. She was neither serving their ends nor assisting herself or others. The ring had shown itself unstable, dangerous. Who could be right to wield the thing? Subverted science indeed!

They each put a hand on the shoulder of the other. They hooked up to the wires of the craft computer, too. They summoned and listened, focused and concentrated.

Time stopped for them, in the sense of how they felt it. Yet the craft showed they had inter-minded for many hours.

While they could reach Andrea, see her, it was as though veils prevented any more. She was stronger now. The distance should not have mattered, with their craft's antennae and their direct crystalo-mechanical link.

This was becoming absurd. They had a-feared to even directly be exposed to Andrea, but they would overcome this. They would prepare more with armor and suggestion, ring's power or no ring's power. Yet first they still had to coax her back to Hilleton. What other possibility was there? Or was all crushed and lost?

This was unfathomable.

The ice stone was the next manoeuvre. They had managed to supplant it in the Lady's domain, at great cost. That 'gift' had been easy to convert to their energies.

Yet firstly, the Lady revered it only as an occasional consultation, and in fact, it had been difficult to generally get it working with any benefit at all. Somehow the Lady used it to her own mental benefit. She was a strong one, with cool leadership abilities that were born of nature, inherent, final, balanced, not prone to madness—something quite rare in any world.

Again the ice stone channelling failed. It would glow and even chime in musical hum, but it was hopeless. Even if they could have bidded it to call the Lady, then what? Urging the Lady who Serves to do their will?

Everything was failing and that expression from Andrea's books "cut the losses" certainly seemed relevant, in the opinion of the second Zordant.

What if they just left Andrea then in the Elysian world and just found new project? Another Hilleton resident? Yet there was nothing to offer, nothing to exchange or receive.

The fist of the first Zordant closed. He was in pain, a headache, very strong. It pulsated to the second, who rubbed at his own head, concerned.

All this expenditure of their mental energies was taxing them crazy.

Scanning the heavens and spatial limits again, they felt hopelessly inclined to simply go on to new places a-far. They set to work on it.

-Ill Traveled-

The Lady who Serves woke up feeling dreadful. First it was a
headache the day before, but then that diminished.

Now she felt a shiver and couldn't stop coughing. Things like this
weren't common at all. Ilric the loyalist he was, had her in bed
and was attending to her. He decanted some water, applied to a
cloth and daubed her forehead again.

Of course the lands didn't need her as such; for everything always
ran so smoothly, but nonetheless the word did spread out when
hours gave way to days, of her being out of service.

Nobody knew what to do.

Herbs had been donated and various concocted drinks, which
passed the taste tester firstly, each time. Enemies were very few
if ever, but the Lady insisted on this practice.

Baric and Ilric compared notes on a day while the Lady slept a
dangerously long time. Her breathing was even, but her face and
arms looked hot flushed.

This wasn't going good at all. It brought into question their own
longevities in their chosen professions. Could anyone
contemplate what to do without her Serving?

"Doesn't anybody out there have any useful information?" Baric
asked with eloquent annoyance.

"We have to keep trying, keeping her cool, towels changed, all
the little things might count. I'll see to having all the foodstuffs
replaced again." Ilric did this to be doubly sure it wasn't a food
supply problem.

With time the word spread far. It really couldn't be kept hidden
from people. Servants and then pickers, farmers and others learnt
of it. The Lady was immobilized by an unknown affliction.

Andrea was really absorbed in her own day to day life, which had the hut as its hub and the fields as the fullest extent. She was withdrawn from so much of the exterior world but did it really matter? She was happy.

Finally though, Alissa brought the news as it happened, with another free picker she didn't know. There were, after all, so many, some of who were itinerant or traveled far about.

In quiet discussion just as two, Alissa recalled from the depths of her mind that the Lady might be served by unknown medicines, of the kind Andrea had mentioned.
"Please Andrea, you must see about your far-land. If there is a way, we have to try. The Lady has served us so long and we know of no other way in our lands."

"Yet I've been here so long! What can I achieve by being back in a wretched place that is no longer mine?"

"Be that as it may, can you not make sacrifice of your own comfort, dear friend?"

The conversation swayed back and forth.

"Can't you understand I'm happy here? Have I not been a good neighbor and resident?"
Alissa understood that she had learnt and adjusted so much, for so long. Andrea had changed, physically and probably in mind too.

"Knowing all this I must still ask you, for compassion sake, to try and you can return here very much quickly to welcome glee. All the people will thank you and hold you in more esteem than ever!"

"Would that somebody else could go."

"Yet whoever has done it? You've always told us so vividly and I've come to believe, but nobody else finds it. Even if I find this last part hard to fathom."

So action is urged and finally Andrea concedes the good it will do and that going back, whilst it might trigger new ruptures in her mental peace again, might be only brief and not of longer consequence, it was hoped.

Inwardly though, Andrea was growing so tired of it all, and having all the old wounds reopening all the time. Would it indeed drive her mad? Just this day, before Alissa arrived, had she been purifying waters with her ring; doing good, here and now, and not in some other place, chasing lofty visions and risking her own sense of life now. Why did it have to come to so much risk again?
She didn't feel much the adventurer in her; she was not some heroine of fables-old. Her knowledge was here and she had all she needed, with great people.

Before setting out, she went to see the Lady for herself, perhaps it could hint at an answer?

She didn't say to Alissa exactly, for nobody truly knew all about the ring, but she thought to test it on the Lady. This seemed a bright and good spark in her mind.

Maybe yet still she could avoid Hilleton.

She was shocked to see the paleness of the Lady, after the journey of three days to be there. Alissa waited in the outer chamber with Baric.

Ilric stayed inside, virtual guard over his titled mistress, a little suspicious of one and all, even Andrea, despite knowing of her close contact and good relations with the Lady from times past.

Andrea used subtlety to caress the cheek of the Lady, in such a way as to ensure her bared ring would touch the skin softly. The ring glowed and the Lady stirred a little.
Sitting for a while though, nothing changed. Thinking and watching, with Ilric pouring water and wiping the brow of the Lady, things dragged on to the point where Baric urged her out to let the Lady rest for the night.

Alissa came in from without and met Andrea's gaze.
So it was, that Alissa felt relieved that now Andrea seemed determined to agree.

The next day she journeyed out. The two women went, but Alissa only as far as the blue field, for as always, she feared to go any further near the groves or trees.

Andrea was alone totally and about to stir mists and possibilities again that didn't invite her thrill at all. She would be alone to see the land she'd left as a part of her cold past. It was not a bad past, but simply not a past she needed or wanted any more. It felt like walking on a grave, blistered memories and ill feeling mocking her.

She stepped through, crawling and feeling at the cave, for it was dark and harder to find the stony steps and tree's-way round the hilly mount. Back to her "far-home." That name was about the only thing which could give her even a beginning hint of a smile, for everything else felt foreboding. Why did it all smell of being so unfair?

-Link-

The Zordants were several quadrants away when the signal came in. The glowing crystal stone, the icy one? Was that not in the accursed Elysian where their fellow laid wasted? They got to wondering. They could see hands on the crystal stone and perceive a voice, although it made not any sense to them. Rapidly the Zordants tried to establish a link, to search, channel and find words. It didn't work, although they did learn that the Lady's plight just might mean Andrea would be back in Hilleton. Luck was turning, it seemed. They broke the link.

They couldn't know that the Lady, servant of her world, collapsed at the ground that same moment. Nobody would ever know it furthermore, but they didn't actually hold much concern for the fact, either way. In the human definition of things, they could be judged heartless, but this was lost on their sense of existence anyway. Information was the true purchase. They were not evil, nor saintly either, but merely practical, trying to reach goals in a cosmic landscape that was slipping away, leaving them in disfavor. All the information from the female had shown them how a civilization not much like their own thought, developed things and approached all manner of reality. It just wasn't like that for them and had never been so.

-

As she stepped through, The Zordants were waiting. It had been hard; they'd really pushed the craft and burnt up a lot of energy chasing up the task, but deemed it a sacrifice that could not be easily substituted for. Trawling around the forest or going into Hilleton's urban dwellings just wasn't going to be fruitful or even feasible. Better to meet her quicker than that or at least scout around. They had half thought she may return via the gateway back to Elysian, where they could not so easily sustain themselves, but then they had equipment this time, if things got desperate. Contingencies really burned at their minds.

This time, the forest had grown haphazardly and not like it once was, so keeping the craft secluded as they touched down was tricky. It was another setback to an otherwise clock-work efficient team. Their minds buzzed in random commune but it tended to disrupt the singular purpose of tasking and trench-coating around the forest. For truly, they were sensing with minds, but flurries of instability weren't helping. The forest was thick, changed, charred, very random in growth and if Andrea was beyond the stone and grove, it just made things impossible. They couldn't decide if she'd arrived, was in town, or what was happening. Confusion was reigning supreme and they had to find her, but also not alarm her. The ring was latent but what had she gleaned from it now? Both their minds were literally burning as never before, losing subtle control. A zillion parameters overweighed their conscious threads and the computer of the craft couldn't help them, now that they were unlinked and outside. They had their mobile consoles but the weather even conspired against them: electric activity was showing above. Was there no end to the problems?

When she did emerge, not near them at all, Andrea was on her guard. She emerged from the cave with the hackles at her neck urging her to caution, all while she envisages her future as a healer in Elysian, the place that will be her peace and purpose. Under the crunch of leaves, she sets out for the direction of down hill and to town. Getting some antibiotic would have to be a start; she didn't know for sure what else to try and get. Wasn't it the miracle cure of the day?

 She kept moving on, peering about between trees and counting her path. She was alert for animals, dangers, problems and just wanted to get to familiar places like her home address and then take the car to a surgery office.
These thoughts tumbled around and annoyed her. She hated having these mundane suggestions and concerns. She'd spent all of a great long time casting all of this away to the dustbins of her mind.

The ring! She could see it on her hand but not under a glove. She must have taken it off. She remembered being in the cave, it being a useful resting spot from the rains after the mountain-edge curves. There she had been, crawling over uneven ground on hands and knees, dirty, feeling ugly and awkward. Sudden realisation told her the gloves weren't at her waist, nor in a small pocket, and in fact she had no pack on her back.

The cave. It must be there or very near! She thought. It might come in handy and it had her notes. It wasn't worth to risk losing it, even if nobody ever came up this far.

Heavier rain was falling and it was agitating. She turned and went back on her path.

On a lower part of the forest, down a hillside but not so far, were two dazed and frantic Zordants. They were tiring from searches and slowed down by swampy ground. Was there any point to this?

Then, they picked up something, or thought it with minds. They moved upwards and found bent leaves and grass. Something or somebody had been here. It was absurd to have to rely on ranger's tracking skills when they had all this advanced gear. The rain had soaked through their consoles.

Brute anger showed on them and was grossly unbecoming. A crude display of what humans apparently did according to the dictionaries they had been given, this was 'venting.' Now their instruments laid smashed on the ground and their gowns made them sweat with perspiration and the humid surrounds. This was like a rainforest now, with plummeting depths here and there, unsteady rocks, balding tops and random patches of heavy woods. Nothing to do now but choose a path. The trails went cold after a few steps. So they couldn't know for sure what was happening or where things were directionally heading. To any critter of the wilds, they might have seemed bizarre, all silvery, slim and tall.

It was important to keep track of the craft. What about subsidence? Thought the second Zordant. Now, they hurried around, circling and then trailing back from where they thought they'd come. The craft had to be zoned-in again. It was their vital reference point in these crude conditions. Who knows what could happen next in this blasted climatic chaos! The rain fell harder and harder, soaking and straining them. It clouded all mental concentration, leaving them with abilities no more than a lowly creature of any forest. They stumbled and stumbled for precious minutes, minutes, minutes.

Andrea was back in the cave. She knew the way like the back of her hand or better. Now inside, away and sheltered from the bucketing torrents of precipitation, she vowed to break the passage back to Hilleton in permanence. Knowing she also has an ally in the Lady, she planned to bargain for the Lady to grant her something else in token of exchange for finding a curative: She wanted the Lady to peer and wipe out the memories of her far-place.

It was so dark, yet despite this she found her backpack and shook off dust and even a lurking spider. It scurried off and she had no time to show fear at all. The glint of the rubeseque was her only lamp. She pondered.

Andrea spent a time near the cave opening, slowing her breath. Then she began mentally planning, and peering out to see Hilleton, but then afraid somehow, ventured back to the shadows of the cave to think still further. It is as though time is passing so slowly.

Ironically, Andrea fell asleep but the ring began to glow large, as though a danger warning. It is mentally connected to her and is in fact warning her not of world dangers, but now turning on its former masters, is foreboding her of the Zordants, approaching, approaching. Something was not right, not quite as it was usually.

Things were quaking in her existence, changing.

 Andrea felt exhausted, confused and slowed down in breathing. The cave was like her bridge half way between places.

In a half-dead trance-sleep she lay. So much had overwhelmed her and robbed her of so much time to relax.

Yet someone else was not resting. Or rather, something: the fires of the ring suddenly charged and ripped out, hurled forth, all a sudden.

Before long, it decimated the Hilleton forest mountains.

Shocking yards upon long yards eyeing out were ablaze a red inferno of sickening crispy towers of embers, strewn torn brushes and branches twisting rippled. A swoosh of infra energy was terrifyingly unnatural in potentiality.

This had the result of warding off the Zordants, who in a bolted run went back, but with one last glimpse, saw that the cave had now closed down with thunderous turning or rubble and clefts of trees, dirt, dust, and more. Unfortunately for Andrea, this meant she was closed in; although graciously they could not know it.

Or perhaps it would not have made any difference.

Struggling for breath and losing her mental clarity, next moment awakening with a sputter, Andrea struggled confused but then thought of the annulus. Yet the ring failed on her, impassive.

She scampered to think of anything, so in crazed rising chill, fears had her uselessly tapping and knocking at the cave's rocky inner walls.

What followed was incredulous, leaving her eyes staring and her mouth agape.

A shrieking screech could be heard and she realised the ring's ability to cut through, pulverising a line of rock, then a circle by the wave of her unsteadied hand.

Unthinking more, she summoned her arms to work, with an incision becoming more. However she was too exhausted to do more. She collapsed to the ground.

Unseen by her though, the grace of Elysian sun burned with the day and connected with the rock. Incredible! It was a fraction of a hole almost leaving no impression perceptible to the naked human eye.

   After very moments of her sitting there breathing, hopes down and all dimming from her eyes, wondering, worrying, rationalizing acceptance of the absurdity of such a deathly place in limbo, yet another event transforms the moments before her...

Moisture forms in the cave, bringing down crystal pure waters that enliven the ring and sear laser iridescence that strikes out in all directions, bleeding the edges of Andrea's eyes, temporarily blinding her.

Things quiver and turn. Rocks move.

She is freed by a shaking of foundations, but broken of bone and lying defeated.

She is not yet dead, but in delirium and with pains beyond belief, lending her to eventual numbness that endangers her very vital processes of breathing and circulating fluids.

Like nothing on earth before, everything else seemed unimportant compared to the immensity of all this chaotic upheaval.

-Debrief-

The Zordant ones stood amidst mess and a metallic disarray.
It was rather a human thing to admit so many miscalculations.
How had they come to underestimate a commune-annulus? Why
was it not theirs to learn? How had a lowly human untapped
potentials that were locked away from their attainment? They had
gifted it away as thankfulness for information gleaned of the
female's world.

Had this entire world, in fact both worlds, been a bane of all
efforts?

Without their assistant pilot, everything had been harder. A trio
of communing minds was always fated to be stronger than just a
duo.

Things, events were screaming out to them of disastrous loss.
What could be forceps-lifted from the clutches of utter defeat
now? The buzz of their bewildered psyches was elemental and
not poised at all. A rain soaking had damaged equipment and
removed their steely determination. Mistakes had given way to
absurdities and bound them to repercussions of their own
formulation.

If a punishment were due, the stupidity was that even it could not
be meted out any more. There were no others! With graftings
and growings, what use was it all? They were stranded and
bereft!

It was a final time to take back an outcome, something
satisfactory. Energies were within that ring and perhaps it could
be unleashed and harnessed, even better than the nucleic which
they had over-run. A horrid eventuation was this unlimited
desperation. To go on was quested.

-Soothing Truths-

In dreams now, Andrea was in Elysian, yet returned back to
Hilleton. To her eventual dismay she would go on to be returned
to her old home, her visage recognized. How depressing to think,
finding herself in the place she had sworn off as no longer hers.
Physically in the present, her body lay there, found by some
searchers. The whole mountaintop was charred, with trees cut,
bent, some limbs handing on at odd unnatural angles. Others
simply lay to waste at the ground.

A fire-force field doctor treats her as a wounded then and there.

"Where" was all she could mutter.

"Where am I? Yes I'm sure you'd like to know what's happening."
The doctor told her some details hurriedly. He had other patients
to attend to back in town.

Press reporters had unfortunately come up and ended up hurting
themselves on hot grounds, not having adequate heat resisting
boots. His work was cut out for him, as it was for all medical
staff at the moment.

The doctor told her of a half burning down in the town.
Unexplained destruction, a kind of once in one hundred years
blaze or something. Nobody really had a clue as to why.
 Many people had been lost.

For her part, Andrea felt grief and could not focus or make clear
decisions. The only good thing to do was sleep. Her clothes had
been changed for her, into a white gown. Her own items were in
a sterile-looking bag at the foot of the basic-constructed rest bed
she lay on. Tied to a corner post.
She was in a makeshift camp, inside a tent.

Recovering quickly, after four days she felt stronger as she sat
herself up on her arms and then turned to put her legs on the
ground. Her head swelling had gone down. Cuts and bruises from
stone fragments would heal. Nothing much more to worry over.

She was alone in a tent with medical supplies. That had escaped her detection before. Hmmm.

 In desperation and with the ring binding her to task, she worked on automatic instincts. Not yet knowing why, but for a vague image of the Lady, as herself but with ebony hair, she saw the tears of one dying, blackening on a palatial floor. Fearing and hating the notion of death, her own death, she plunged into action, stealing a medical bag and carrying it back, stumbling, circling. Adrenalin was her friend as she took all-force in her to go back up the mountain.

Digging at rubbles near some fragments of stones, she took a guess and walked around until nearer a coverage of ember-blistered burnt trees. A dark foggy surround made her smile. So she dragged the weighty kit forward. "By ring and by me, we will succeed" she whispered to herself. The kit grew heavier but she began to see fields and nothing more of the fiery plain. Elysian sun glared down on her with ferocious heat. How relieving a vision before her it truly was! A tear of joy rushed down her cheek and she gasped a small grin.

The only problem was, how to pull this weight and get going. Her mind had a fog lifting from it. She knew why she was here and could see a future for herself, short term and long term. Now first to task!

She sat to take a rest after some minutes pulling and walking unsteadily. Maybe her recovery wasn't as complete as she'd wanted. At least she'd gotten through and away, but now her arms ached. Muscles groaned. Newfound strength just wasn't going to be sufficient for this, in the circumstances.

So it was in untold minutes, he found her, truly a moment of scrcndipity.

It was a lumber worker, Rementrium, who has gone mad and now walked idly for hours.
"Fair hail to you, woman."

She turned, straightening up from her hunched pose and stopped trying to pull.

"That be sure a heavy thing you have there. What is it exactly? Need you a hand?"

"What luck, a helpful fellow!" thought Andrea. She smiled and pushed back her hair. "What is your name?"

He told her and they nodded each to the other. He had a broad smile. Urgency was more her mood than anything else. To get this thing going and help the Lady!
Perhaps direct was the best approach...so she told him all the details.

He took the load and dismissed her volunteering to carry one end with him at the other. "I've lifted heavies all my life, this is not much at all to me!"

Jolly fellow for company he was, although a little difficult to keep up with! He had great strides but after a while slowed enough, perhaps tired or in deference to her own pace.

Rementrium knew of the yellow fields and brought her back by cool of night.
He nodded to the old couple, who smile back at him.

Although words were brief and the morning passed quickly, it seemed there was something more here than simple acknowledgements. Were they more acquainted, the couple and this man, this Rementrium?

As it was, he told Andrea he must "lumber again" and Andrea sensed he was their lost son, or something... maybe he had wanted to see them again after so long, once he'd heard her story. The medical bag didn't concern him much at all, but having Andrea there and then gave him reason and compass to meet the couple and he seemed to know the way quite easily for a man that wandered about every place.

He didn't lumber again much: Rementrium visited the very next day and cried, broke down, telling her that his parents indeed didn't remember him, following a tragic accident. It had been long before that he'd felled a tree, leaving them both with something like concussion.

He had been showing them the labors of his new mastership after being a "new called," which Andrea likened to an apprenticeship. All the drama of the accident had put a dampener on his professional skill, but as was the way in this place, things were set in stone so much as people's doings. Nonetheless the experience had marked him. He had something of a jolly craze in him. She got to wondering though that somehow the lumbering occupation was but curse and grace, for it gave him a purpose and focus.

Rementrium also mentioned that in his travels, which had gone on for more than 30 years, that he remembered seeing a strange craft deep in sky.

Andrea paid vivid attention and asked more....
Apparently, a gleaming one had stepped out, only to suffocate in the rich airs.

"I was struck bizarre by it. My tree lay ready to be stripped and prepared for carpenter's working, but here was something that had fallen from the sky. I just stood a-gasp and amazed. The best thing to do seemed to be to watch."

He told her of the detail of their appearance and odd boxes they held. He couldn't quite remember how many might have been there that day, or how many suns ago it had occurred.
He scratched his head trying to think of more.
Andrea waited. She got him a drink of water, very fresh.
He went on: "When I saw them coughing, heaving double over, it made me very much afraid. I didn't want no trouble or responsibility. Perhaps they were Lady's men, how could I know? I'm a simple man, so I ran away, very troubled by it all."

Lastly he described the first figure, the one truly that seemed doomed to a worse fate than his colleague had collapsed just as he turned to leave from behind his tree of hiding. All the beings had glowed with a glorious power.
They had destroyed a field of good-yielding fruits! Rementrium considered this probably more important. He backtracked his story, saying "No no, it was when they first landed or crashed...I

had a hovel which I had been using as night shelter. It all got crushed. Luckily I wasn't inside but it seemed so shocking to see good lands broken."

After, a scar had been left on Rementrium.   That is, the event left him too afraid to ever set home in a permanent place anywhere again. Sleeping as a camper was all he could do.

'That explains at least why you couldn't sleep in the barn last evening then', Andrea thought.

-Inquisitive Mind-

She came to terms with what everything meant. She imagined
and reasoned, sifted through it all and came to see the possibility
that the Zordants not only harnessed a ring that they only partly
understood, but that they had a kind of shadow power over the
world she'd come to know as Elysian. That world seemed almost
magical, an alternate medieval but permeating the energies that
seemed to unlock powers unheard of in modern Hilleton and her
old world. She wondered. Why can't anybody just talk straight
and upfront? Zordants were just like all people, hiding everything
and causing so much tangled mess.
Alternatively, was Elysian something else, something that the
Zordants had wanted but could not bring to heel?

Realization soon became her. She had to find out the answers
from the source.

After so long a time she went again to the forest. Crossing over
felt at once right and wrong, to her instincts.

Nonetheless, it seemed to come to her that things had to be ended
properly.
In almost a haze of unconsciousness she dutifully trotted down to
her home in town. Then, she went across to the salon and
declared she was taking leave from her job. Judith had been
startled to see her, then stoically resigned. It would be the end of
her employment. The air itself spoke so.

So it were, that in the course of some days she found herself
scouting through the area, trying to understand things further in
the forest.

At some point, The Zordants found and met her, quite dishevelled
looking. "Andree-ah," called the first.

She told them what she thought and what she had learnt. They
didn't seem so magical this day. It was more a meeting of equals
this time.

Quizzically they asked her if this is what she truly believed?
They then polished things off by telling her that if she believed it,
then she had already made it true.
"There is nothing more to say," the second said to her
telepathically, with a sadness almost imperceptible.
They neither elaborated nor helped her to understand.

After they left for their craft again for "repair and recuperation",
she felt different, as though her mind was more open, and the ring
more dull.
It wasn't worth contemplating. All that mattered at this moment
was understanding, putting to rest all the doubts and quirky
happenings, that had re-colored the fabric of her being beyond all
recognition.

She gathered near to the great stone and peered through, at the
edge of both worlds.
   She could see nothingness. Curious, or even a little alarmed, she
crossed the division of worlds and entered again into Elysian, sure
enough.

However, she wondered where she was, for this time, she saw
before her a world which appeared empty of life. No people, only
fields lying in a steady state. Unchanging. Going forward, she
walked around wondering and her mind seemed to teem with
thoughts.

In despair at the hot sun, she cried out in low-register voice,
"Noooo!" Imagining that her world was evaporating.

Her world?

Did she even dare say that?

What concoctions of puzzles and non-informations had the
Zordants given her? Never direct, never enough from them!

She felt parched and ran, running for life and purpose...but there
and then slowed herself, feeling defeated and betrayed. What
was this? The ring bore dull as she gazed on it. Her breathing

labored as she urged it to calm, while her temples still pulsed thick blood under beads of sweated skin.

Perplexed and in a shrug, her eyes scanned around more carefully, squinting for details afar.

Noticing a large lagoon she had never reached before, let alone observed, she shrugged shoulders and made her way towards it.

Distant tumbles, like waves could be heard. Hmmm, Where IS the coastline? She had never confronted this question before, in Elysian. It had never seemed appropriate or relevant. Whatever, but it wasn't at all was it?
So now at the Lagoon, puzzled mind, she bent down fully to the ground crouching, and to find coolness dipped her head into the water, throwing away even the question of whether it was potable. She proceeded to rinse her face and then cupped her hands to drink.

Nothing unusual, everything fine as it should be.

Time to think again and perhaps even worry. Feeling overcome, she lay on the ground and slept some hours.
The caresses of the airs and gentle heat touched her gracefully, though she did not dream.

Stirring from the absolute silence, she sat up with a bit of a shock. She looked around, staring with eyes, reacquainting her mind to the present.

With a sigh, she considered. She couldn't stay here, she knew this true.
Not with this emptiness everywhere.

Her pulse quickened, as if hearing her concerns. The sun glowed hot above, mid-day.

 She then sat for untold hours.

It was broken, the silence. Softly on a breeze, she heard talking and wails. Her ring was gleaming, reddening, warming, as she looked at it.

She walked towards the noises, back on her own footpath, and then taking breath, went to a run.

Miraculous!

People!
Again she found people. It did not occur to her at the time that once again, she was finding glimmers of connections. A lagoon? Was it coincidence that its waters, on touching the ring, had preceded the event of returning people? She did not think this for now though.

 She said hello's but got back their stares and smiles. They worked on moving stones, walking, talking, all the regular things.

Not really focused on them much more, she moved quickly away.

Andrea was on her way, going back to the blue field, then the yellow field. She observed insects and saw a horse. Life was here. Good. As it should be.

Timelessly, merriment filled her heart with joy.

She never for a moment thought delusions were racking her. She'd long given up on such feeble rubbish.

Now her mind felt scientific and she wanted to think.

Satisfied, she did the unthinkable, and actually led herself back to Hilleton and wrote down all that she could remember, burning her brain to note what had happened and look at other notes she wrote many many days before.

This was assuming she still had a home standing, after the calamitous fires. Foresight was a luxury at this stage. Putting it all together, all the lost thoughts and unchained happenings, seemed important, despite the puzzles the Zordants always left her with.

Were they incompetents or holding back?

Was it even worth assuming they were so intelligent?

Had they stumbled on all they had and not so much 'invented' it all?

Rising skepticism was just another metaphysical walk, perhaps. Had the Zordants attempted to control the lands of Elysian, as though a new home, only to find it impossible to reside in it? Were they stranded from another world, unable perhaps to use Hilleton and beyond due to its over-sophistication?

Twin worlds that doomed them to having neither one place nor the other?
Yet if any of this were feasible, why had they given her a communications ring? What could they gain from her? A few scraps of general knowledge? To what aim?

Could she be free of them and truly find her own destiny, make peace and find posting in Elysian with the Lady who serves and the ever expanses there, in silent solace-- a restful peace, inner purpose more than she had ever imagined she could in simple-life Hilleton??

Did the Zordants defy all logic that her world's people could understand?
This was all so hypothetical but it all fitted and it was all she had. Her determination was to be as she would be, as she designed, and to be controlled by nobody! If that meant yet again the discomfort, then so be it.

She was so tired of the torment, tired of all of this, and couldn't trust much at all now. She wouldn't let things pull away from her any more. She had the will to be, and wanted to make sure that nothing would keep on ripping up her chosen life. Now to bridge the gaps and piece it all cohesively at last! Finding a place of solace would let her put an end to this. Elysian.

This was where her thoughts rested. No more feeling fragmented across spaces, dizzy and scratching at answers, everything disturbed over and over in a repetitive stink!

-The Return-

After a doze, she rose. Upward she marched in fine boots and practical skirt with stockings and good coat.
On the forest tops again, the stones loomed large to Andrea's perception.
Questions still remained for her, but she'd learnt things too. The motivations of people—and Zordants -- were as always, a mystery.
It was her world, the present as she knew it, home. Hairdressing, solace in her dwelling-home, all that and her work friends. Yet was that all? Things had changed. New channels had opened.
She wouldn't tell them of the crystal lines she had gazed at in the microcosm of the ring. They didn't seem to hear of it. To them it was a distress beacon of communication and no more. Photic energy to signal beyond star-distances?
Yet it aligned with her, and she knew it had powers in it, more, that she'd seen, felt, embraced. Unbetold more could be inside to discover, perhaps too.

Then she HEARD them.

It was telepathic, somehow. It had never happened like this before. The Zordant two were concerned about her 'bond' with the ring and the wounds she had suffered. Didn't they see? She had recovered from them all, given time.

Andrea understood now. The ring wasn't apart from her. It was a part of her, innermost. From the time of the light and fire the first time, she had felt a surge of charge across her. It was spine-tingling and almost too much. She subconsciously protected her thoughts from the Zordants. They must have known. Their gestures and expressions gave away their uncertainty now about the ring.
It wasn't just their creation. Had it ever been? It was hers. Perfections swirled in it. No, maybe not perfections but potentials.

She did want to tell them at least this. In a flash, she felt irritated. When were these high ones ever straight with her? She had to piece it altogether, it was instinctual. She represented this earth and had been fair-handed. She, the quiet woman, the diplomatic. Things beyond her had become her. She had grown but had to stumble her way and only by her own efforts had anything been gained.

Was anybody truly thinking beyond, beyond their personal selfish skin?

Waiting, she calmed herself. These thoughts blazed at light speed through her. They...they, were too self-absorbed to know of it. Physically approached, now present before Andrea's many times strengthened and tanned new self.

In the moment, in such fashion, They conveyed messages back and forth. The leading Zordant and her. The other looked on staringly, intently. Not with judgment. His thimble and thin features had hidden strengths. She knew it. Reflecting off his gaze was also the recognition that she had changed herself. With a tinge of smile she continued on.

The Zordants turned to each other for but a moment. They were communicating silently, perhaps mentally again. It was something she never could know. Their wrist bands at the ready, the second Zordant held out his arm, after touching his wrist band.

"Andrea, we would like to free you from the ring now. You have a good life to live, there is no danger for you now." They did not feel they could learn or exchange further with her.

Despite what had transpired for the minutes, Andrea was shocked. After all she'd gone through, this dismissive objectivity they displayed only served to truly stun her. The opening of her mind and finding of more purpose than had ever dawned, was ... blessing. Would she just not see them again? Part of her thought to learn more, but more intimately she felt the ring was her tower of strength. Everything was at risk; the foundations she'd laid and the life she'd built with her own herculean determinations despite setbacks and stumblings.

So next she did something she had never done before.

She shot her mind at them. A push. Their heads instinctively turned and chins moved up. Their eyebrows frowned. Listening? Knowing?
She conveyed to them that the ring was not an invasive influence, but had helped her, lifted her.

Concerned emotions stirred in them. Telepathics was not for human folk.

She was sniffing the air through her nostrils with controlled haste. Rising intonations of deep venting and before she spoke, they felt the charge of vexatious energy from her. Unused to being challenged, they just froze and lost normal state of 'situational calm' as they programmatically knew it.

Perceptibly something had changed forever, as the atmospherics themselves would attest, were they to have voice to speak.
As before a storm, an incredulous calm loomed mighty. All waiting.

-Chasm-Hanger-

Gem of gem, banded circle, never ending, was of her, and her of it...such simple truism filled her depths...to a destiny.

"You can't do this to me!!!" Screamed Andrea, in a blood-curdling rage. Being told the ring and her would be parted was beyond cosmic distance in possibilities, beyond it all and forever more.

Redness raced down from that rustic ring and encircled her gleaming burning rubesque, true to scene and hue. Reaching from her legging brace, Bending spine she snaked out a piece of silver shining, and slid it up her thigh, then torso, to beating beat and even nether reach of her carotid region, slowly, as she yet inhaled. Filling her chest with chilling airs, a glare in her eyes of utter pre-determination and browed vexation, she lifted up her head again tall. Then, producing gemmed dagger, the airs shook. She thrust back her arm and heaved, plunging it into space of gusts, rushing past and then down. Down, down, down...pounding in a thunderous thud into barren earth and ripping a crevasse. Busting boulder and rumbling rubble torn at the fabric of it all and no-one, man or Zordant, could bear down on her any more...

(End)

(Intentionally blank)

Author's note: This story to be continued.

Many thanks for reading!